to ... Bill Copeland

MW00936493

# The Apostasy

Bill L. Copeland

**The Apostasy**

© Copyright 2006 by Bill L. Copeland

All rights reserved. No portion of this book may be reproduced in any form, except for brief quotations in reviews, without the written permission of the copyright holder.

This is a work of fiction. Any resemblance to any person or persons, living or dead, is purely coincidental.

Scripture references are taken from the King James version of the Bible.

Library of Congress Cataloging-in-Publication Data

Copeland, Bill L. 1948-
The Apostasy / Bill L. Copeland

*Cover art by:* Fariad at wildlandimages.com
*Printed in the United States of America:* Wirz & Company Printing

# Acknowledgments

First and foremost to my God, who compelled me, the guy who failed English throughout all my schooling, to write a novel of all things. Without Him, and the supernatural direction of the Holy spirit, this book would never have happened. It has been an amazing and difficult journey and yet one that has caused me to grow so much closer to my Lord Jesus Christ.

As I began to write the first stages of this book, God brought across my path and set before me strangers, people I had never met before and have not seen since. These people came from different walks of life and professions, some from the intelligence community here in the United States and the Middle East. They all gave me information that the Lord wanted me to include in the book. Most of them would not want me to mention their names, but God used them and they know who they are.

In the beginning were two people who from the start prophesied this book would be a success. They read and reread my first drafts and offered suggestions and advice that encouraged me greatly. I also recall feeling their prayers. God bless you, Ron and Gladys Dudley.

My gratitude to James Vowell for taking my manuscript and cutting out all the useless fat and bad grammar and making it look like a book.

I cannot fully express my gratitude to my friend Deanna Dunn who did the final editing and whose revising and rearranging made this book what it is today.

And finally, I would like to thank the one person who has stood by me steadfastly through it all. She is the love of my life, and I dedicate this book...

...to Barbara

## AUTHOR'S NOTE

Although the scenario of this novel follows the timeline of a pre-tribulation rapture, it is not the author's intent to exclusively promote this theory. Rather, the characters and events in this novel could fit accordingly in a mid-tribulation or even later rapture.

In the skies over earth in the late 1940s, spiritual entities began spreading the seeds of deception. These dark forces made contact with their human counterparts in the government and the media and together they perpetuated the deception in the minds of the population. Over the following decades mysterious manifestations in the air, along with the deliberate disinformation about them, have created misleading beliefs.

Now, after more than 60 years, the conspirators are ready to attack and accomplish their goal. The extraterrestrial illusions have trained the people of the world to react in a certain way to a concluding great delusion.

Mankind is now conditioned to accept the ultimate lie.

# Apostasy
*(falling away)*

*Now we beseech you, brethren, by the coming of our Lord Jesus Christ, and by our gathering unto him.*

*That ye be not shaken in mind, or be troubled, neither by spirit, nor by word, nor by letter as from us that the day of the Lord is present.*

*Let no man deceive you by any means; for that day shall not come, except there come the falling away first, and that man of sin be revealed, the son of perdition.*

— II Thessalonians 2:1-3

# Introduction

As a Christian growing up in the church, whenever I heard a minister teach on Thessalonians 2:1-3, he would most often explain the "falling away" as a gradual moral decline that would happen to the church in the days before the Rapture.

The Greek word translated here for falling away is "apostasy" which means an abandonment of one's religion. In the original Greek text, the definite article "the" is used referring this apostasy to a specific event, not some vague or gradual deterioration over a long period of time. In the Latin text, the word "rapere" is used to describe this apostasy. *Rapere* is the root for *raptor,* describing the kind of animal that strikes quickly. It is also where we get the word *rapture,* that sudden event that will happen in the blink of an eye.

After studying this scripture for many years I have come to the conclusion, as with some others more learned than I, that this apostasy the Apostle Paul tells us about here in Thessalonians is a quick and sudden, world-shaking event that will have a devestating effect on mankind. That it will cause many who are not grounded in their faith in God to abandon it.

Paul does not tell us exactly what will happen to cause this apostasy that will usher in the appearance of the anti-Christ, but he does give us a clue later in the same chapter. In verse nine, he tells us this apostasy will be part of a series of "signs and lying wonders." Then in verse eleven, he states that it will be a strong "delusion."

This book is a possible scenario about the times we live in and how we are being set up by the devil for his soon-to-come great delusion. The delusion that will not only usher in his man of perdition but cause many to lose their faith in God, create unbridled persecution against Christians, and even explain away the miracle of the Rapture after it happens.

God compelled me to write this book. Using prophetic scripture and the thoughts He has given me, I present it not as if this is exactly what is going to happen, but to warn Christians that *something* is going to happen. And when it does, we need to be prepared and aware of this delusion. We must not allow it to cause us to lose faith in what God's Word says, no matter how real and terrible that delusion might be.

Those of us who have a solid personal relationship with Jesus Christ should not fear the coming days before His return. We know that He has assured us that, "He will be with us always, even unto the end."

Bill Copeland
September 2004

*In that day shall there be an altar to the Lord in the midst of Egypt, and a pillar at the border of it to the Lord. And it shall be a sign and for a witness unto the Lord of host in the land of Egypt, for they shall cry unto the Lord because of the oppressors and he shall send them a savior, and a great one, and he shall deliver them.*

— Isaiah 19:19, 20*

**3017 BC Midnight …**
The great pyramid, on the borderline
in the middle of what will someday be
Northern and Southern Egypt

# Prologue

IT ROSE OUT OF THE DESERT SAND, soaring up to the heavens, huge, massive, more than 450 feet tall. It stood alone and silent in the midst of the dark open desert. Constructed of stones, some weighing over 70 tons, the engineering of the pyramid would not be matched even in a technical, modern world, 5,000 years into the future.

Some would try. They would attempt to make copies of it, but their efforts would always fall short of this marker's incredible

*__Author's Note:__ In the original Hebrew language, the numerical number of the letters in these verses add up to the exact height in primitive inches (5449) of the Great pyramid at Giza in Egypt.

construction. The four sides of the pyramid were covered with polished white limestone from top to bottom. From directly overhead, the light of the full moon reflected off the monument with a brilliance that cast a pillar of white light high into the sky. The stream of light pierced heat waves radiating from the desert and floated skyward into the night. The atmospheric effect made the stars appear to shimmer.

From out of the eastern horizon, a row of lights appeared, brighter than the stars and much closer to the earth. They descended slowly, threateningly, in a straight pattern until they came to hover above the glowing pyramid. Other lights of different shapes and colors shot from over the four corners of the dark, silent sky to join these lights. Some swirled around, while others darted off at odd angles. Certain lights appeared tubular in shape, while others looked like brilliant silver saucers. Passing overhead in wide circles the lights, one by one, began a slow descent to the side of a high sandy ridge, not far from the pyramid, that stood like a white mountain.

In their stately descent, the lights blurred and metamorphosed into the crisp shapes of large winged, black beings. The supernatural entities appeared human in form, with heavily muscled arms and legs. Scales covered their shoulders and climbed their long necks to form heads like those of vipers. The ominous dark creatures, long tails trailing behind them, glided downward through the night air with outstretched wings like birds of prey. Landing, they settled folded pinions to their backs, stamped clawed feet and walked awkwardly about to form into groups.

They sat quietly ... waiting.

Several hours passed.

Except for a slight rustle of wings, or a low murmur of short conversation heard floating across the still night air, the groups of black spirits did not move.

High in the sky, again from the east, a radiant light appeared and began its ponderous descent. As it drew near the waiting group on the desert floor, its brightness became overwhelming in intensity, with brilliant, sharp rays of light streaming out in all directions.

The desert lit up like sunrise.

The black creatures cowered against the hot sand, bowing their heads and shielding themselves with their wings. The onslaught of radiant energy was like a brilliant star as it regally passed over them. Not one of the dark spirits dared look at it. The glowing point of light then floated over to sink behind the ridge, its brilliance now shielded by the tall sand dune.

A few among the black horde gathered on the desert floor cautiously lifted their heads to stare with beaded red eyes toward the ridge, its long, distinct crest silhouetted against the now fading light. Whispers of vapor began to curl upward from behind the sand, the fumes swelling into billowing gray clouds. As the thick smoke moved skyward, twisting and writhing, an iridescent red glow appeared against it, as though reflecting a large fire. A black profile slowly began to rise over the crest of the ridge. As it ascended, regal and majestic, its form clarified as separate from the glowing background.

A dragon: huge and menacing.

The full image of the beast finally stood atop the ridge, its head swiveling, searching in all directions, like a predator on the prowl. With spread wings, the giant reptile glided slowly forward, hovering just above the ground, until it stopped in front of the groups of black creatures that had been waiting. The monster stood about thirty-five feet tall. Its torso was human in form, with powerful legs and arms that ended in thick, cruel claws. The head was oblong and wicked looking, shaped like a venomous snake, with two large pointed horns thrusting from each side above pointed ears. They were followed by other smaller horns that trailed down his head and back. His sneering mouth was full of sharp, glistening fangs, and sinister eyes glowed with an intense yellow light below a dark arched brow. The dragon's massive body was covered with leathery red scales that reflected the moonlight. The horny, shining plates covered him from his head to his massive tail, which writhed like a snake.

For, like that earth reptile, who once had this same form, this was that great serpent, Lucifer.

Lucifer — the Devil, Satan, the adversary of the Most High God, ruler and god of the earth and its skies. The black creatures before him were his fallen angels, spirits, and demons.

Satan pondered the groups before him, probing, measuring, weighing each individual. Satisfied with the gathering, his egg-yoke, glossy eyes lifted to the dark horizon, his head swaying toward the east whence he came. Eyes hooded, he focused into the distance to that area near the Euphrates River where the Garden of Eden had flourished. Lucifer sighed as he relished the memory of his act of deceiving the woman and causing the man to disobey God. Thus, bringing the curse upon all mankind.

It had been his greatest triumph thus far.

The enmity on earth between himself and God had started then. And because of that fall of man, the Lord of heaven had made a vow to Satan. God's seed, a man, born of a woman, would someday come to redeem mankind.

The dragon clenched his sharp fangs and snarled with smoldering anger.

No, it would not happen. The devil's own seed, through a woman, someday would enslave man, beginning the culmination of Satan's plan to set up his kingdom here on earth.

As the dragon restlessly stood in hostile discontent, his hate-filled eyes wondered across the desert sands and gazed upon the pyramid. He growled as he cursed its magnificence. The groups of nomadic hu-mans that sometimes passed by the pyramid would marvel at it and wonder who had built it, for no one knew.

But Satan knew.

The glowing white pyramid was an altar to the God of heaven, built by one of the hu-mans from the generations of Adam. Enoch, the one who had "walked with God," had become privy to the divine secrets, to supernatural knowledge that had enabled him to construct the pyramid. Satan knew the white stone pillar standing so magnificently in front of him was a testament from God to the hu-mans on earth for now and forever. He knew the pyramid would play a part in God's plans in the last days. Satan knew he dare not try to destroy it, but what if …

As the dragon kept looking at this altar to the Lord, the end to a plan started to form in his mind — a plan for his seed, his man of sin, in the end times. A deception he had already conceived that would use the abilities of his demons to alter form and appearance, to seem what they were not, and linger to do his will. To deceive, to confuse — to cause many to reject the very idea of a loving God.

It would be the climax of Satan's scheme over the centuries, to thwart God's plan of salvation for mankind.

As Satan continued to glower at the pyramid, he thought about the secrets hidden in that pile of rocks. He wondered what God planned for it, in the future, in the end times?

Someday, a culmination of his on-going battle with the Lord of the heavenly hosts would come. When he defeated the most-high God here on earth, he would then set up his kingdom. It would be so. Because of his power to deceive man, a total abandoning of faith would occur. All of what the Most-High had hoped for, for mankind and this world, would end in ruin.

The devil stared at the radiant marker, his hot yellow eyes glaring intensely as his mouth formed an evil sneer.

He would use this monument, this pillar, this altar. He would corrupt it as he worked at poisoning everything else the Lord had placed here on earth. Yes, the dragon decided, he would make it the symbol and seal of his kingdom on earth. "Yes," he hissed. The idea swelled in his mind, and his eyes glowed as he relished the thought of it.

The dragon tore his eyes from the pyramid and returned his malevolent gaze to the black hoard before him. Hundreds of neon red eyes watched him silently, awaiting his command.

He would begin his plan now ... and when the time came, he would have the people of earth prepared. His dark angels would cause a deception of quick and immediate confusion that would be amazing ...

It would be terrible ...

And it would work!

The dragon's head swiveled as he looked over his followers. A boisterous laughter roared from his mouth, sending shock waves of sound across the desert, startling even his demon hosts. They cowered in fright and looked up to their lord.

The dragon then issued commands for the beginning of his Great Plan.

# PART 1

# The Beginnings

*And I will put enmity between thee and the woman, and between thy seed, and her seed; he shall bruise thy head, and thou shalt bruise his heel.*

— Genesis 3:15

**December 25, 1963**
Early morning … a convent high in the mountain forest of northern Italy.

.............................................

# Chapter 1

DURING THE NIGHT SNOW FELL, blanketing the forest in a shroud of white. The smoke-grey sky was barely visible through thick clusters of dark, barren trees. Other than a snowflake floating downward now and then, the air in the woods was still. No bird flew, no animal moved. The black and white forest was ominously silent.

Amid the trees, in a small clearing, stood a large three-story structure, a massive castle of grey rock. The citadel looked deserted, but it was not. Inside its 300-year-old walls lived more than fifty sequestered women — nuns and novices set off and apart from the outside world. The few inhabitants of the surrounding countryside seldom saw the occupants in the convent. The neighbors were, for the most part, shepherds, and not one of them ever ventured near the solemn-looking structure.

The shepherds were a superstitious lot. Through the years, stories of supernatural happenings had been told about the area around the convent. Witches, demons, ghosts, and devils had been seen countless times, by folks of good stature and sound mind.

Except for a yearly visit by a few nuns from the flatlands, no one ever came around. To the villagers, fear always seemed to hang in the heavy air of the forest that surrounded the convent.

Amid the dark trees, a figure of a man suddenly emerged and stared at the convent. He wore a long, dark topcoat, with his hands shoved into the side pockets. A black fedora covered most of his grey hair. His face bore many creases, like the jagged lines on a battle map. His eyes — shining, piercing, blue diamond eyes — had witnessed countless events over many thousands of years and spoke of great wisdom. Although possessing a name, he was generally known as "the Messenger."

An invisible — and sometimes visible — observer of life on earth, the Messenger was not of this world. His deep voice resonated when he spoke:

> **One of the final stages of Satan's 5,000-year-old plan for his kingdom on earth will start here. This is the first of many occurrences that will take place in this concluding time of mankind. The people will be known as the "Terminal Generation," a generation that will lose its spiritual equilibrium with God and start to invert His values.**

The Messenger paused for one last look at the convent, his brilliant blue eyes searching as if they could pierce the stone walls. He then turned and walked away, disappearing into the forest.

Morning sunlight filtered through the grey clouds and snow-covered trees and streaked the walls of the convent. The sunlight also angled across several windows of a chapel adjacent to the convent. Inside the chapel, candles flickered. The stone interior was bare except for a large wooden crucifix hanging on the chancel wall. Rays of sunlight slanted through the windows, illuminating particles of dust floating in the air. The light sent long silhouettes of the window frames across the stone floor and up the opposite wall. Two rows of rough wooden benches filled the room, with an aisle down the middle. The chapel felt gloomy and cold, like a tomb.

At the front of the aisle, a woman knelt in prayer.

Her black veil and habit were meticulously clean and pressed. The bulky garments hid her well-shaped body and long legs. The proportions of her face and high cheekbones showed a Roman heritage, for she had been born to an aristocratic Italian family. Her eyes, now closed as she bowed her head, were the color of the clear sky, and they usually gleamed with defiant authority. Her once-beautiful hands, folded in her lap, were beginning to look worn from a lifetime of hard work.

Ann Stefannelli, Mother Superior of the convent, felt every year of the heavy responsibility.

The subject of Ann's prayers this morning was the same as it had been every morning for almost a year. A continuous feeling of dread had come over her, and no matter how she prayed she could not rid herself of it. She had sensed it in the other nuns, also. She suppressed these thoughts daily — continuously — trying to displace the horrible sense of fear onto something else, anything else. How could evil possibly exist here? This place was property of the church. The work of God was performed here. Yet, no matter how she tried, an intense sense of danger filled her every thought. Everywhere she went inside the convent she felt the presence of evil.

The calm and peace of the convent had evaporated. She wanted to escape, to flee, to run away, to feel peace again — if only for a moment. But her pounding heart reminded her she would not, could not, forsake her responsibilities.

So, as she had for so many mornings, she bowed her head, closed her eyes, sighed, and prayed to the Lord for peace. Peace for her, peace for her convent.

The heavy back door of the chapel creaked open, interrupting Ann's thoughts. She heard footsteps in the aisle behind her. Someone had come in during her prayers. This was odd. No one had ever bothered her during prayer time before.

"Mother Superior," whispered Sister Bregga.

Ann did not respond.

"Mother Superior," the young woman urged.

Ann slowly lifted her head, focused her brilliant blue eyes on the crucifix.

"Yes?" Ann replied.

"Mother Superior, Sister Volonte told me to bring you immediately!"

Sister Sarah Volonte was the only certified nurse in the order, Ann remembered with alarm. She rose, turned, folding her arms into the sleeves of her black robe, and studied the young nun. The novice trembled under her grey clothing, her face a mask of fright.

"What's wrong, child?"

"It's ... it's ... Sister Mary," said the young nun, her eyes dropping to the floor, unable to look directly at her Superior.

"What about her?" Ann asked.

"She's having a baby."

SIX THOUSAND MILES AWAY on an Indian reservation near Red Bluff, Oklahoma, at exactly the same time as Sister Mary's delivery that Christmas night, Linda Allen was also having a baby.

Married less than a year, Jim and Linda were very excited over the arrival of their new son. Jim was full-blooded Cherokee, with many relatives living in the area. Linda was Caucasian; her widowed mother lived in town. Linda, her mother, and all the Allen clan celebrated Christmas that night, elated over the new addition to their family.

Grandpa Karrel Allen was especially proud of his new grandson and namesake, John Karrel Allen.

**December 26, 1963 – 3:12 p.m.**
Mountain forest in Italy
on the road 10 miles
from the convent.

A black Cadillac limousine crept along the narrow mountain road. More snow had fallen during the night, and fog draped like a grey shroud over the forest.

Two people rode in the front seat, a male driver and a woman passenger. The woman was middle aged and wore a nurse's uniform under her winter coat. The driver, dark complexioned and husky, was chauffeur and bodyguard to the single occupant in the rear of the limousine.

The man in the spacious back seat made a stark contrast to the two people in front. He would have stood out in a crowd of thousands.

The lone passenger, who looked younger than his fifty-seven years, had an air of absolute authority and radiant power about him. At 6 feet 9 inches he towered over, — and intimidated — most men. His large body, broad shoulders, and wide chest matched his height. He wore a custom-tailored suit, midnight-blue with a rich purple tint, a matching silk tie and shirt. His supple skin was light bronze. His hair, combed straight back, gleamed jet black. Sharp lines in his face were bold and accented, as if chiseled from granite. A hawk-shaped nose loomed above his cruel thin mouth.

Some might call him brutally handsome, but what frightened men and women most were his vibrant jade-green eyes. Extraordinary submissiveness seized nearly everyone who looked into them for more than a moment.

Frank Pettinati posed as an envoy for the Curia, the administrative arm of the Catholic Church. A strange role, for he was farthest any man could be from religious. However, he was on a personal task, one on which his destiny depended, and he would do anything, no matter what, to complete his mission.

Frank pressed back into the leather seat, held his head up, and looked out the window at the snow-covered forest. What he had to do today would be simple. He would play his role and take what he came for.

*If my little charade doesn't work*, he said to himself, eyebrow arching as his eyes narrowed in determination, *I'll take what I want anyway*.

Frank was a man of a thousand desires. Whether it was his sexual appetite, material things, or anything else that pleased him, he was accustomed to getting what he wanted.

The Cadillac arrived in a small village. The only person in sight was an old man sitting in a chair, reading a book in front of one of the hamlet's few buildings. He was dressed in a brown winter coat, a leather-and-fur hat with floppy earflaps perched on his head. The limousine's tires crunched to a halt in the snow in front of the old man. Frank rolled down the window and leaned his head out.

"Bon giorno, signore," said Frank, his words turning to vapor as they hit the outside air.

The old man looked up from his reading and stared for a moment at Frank. "Bon giorno," the old man said without emotion. He rolled a cud of chewing tobacco inside his mouth, adding more stain to his full white beard, as he stared at Frank.

"Excuse me. I wonder if you could tell me how far is the convent la casa?"

The old man broke his stare after a moment, his eyes traveling down the long automobile. He leaned over to spit a stream of brown juice. "About 2 kilometers, signore," he said, nodding up the road, resuming his study of the stranger.

Frank sensed hostility from the villager but was about to tell him thank you anyway. Then, looking around, he began to wonder. "Are there no other people here, signore?

"They are all hiding in their houses. They are afraid."

"Afraid of what, signore?"

"Banshees, ghosts and demons … evil spirits." The old man

chewed his tobacco and assessed Frank's reaction to his words. "They made quite a ruckus last night, flying around, howling, and carrying on. Between that and the wind blowing, it has everyone scared."

"Evil spirits?" said Frank, lifting one eyebrow. "But you are not afraid, signore?"

"I am not afraid of such things."

"Non capiso? Why not?"

The old man reached inside his coat and brought out a silver Christian cross that was hanging on a chain around his neck. He held it in front of himself in Frank's direction, as if in a gesture of warding off evil.

Frank glared at the cross as he leaned back from the window. "Ah, si signore, I see." He smirked as the tinted window closed.

The car pulled away. The old man went back to his Bible.

ANN STEFANNELLI STOOD MOTIONLESS at the third-story window of her office. Long shadows stretched across the snow-covered forest. The landscape looked cold and forbidding. It was not, however, as remotely chilling as the fear and uncertainty that gripped her heart.

Yesterday had been a nightmare. She would never forget the shock, much less the confusion and unbelief, as she rushed to the room of Sister Mary Giuffre. Mary had been with the order for two years and was still in novice training. When Ann arrived at the doorway of the young sister's room, Mary was lying on her bed with an exposed belly that most certainly contained a baby.

Sister Sarah Volonte scurried about the room, getting ready to assist with the coming birth. She was helped by two other sisters. More nuns stood stone-faced in the hallway like spectators at an accident. Panic was palpable in the room and, if Ann guessed correctly, the baby was coming soon.

As Ann walked in, Sarah stopped her work briefly, her eyes rising upward and locking on Ann's. For a moment, the critical question flashed in silence between them: How could a woman, sequestered away from any outside contact with the world for more than two years, become pregnant? Neither had an answer, because there simply wasn't one.

The convent was in a remote area and the outside windows and doors were always locked. Could a man somehow miraculously slip in and out under such daunting circumstances? If so, how could it have happened without anyone noticing? If someone had impregnated her and she knew it, why hadn't Sister Mary told anyone? Mary apparently kept her incredible secret hidden under her loose clothing, but why? What was the reason for it all? Ann's thoughts were in disarray.

Sister Mary's eyes were closed, and she was delirious with pain. She screamed out — cries that to Ann were more yells of terror than pain. Ann's eyes widened with fear as the screams became more hysterical. Shrill, piercing cries echoed down the hallways, flooding the convent with ever more dread.

At the time, Ann told herself that the answer to the frightful mystery could and would have to wait until after the baby was born.

That was yesterday.

Spellbound, Ann now stared at the snow glistening on the tree branches outside her window.

*Today is another day. Today is the day they will bury Mary.* The baby boy had come, and Mary had died giving birth, never uttering a word. The incident was a paradox of troubling and unanswered questions. Moreover, Mary, the only source of those answers was gone forever, sealing off any reply to Ann's questions.

Since yesterday, no one in the convent had spoken about the birth. It was too hard to think about it and Mary's death. Through the night, the cold air outside the convent had blown and howled relentlessly, the wind filled with the sounds of eerie screaming, as if echoing Mary's torment. To Ann, it seemed like a taunting after the day's events.

Ann pressed the long fingers of one hand on the cold glass of the window. The sensation was as chilling as the reception of her telephoned report of the seemingly miraculous and literally inconceivable birth to her superior in Rome. And who could blame him? It was unbelievable that a woman, showing religious devotion and supposedly a virgin, had given birth to a son. The fact that it had happened once before in history, and by another virgin named Mary, was not lost on Ann. What had they thought of this in Rome? To her surprise, her superior hadn't really commented on the strange situation. He just said that he would send someone for the baby.

Ann then remembered that Mary Giuffre had come from a Jewish family. She strained to recall from the outer edge of her mind a Biblical foretelling long buried from the education of her youth. Suddenly her concentration was broken by movement through the distant fog. It was a vehicle, a long black car, coming up the snow-covered road to the convent.

Well, they certainly came quickly, she thought.

The limousine pulled up in front of the convent's main door and stopped. Ann watched a chauffeur and a woman get out. The chauffeur opened a side door and a big, well-dressed man stepped forth. Ann closed her eyes and sighed deeply. She turned and sat down at her desk.

Frank stood by the car and arched his back, then stretched his legs, his eyes disecting the area. It had been a long, dull journey, and he was anxious to get the next part over with.

Looking up, he noticed hordes of black-winged demons lined up on the peaks of all the convent roofs, like rows of birds on a telephone line. The horrid creatures sat motionless, staring at Frank with piercing red eyes, knowing who he was.

Of course, he nodded slyly, there would be "angels heralding the advent." They were the cause of the clamor last night that the old man back in the village had mentioned.

"Announcing ... the birth ... to the shepherds," he chuckled to himself, looking to see if the nurse or the driver saw the demons. But of course, they did not. Only he could see them. Looking back up at the demons, Frank solemnly met their fiery gaze. Yes, they knew why he was here.

Frank tightened the knot in his tie and slid his hand down his suit coat. He gave a heavy sigh.

The driver and nurse stood by the car, glancing around at the convent and woods. The driver broke out a pack of cigarettes and offered one to the nurse.

"I'll call you if I need you," Frank said. As they lit up, he walked to the front door of the convent.

Frank stared at the ugly grey walls; he hated any religious buildings, especially churches. He sometimes fantasized on the idea of burning churches. Someday, he thought, he would fulfill that urge. As for now, he needed to bear the repugnance he felt at this place. A mental transformation came over Frank as he knocked on the convent door. He became a gentleman.

A nervous nun ushered him into the Mother Superior's office, a room far better appointed than the bleak foyer and halls he had just walked through. It felt cozy, with light-colored wood on the walls and a large rug covering the floor. A panoramic view from the windows showed the surrounding forest. Seated behind a large wooden desk, the Mother Superior rose in greeting. *She does not look like she's having a good day,* Frank thought.

"Signore," said Ann with a slight bow of her head. "I am Sister Ann Stefannelli."

"Good afternoon, signora."

At first, Ann was impressed by the air and presence of this large, good-looking man. Suddenly, however, she sensed that a wild beast had just walked into the room. She looked at him with hidden trepidation, then quickly gathered her senses and came back to the situation at hand.

"Please be seated," she said.

"My name is Frank Pettinati, and I am from the Curia."

"You have come for the child I presume?" she said, feeling uncomfortable and vulnerable from the intensity of his green eyes.

"Yes, signora, I am charged with finding the boy a good home."

"You know, then, that the mother had no living relatives?"

"Yes," Frank replied. "Is it true the mother was a Jewess?"

"Yes. Is that important?"

"Well, yes, but just for the birth record."

"Of course," Ann said. She bit her lip and turned her head to the window, sighing in distress.

"I do not know how to explain this birth," she continued. "We have many unanswered questions here. I can't even begin to sort this out." She rose from her chair and walked to a window, finding it hard to endure the evil she sensed radiating from Frank.

"We are burying the mother today," she announced as she looked out over the forest.

Frank's right hand tightened into a fist as he studied the woman's back. He had expected an emotional reaction from the nuns, and he was prepared for it.

"Signora, please let me say, first of all, that Cardinal Vincenzoni sends his deepest concern for you and your sisters here. He has instructed me to render to you any help you may require. He has also asked me to tell you he is personally recommending a commendation to your already outstanding record."

Ann could not believe her ears. She was speechless. Since the baby's birth yesterday, she had been troubled by what her superiors might think. She had never heard of Cardinal Vincenzoni, but then she could hardly expect to know all of the cardinals' names. But this, this was like they were giving her a reward, which was the last thing she cared for. What she wanted were answers. She finally found her voice as she turned to him.

"I do not understand any of this."

Frank looked her up and down, noticing her body movements under the black gown. The fiery look on Ann's high-cheekboned face intrigued him. He wondered what it would be like to... For a few seconds he toyed with a scenario of lustful images.

Suppressing his overactive desires, he returned his mind to the task at hand and turned up the charm. "Please, signora, do not trouble yourself with this mystery. I can assure you Rome will make no inquiries. It is best, I think, to put this all behind you and to simply go on with your work here. What good would any further investigation be at this time? As you have said, the mother is dead."

*Well, that's easy for Mr. Fancy Suit to say,* thought Ann, her head turning once more to the window. He didn't have to live with more than fifty other women who were wondering what in God's name had happened here. Moreover, he didn't have her nagging suspicions that something was terribly wrong about this whole affair. Something strange was happening here, she felt, something that was evil and out of her control. It was dark and powerful, and it was rushing past her like a runaway horse.

However, Ann sensed her superiors had already swept the matter aside. They did not want annoying events like this one to become public. She had witnessed similar coverups before.

"I see. I guess there is no more to be said," she said, capitulating outwardly but not in her heart. "I will have the child brought to you in the foyer." She gave Frank one last glance, then faced the window. She looked out at the dark trees standing in the pure snow. Things do not always appear black and white, she said to herself. Sometimes God does not give us all the answers to our questions.

"Good day, Mr. Pettinati," she said finally.

"Thank you, signora." Frank stood to leave.

The front door of the convent creaked open and Frank stepped out with the baby in his arms, wrapped in a blanket. The boy was asleep, but just before he handed him to the nurse, the baby stared at Frank with wide-open eyes. Yellow eyes, like twin burning suns. Yes, thought Frank, he has his father's eyes.

From her window, Ann watched the black limousine move down the forest road. To her amazement, she began to feel better. She sensed that the wicked presence in the convent was gone. The dread that had surrounded her and the convent for so long was dissipating like a fog. Her blue eyes trailed after the black automobile as it disappeared into the distance. Dread had left in that car.

As the Cadillac moved down the road, Frank relaxed. The baby was up front with the nurse and sleeping again. After closing the private window between the front and the rear of the luxury car, Frank stuck a cigar in his mouth and savored its taste. At the end of the cigar, a small flame suddenly arose as if by magic — with a flicker out of thin air — and an ash began to grow.

Frank Pettinati was not his real name. He had been born Sergio Morricone in 1907, the child of a farmer and his wife in a small village in southern Italy. From early childhood, Sergio had been obsessed with the pleasures of life — money, power, and all the things you could possess with them. Now, at age 56, he was one of the wealthiest men in the world.

As a boy, he had wanted to be a chemist. In school he studied everything he could find about science. By age seventeen, he was working for one of Italy's largest chemical companies.

During World War II, the German Army occupied Italy. A German chemist, visiting his company, noticed Sergio's talents. He was especially interested in research Sergio was doing with a chemical compound called Zyklon B. The German, Hans Meyer, would become instrumental in Sergio's life. He invited the young man back to Germany to work on some special research projects, and Sergio eagerly agreed.

In Germany, Sergio lived with Hans on a large estate outside of Berlin. Meyer, it turned out, was a general in the Reichsführer der SS, Heinrich Himmler's personal staff. In addition, Sergio learned, Hans had mystical powers, achieved by practicing in the realm of the occult. In the following months, Sergio worked with Meyer in the laboratories of the Reich's main security building on the Prinz-Albrecht-Strasse, the headquarters of the SS and the Gestapo. Working together, the two men developed a new poison gas made from Cyanide, Zyklon B, and Malathion. At the same time, Hans taught Sergio about the god of his world, Satan. Hans told his protege about the power that could come to those who worshiped and served Satan. Over time, Hans introduced

Sergio to many influential and powerful men in Germany and Europe, who belonged to numerous secret societies in the occult. Before long, Sergio grew his own powers of darkness until he had surpassed even Hans.

One night, in an occult ceremony in Germany's Black Forest, the lord of darkness, the devil himself, appeared to Sergio. Satan gave Sergio the power to create FIRE, and he promised him that he would live forever and never grow old. The devil also told him, that he, Sergio, would be part of a three-point power structure that would someday rule the world. Years would pass before Sergio would understand fully the implications of the promises given to him that night.

As a prince of evil, Sergio grew to hate God's chosen people, the Jews. One day when he and Hans were testing the poison gas on a group of mice, Sergio asked, "What are you going to do with this stuff, Hans?"

"Kill Jews."

The limousine hit a bump, and Frank popped out of his past. He often wondered what some of the people he associated with now would think if they knew of his wartime activities. However, no one would ever know. He had worked long and hard to cover his tracks.

As the war ended, Meyer and many of the industrialist friends were on the list of war criminals. Before facing trial, many of them signed over their holdings to a man named Frank Pettinati, who was in fact Sergio. They had done so on Frank's promise that he would return their fortunes when they desired. Instead, Frank stole it all for himself. Through systematic deceit, intimidation, and murder, he held on to all the factories, businesses, real estate, and bank accounts. In the two decades since, he parlayed those holdings into an immense worldwide financial empire. Meanwhile, Satan taught Frank the role he would play in the plan to create the devil's kingdom on earth. Frank became so powerful, both financially and supernaturally, that he now feared no man or country.

This baby in the front of the car represented the beginning of Satan's kingdom on earth. Frank had been waiting for the start of these events for a long time. They would change the world forever, and as they happened, Frank would be part of it. The baby boy would be part of it.

His lord Satan would be the third part of it, a trinity that would someday soon set up its kingdom over the entire earth forever.

As the limousine traveled through the forest, the Messenger stood by the roadside and watched the car travel out of sight.

**There is a secret group, consisting of ten men who rule the world. They claim to be mystical guardians and divine rulers of mankind. The men call themselves the "Circle." Their secret symbol, down through the ages, has been the All-Seeing Eye of the pyramid.**

**Over the centuries, these men have consorted together, amassing wealth and power beyond that of most nations. Although the individual men in this group have come and gone through the years, their number and objectives have stayed the same throughout the centuries. They are not known by the public generally, nor do they appear on the list of the richest men in the world. They keep their identities secret along with their actual wealth.**

**They are kings, although their kingdoms have no borders. They are internationalists. They have no loyalty to any country. Their ultimate goal is a New World Order, ruled by Satan.**

**This plan, for the devil's kingdom on earth, began more than 5,000 years ago on the plains of Shinar, in what is now the country of Iraq. It started with a man named Nimrod, who built a tower. The tower of Babel was built to commemorate the first adulterous religion against the true God. From that beginning, through the centuries, a conspiracy of secret societies, coupled with the worship in the occult, have worked toward a common goal, to set up Satan's kingdom on earth.**

**The men of the Circle accept Satan as the one and only true**

god. They consent to blatant occultism and reject the absolutes of Christianity.

They claim that they work to better mankind, but in reality, they view most of humanity as useless eaters. They control governments; create wars, famines, and diseases; and direct the financial rises and crashes worldwide.

These ten men are supported by many secret societies around the world, each having his own place in the New World Order. Some of these groups are centuries old and claim to possess religious relics of great power, like the robe that Jesus wore before he was crucified, or the spear that was used to pierce his side on the cross. Others claim to have the cup that He used at the Last Supper. These items are thought to bring power to any world leader, and have caused power-hungry men like Napoleon and Hitler to seek them down through the ages.

The Circle meets several times a year in secluded locations, usually resorts or private estates. Plots are hatched, and events are orchestrated. Masks, ruses, and treachery are their tools — used for whatever they desire accomplished worldwide.

It matters not whether people believe, or disbelieve, the Circle exists. These men control the lives of everyone on earth, whether they believe or not.

The people of the world assume they control their own destinies. They think they have the freedom to choose their own leaders. It does not matter which political party they choose; the Circle controls all sides. They pick the leaders of governments, they control economies, and soon they will cause the world to forget the living God, and worship in a single worldwide unholy religion.

One of the ten men of the Circle is Frank Pettinati.

Tomorrow Frank will announce to the Circle the birth of the future "New World Leader" anticipated for centuries. His name will be Denzel Marduk.

There will be rejoicing and much anticipation within the group. They will set long-laid plans into motion. Ideas will emerge and

**events will take place in the coming decades that, later on, people will look back and say that they marked the start of the age of lost innocence. It will be the beginning of the "Terminal Generation."**

**In November of this year, 1963, the Circle made an example out of one who refused to ally with them. They spilled his blood on the streets of Dallas, Texas, in a military-textbook three-point ambush. The blame was expertly placed on an innocent patsy.**

**But those who know the truth understand its meaning: That those who resist the Circle are dealt with harshly.**

The Messenger turned his head slowly and gazed at the forest for a few moments. Piercing blue eyes searched the snow-covered ground and trees. He walked into the forest and faded from sight.

*And the ten horns, which thou sawest, are ten kings, who have received no kingdom as yet, but receive power as kings one hour with the beast.*

— Revelation 17:12

*And the King shall do according to his will; and he shall exalt himself, and magnify himself above every god, and shall speak marvelous things against the God of gods, and shall prosper till the indignation be accomplished; for that which is determined shall be done.*

— Daniel 11:36

# Chapter 2

**11:37 p.m., June 10, 1967**
Red Bluff, Oklahoma

.............................................

RAIN HAD BEEN FALLING most of the evening. The roads were wet and slick from the summer's first down pour. The horizon stretched out endlessly and was dark except for the blurry lights of town on the distant horizon.

Bright headlights of an old pickup pierced the darkness of the two-lane blacktop road that ran across the sand-covered wasteland. Inside, Ron and Linda Allen snuggled close, enjoying the drive home after dinner and a movie in town. Little John was at Grandpa

Allen's tonight, like almost every Friday night. Grandpa enjoyed baby-sitting the four-year-old, which gave the young couple a night off together, although they missed having their little son with them, even for one night.

The pickup started up a hill and as it moved near the top, angels from heaven drew close by.

Cresting the hill, the truck passed over to the Other Side, carrying Ron and Linda away, forever. The drunk driver hit them head-on at over ninety miles an hour. In the moment before the thunderous collapse of metal on metal, the instant Linda recognized the inescapable conclusion of the approaching encounter, she experienced a flash of gratitude that Ron would meet Jesus with her. And that little John would not yet. Her sweet boy, the embodiment of their love, a part of them carried into the waiting future.

Rain beat against the blacktop. Water ran in streams from the top of the hill, bubbles like large tears at their ends. Some of the streams swirled around a pair of black shoes worn by the Messenger. Lightning flashed to expose his dark form for a moment as he looked toward the top of the hill.

**Why do good people die young, while the wicked seem to prosper? It is an age-old question. Nevertheless, unlike nonbelievers, those who trust in the Lord live and face death with his promises of comfort, hope, and eternal life with God in Heaven.**

**For everyone, the choice is theirs.**

The rain continued, lightning cracked, its light flashing on the spot where the vanished Messenger had stood. Thunder walked the sky as though trying to follow in his footsteps.

**6 p.m., June 11, 1967**
Estate owned by Frank Pettinati
outside London, England

THE LUSH AND EMERALD GREEN countryside was succumbing to nightfall. A light mist coalesced into rain.

The estate lurked away from the main road, hidden by large trees. A massive structure of dark red brick with a white-colonnaded portico bisecting the front, it stood vanguard to a dark woods that haunted the mind like an army of trees waiting to snag the unwary. Old World shadows hung heavily around the mansion, like black shrouds draped over a casket.

The large main building was flanked by small servant houses, horse stables and barns. Although it had a state-of-the-art high-tech security system, along with seven armed guards, the estate and grounds appeared sedate in the softness of falling rain.

In the night shadows across the road from the estate's main gate, the Messenger stood watching. Droplets of water fell from the bleak sky and clung to his dark hat and shoulders as he stood with his hands tucked into the pockets of a long coat.

**A man named Solomon once said, 'It is wise to fear God, and to depart from evil.' The men meeting here tonight choose to deny God, and they love that which is evil. They have come to pay homage to the child, to the 'New World Order Messiah.'**

Headlights pierced the gloom and from out of the night a pair of matched Rolls Royce Silver Shadows appeared and quickly swept past the Messenger. The estate's iron gate was suddenly bathed in light as the cars waited before it. After passing through security, the two automobiles moved slowly up the curved, cobblestone driveway to the front of the house to stop in front of the main door.

Four men stepped out of the rear automobile and quickly positioned themselves in a four-point perimeter around the first Rolls Royce. Dressed in black business suits and bowler hats, they looked like businessmen found in London's financial district. Their appearance was a disguise. Highly trained security guards, each carried a custom-made Uzi machine gun in a special holster under his suit jacket.

The chauffeur stepped out of the first car and opened a back door. Three well-dressed men emerged and walk to the rear to retrieve three boxes from the trunk. Each carrying a box, they approached the front door of the estate.

The old house had a large study with walnut-paneled walls, one covered with paintings. Oils of mist-shrouded landscapes and shadowy hunting scenes. Floor to ceiling shelves covered two entire walls, filled with thousands of books. A fire roared in a stone fireplace on one wall. Four leather chairs were positioned in a semi-circle facing to the fire. A massive burled walnut table waited close by.

Frank Pettinati sat in one of the chairs wearing black dress pants with a white open-collar shirt, purple ascot, and a steel grey smoking jacket. He was reading the London Times; the front-page headlines read, "Six-Day War Over, Israel Captures Jerusalem."

A butler appeared at the door of the study.

"Your guests have arrived, sir."

"Send them in," Frank said, lifting his eyes from the paper. "And, Charles, bring Denzel down in ten minutes."

"Yes, sir."

Folding the newspaper and laying it aside, Frank stood and prepared to welcome his guests.

Moments later the three visitors entered the study.

"Gentlemen," Frank said. "So good of you to come. You may put your gifts here on the table."

The first man was visibly English in appearance, in his mid-sixties, with white hair and a neat white beard. With his ruddy complexion and black English-cut suit, he looked like a Member of Parliament.

"Sir Orville," said Frank, shaking his hand. "I am so glad you could come."

"Yes, well,we figured it was about time we met the boy."

The second man was large and heavy, his head bald. He wore a brown suit and a turtle-neck sweater. He spoke with a German accent as he shook Frank's hand.

"Yes, Frank, it is time we came."

"I agree, Herr Mannstein."

The third man was tall and distinguished. His hair was black and his appearance wholly American. He wore a three-piece, dark-blue suit and a red tie.

"It's nice to see you again, Phil," Frank said. "Come gentlemen, sit by the fire and take the chill off."

When they were seated, the Englishman asked, "How are you doing these days, Frank?"

"Wonderful, couldn't be better. Right now I am making preparations to move, with Denzel, to live in America."

"Excellent," said the American. "And how is Denzel?"

"Doing great," Frank answered. "He likes it here, and I have already started his formal education. I hired an excellent tutor. He has Denzel working at the fifth grade level."

"My word," said the German excitedly. "And he's only four, right?"

"Yes. He is quite intelligent."

The butler appeared at the door.

Next to him stood a small boy dressed in a black suit, white shirt, and black tie. His curly black hair, blue eyes, and plump face should have made him cute, but an evil stare preempted any notion of childishness. Something about him exuded the sense that he knew all.

The boy swaggered into the room.

"Denzel," Frank said, "these gentlemen have come to meet you." The three men stood as if a king had just entered the room. Each one bowed as Frank introduced them.

"This is Sir Orville, Mr. Mannstein, and Mr. Anderson."

Denzel said nothing as he eyed each man separately.

Clearing his throat to arrest the boy's attention, the Englishman spoke first. "I hear you have started schooling, Denzel."

"I like school," the boy replied in a small, but dignified voice.

"Tell us Denzel," asked Mr. Anderson, "what else do you like to do?"

Denzel pondered for a moment. "Uncle Frank gave me a horse and I ride him everyday."

"Excellent. And have you fallen off yet?"

Denzel answered with frown, "No."

All the men laughed.

Denzel did not appear amused.

"Come," the German said, "we have brought you gifts." They all moved to stand around the table.

Each man presented his offering in ceremonial fashion to Denzel. Each gift rested in a stained-oak box with a hermetically sealed glass top.

The first was a twelve-inch cube and held an old silver cup lying on a bed of red velvet.

The second box was two-by-two-feet and six inches deep. It held what appeared to be an old cloth robe, grey in color.

The third was about four feet in length and eight-by-eight inches square. It held an ancient spear. The wooden shaft was dark with age and broken in three pieces. The tip was dull silver with the carving of an eagle where it clasped the wood.

Frank stared at the 2000-year-old relics in amazement. The three boxes held the Holy Grail, the Robe of Christ, and the Spear of Destiny. They all radiated powerful energies. He had known of their existence, but never before seen them. To have them all together for the first time in history awed even him.

Denzel studied the contents of each box for a long time. The color of his eyes turned from blue to a vibrant yellow. As the three guests looked into his eyes, they felt overpowered, as if they were looking into the eyes of an ancient predator. Each feared the boy would turn his gaze on him. Each barely suppressed a sigh of relief when Denzel was escorted from the room.

"Those eyes!" exclaimed the German as the men sat around the fire sipping brandy. "Has he shown any powers yet?"

"No," Frank said. "I do not expect him to show his powers until he is grown, but I sense what is not seen."

"Do you think he understands the importance of these boxes?" asked the American.

"Napoleon, Hitler — many men through the centuries have tried to get their hands on what is in those boxes," Sir Orville said. "No one man has ever possessed all three at one time."

"I assure you, gentlemen," Frank said. "Your people have done the right thing. It is the destiny of the relics that they belong to Denzel."

The three men nodded in agreement. The German then noticed the newspaper next to Frank's chair. "The Jews are saying they are finally a nation now with the capture of Jerusalem," he said. "You know they will make it their Capital."

"Yes, and now they have the Sinai, the Gaza Strip, the West Bank, and the Golan Heights." Sir Orville said. "The Arabs have lost a lot."

"My sources tell me the deserts are littered with hundreds of thousands of army boots," the American said. "The Arabs shook them off their feet so they could run away faster. The Jews killed them like fish in a barrel. Who would have thought such a thing could happen!"

"Someday, my friends," Frank said, "the Jews will be driven from Palestine forever. They will be annihilated completely and Denzel will do it!"

"Ah, the prophet has spoken," Sir Orville said. "I only wish I could live to see it."

"Maybe you will," Frank said with an evil smile. "I know I will be there to see it. Believe me gentlemen, it will happen."

Later that evening the three men left. After saying good-byes to Frank, they stepped into the car and rode down the driveway into the darkeness. The three men were all wealthy, highly intelligent and well-connected. They had all risen to the top of the financial and academic world. They were cunning and shrewd and had achieved the highest positions in several secret societies.

The three felt they had made the right choice in giving such powerful gifts to Denzel.

In their opinion, they had acted well. They had used good judgment. They were, in their own eyes, three wise men.

*For you see your calling, brethren, how that not many wise men after the flesh, not many mighty, not many noble, are called: But God hath chosen the foolish things of the world to confound the wise.*

— 1 Corinthians 1; 26-27

# Chapter 3

**August 3, 1977**
Cordoba, Arizona

.............................................

THE TANGERINE-COLORED STONE mountains of Northern Arizona are unlike any other formations on earth. They stand out with artistic boldness in a blend of desert colors, evergreen trees, and cotton-like clouds in a vibrant blue sky. The air is crisp and smells of pine.

Cordoba, an artist's town full of tourist shops, art galleries, and expensive restaurants, is a mecca for celebrities. Many wealthy people have homes in the area.

But to people of supernatural discernment, the area has an eerie feel. It is a small stronghold of demons.

In the summer of 1967, Frank Pettinati brought Denzel to America to live on his 1,000-acre estate on the outskirts of Cordoba. He wanted the boy to grow up in the openness of the American southwest, while at the same time exposing him to the upper levels of society. Cordoba seemed the perfect place.

Frank hired Karrell Allen, a middle-aged Cherokee from Oklahoma, as foreman of the wranglers who tended the estate's large herd of Thoroughbred horses. Young Denzel had one passion, which was riding horses. Allen came highly recommended, for he practiced the old ways of raising and training the animals. The foreman lived in a small house on the estate with his grandson, fourteen-year-old John Allen.

Pettinati's villa stood pristine and gleaming in the wavering heat waves of the noonday desert sun. White stucco covered the outside walls, and large green plants grew everywhere in giant pots and planters scattered around the main house. A tall, white stucco wall enclosed ten acres of manicured lawns and gardens, horse stables and riding areas.

On top of one of the reddish, rocky hills overlooking the estate, the Messenger stood, contemplating the expanse of the magnificent estate. He wore light-colored khaki trousers and shirt. A wide brim safari hat cast a dark shadow across his eyes.

**The strategies of the ten men in the Circle are in their second decade in creating the way for the coming New World Order. The young people of the 'Terminal Generation' are beginning to fall into the pleasurable pre-occupations offered to them at every turn in their development. It is part of the plan to lower their mental defenses. Their education is controlled more and more by the government, instead of the family unit. They are kept ignorant with the poor education in the public schools, which, when they become adults, will impair their awareness of what their government is doing. They are offered easy credit and welfare to create**

**constant self-indulgence, which also creates personal data on their lives that is recorded in vast mainframe computers for rapid retrieval and manipulation.**

The Messenger turned his head toward two dust trails streaking across the desert floor coming from the east toward the estate. From this distance it was clear they were horses running at full speed. To the human eye, the riders were too far away to distinguish, but as the diamond blue eyes of the Messenger steadily focused on them, he knew who they were.

**The messiah of the coming New World Order lives here. His development is on track and being formed at this time.**

The noise of the horse's hooves pounding the ground was deafening. The chestnut and dark bay Thoroughbreds were running at top speed, their leg movements like pistons in a flesh-and-blood racing engine propelling the sleek animals across the high chaparral. Rooster tails of sand billowed behind them as if they were dragsters speeding across the salt flats.

Two teenagers appeared molded onto the horse's backs as they raced side by side across the open desert. The hair of the two boys flew back wildly. Their faces were masks of determination as they spurred their mounts on in a contest to see who could make it through the estate's main gate first.

With thundering steel-shod hooves and the powerful gale of a desert storm, the two speeding horses flew by a pile of flat rocks, disturbing a rattlesnake coiled in the noonday sun. The reptile raised its head and rattled its tail, but its antagonists had already disappeared over a crest, leaving only chunks of dirt on the ground as if they had fallen from the sky.

Down the other side of the slope the two horses raced, then broke out in a neck-and-neck charge in a straight line across the desert floor. The Thoroughbreds stretched their long legs as they ran, rocketing through scattered sagebrush and passing saguaro cactus pointing up to the blue sky like green fingers.

The gravel road that lead to the main gate of the estate was now visible to the young riders. They both kicked the sides of their speeding mounts, summoning up the last remaining power in their lathered horses for a burst of speed.

The racing horses moved in unison, their hoofs pounding onto the desert road that lead straight to the gate, now only a eighth of a mile away.

"Fifty on the bay," said Frank, standing in the courtyard near the main gate. He was wearing a white dress suit and a broad-rimmed white planter's hat that made him look like the owner of a pre-Civil War plantation in the South. Frank never seemed to age, and an air of power and authority always surrounded him like natural cologne. He chewed on an unlit cigar as he talked to Karrell Allen, who sat on a horse, his right arm lazily draped over the saddle horn.

The Indian foreman was dressed in tight Levi's and a bright red western shirt, a wildly colorful bandanna hung loose around his neck. He wore custom-made cowboy boots with Spanish spurs that looked large and dangerous. Long white hair tumbled out beneath a tall, grey Stetson and framed an intelligent face, covered with creases and richly tanned like worn leather. From the Native American's strong, handsome countenance, dark opal eyes seemed to assess all the many aspects of life.

The two men had turned from their conversation when they heard the thundering hoof beats of the approaching horses. They both watched as the horses stampeded up the road toward them. Although Karrell was not a betting man as a rule, he usually could not resist taking Frank's offer when the two boys raced, even though their wagers were always conspicuously made on the horses, not the riders.

Karrell stretched his lean body tall in the saddle and looked down the road; his eyes squinted in appraisal as he focused on the fast approaching horses.

"Fifty on the chestnut," he drawled, the words slipping out the side of his mouth past a dangling cigarette.

Denzel peered from the corner of his left eye at John on the horse next to him. They were in a dead heat, neither one able to pull even slightly ahead of the other, and now only seconds away from the gate. Unless something happened, the race would be too close to determine a winner.

Denzel suddenly swiped his horse toward John with a hard sweeping blow, trying to knock him out of the race. John saw it coming and swerved his mount to avoid contact. Denzel's act had the opposite effect than what he had anticipated. His horse hesitated unsteadily for a moment—enough for John to clear the gate first.

Now in the courtyard, the boys leaned back in their saddles and struggled to rein in the live rockets beneath them. The horses pivoted in circles, rising off their front feet in high steps, settling down amid the dust cloud that had finally managed to catch them.

Denzel aimed a hateful glare at John, then jumped off his horse before it had stopped completely. He stomped off toward the house in a huff, leaving the panting horse loose.

"Hey," John yelled. "You need to cool your horse down."

Denzel kept walking but yelled back, "Why should I? He lost didn't he?"

Frank looked at Karrell and handed him $50 from a wad of bills he'd pulled from his pocket. "I'll talk to you later," he said. He followed Denzel into the big house.

Karrell rode over to his grandson. John had grabbed the reins of Denzel's horse to walk it with his to cool them down. They continued in silence toward the stables.

As they rode, out of the corner of his eye, Grandpa Allen watched his grandson with hidden amusement and pride. The boy was tall and strong for his fourteen years. He had his mother's light skin and blue eyes, and his father's Native American facial features, framed with long black hair that hung past his shoulders. His young face resembled that of Hollywood actor Jeff Chandler, a resemblance the old man kidded him about occasionally.

"You looked real western out there riding that race," said Karrell. "Like that cowboy in the movies?" The old Indian feigned forgetfulness, squinting upward to the sky as if the answer were written in the fluffy clouds. "Ah, what's his name? Oh yeah, Chandler."

"Aw, Grandpa," John said. "Don't you start with me. I get teased enough at school over that."

"I bet the girls do not tease you," the old man replied.

John watched his grandpa, with his admiration hidden, as the old man he loved so much opened a gate on horseback. John thought his grandpa, unlike most people who looked uncomfortable in the saddle, only looked natural on a horse.

Riding into the corral, the old man and his grandson stepped off their horses and started to remove their saddles and gear.

"Why is Denzel so mean, Grandpa?" John asked. "He's always trying to cheat or do something dishonest."

"Men can be like water in a river, son, flowing in the direction of least resistance. So you have crooked rivers, and men that do not desire to live straight. If a man does not choose to live within God's commandments, he will start running crooked also."

"You believe in comparing everything in life with what God wants us to do, don't ya Grandpa?"

"It is the secret to true happiness. When your grandma was alive, we went to the church on the reservation. I learned the wisdom of the Lord then, and now I read His wise words every day."

John knew Grandpa was referring to the worn Bible on the nightstand in his bedroom. Next to it was John's favorite picture of his grandpa; sometimes he went into the room just to look at it. The photograph showed a cocky, twenty-two-year-old Karrell, dressed in jeans and a T-shirt with a pack of cigarettes rolled up in the shirtsleeve, a cigarette dangling from his mouth. His arm was around a pretty young woman in an Indian dress, who later became John's grandma. They are leaning against a '48 Ford pickup.

The picture had been taken after his grandpa returned from fighting the Japanese during World War II. John wished his grandpa talked more of those times, instead of just going to church.

Karrell Allen had lived an interesting life, and John respected him more than anyone he knew. His grandpa had taught him many things. John learned from Karrell all he knew about training horses in the old way. He had learned to do it slowly, rather than rushing through as everyone wanted to do these days. Karrell had taught him how to live off the land, about his Indian heritage, and to be respectful to the land and to people. That meant being honest and upright in everything you did. They were the values John had learned to live by.

The old Indian veteran had also instilled in John a zealous love for his country, to the point where John had already decided he wanted a career in the military. However, when his grandpa talked about God, John wasn't much interested and he had his reasons. They were set down deep inside him. Although he thought about those reasons often, he never spoke about them to anyone.

Not even his grandpa.

As they removed the tack from the horses and allowed the animals to roam free in the corral, Karrell turned to John with a smile that did not hide the concern in his eyes over the boy's silence in not pursuing their conversation.

"Well, I've got to check that mare in foal. I'll see you later, son."

"Okay, grandpa," John said as he watched the old wrangler walk out of the stable, jingling spurs trailing him out the door.

A few minutes later, Denzel ambled into the stable where John was cleaning tack. He was as tall as John but thinner. His dark curly hair was cut short in contrast to John's long, flowing black mane. His aristocratic young face always looked sly, a devious smile twitching the shapely lips. As though he knew something no one else even suspected, something he'd never condescend to tell.

"Whatcha doin', Tonto?" It was the nickname Denzel used when he wanted to taunt or cover his anger toward John.

"What's it look like, egghead?" John said, holding out the bridle he was cleaning. His taunting name for Denzel came from the fact that Denzel spent most of his time studying with the special tutor on the estate, while John went to public school.

The only education the two boys shared was a weekly practice with a fencing instructor. Fencing was part of the aristocratic education Frank wanted Denzel to master. John was a convenient adversary, usually losing to Denzel's superior ability, honed over years of practice. Denzel liked winning at everything, and it made him insanely mad whenever he lost, especially to John.

"I would have beat you today, if my horse hadn't stumbled."

"You lie," John said. "You tried to ram me."

Denzel shrugged his shoulders, realizing John knew what he had done. "Sometimes it pays to lie."

John just stared at him.

"You are such a goody two shoes," Denzel said. "You need to lighten up a little."

"Why? Because I don't lie?"

"Hey, my Uncle Frank says if you're going to go anywhere in this world, 'you gotta do what ya gotta do,'" Denzel said. "And look at him, he's like a godszillionaire!"

"Money isn't everything in life, Denzel," John said, starting to clean his saddle.

"No," Denzel said, picking up and studying the bridle John had just cleaned. His eyes narrowed. "There's also power."

John stopped working and stared at Denzel. Sometimes he got the feeling his friend was really weird, in a scary kind of way. *Heck,* John thought, starting to polish the saddle again while watching Denzel wander around the stable. Sometimes he even wondered if they were really friends. It seemed like most of the time they were at odds in some type of competition.

"Hey, John," Denzel whispered, searching around to see if anyone was in earshot. "Let's check out those abandoned gold mines tomorrow, huh?"

"No," John said, rubbing the saddle a little faster. Denzel had been after him for weeks to explore several abandoned mines they'd heard about. They were far back in the rugged mountains north of the estate. Both his grandfather and Denzel's uncle had forbidden them to go anywhere near the mine. They had warned the boys of hidden tunnels and shafts that webbed the area. It was a dangerous place.

"Go with me and I'll give you that silver bridle of mine you've been admiring. You could give it to your Grandfather for his birthday next week."

THE MORNING SUN WAS A BLINDING, white shape in the cloudless blue sky. Its streams of brightness and heat reflected off the rugged terrain of reddish rocks and the cream-colored sand.

John and Denzel, dressed in T-shirts, jeans, and cowboy hats, rode their horses single file up an incline on the side of a rocky hill. The trail was overgrown with sagebrush and hadn't been traveled in decades. Nevertheless, it had obviously been carved out of the mountain by human hands. It would certainly lead them to one of the old mines.

John turned in his saddle and looked back. Denzel grinned at him in triumph. Turning forward and adjusting his seat, John stared ahead with a deep sigh. He had not slept well last night, regretting giving into Denzel's bribe. But, now that they were out here, "in the forbidden place," he had to admit to himself he was excited.

Earlier that morning, John had made lunch and packed some extra gear and a rope just in case of trouble, while Denzel had just jumped on his horse and rode off without a care in the world.

John led them up the trail for another twenty minutes when suddenly Denzel shouted, "What's that?" He pointed toward an old iron door sunk into the rocky mountainside.

The boys rode to the spot. Quickly dismounting, Denzel ran over to the door and studied it, tugging at an old padlock on the handle. John watched with amusement as Denzel ran back to John's horse and retrieved a crowbar out of his saddlebags. He was soon feverishly prying the padlock. John had never seen him work at anything so hard in his life. The lock broke under the force of the tool. Denzel tossed it aside and began to tug on the door.

"Come on, John, help me."

John lifted a leg over his horse and slid off, landing easily on the sandy ground. Walking over to Denzel, he picked up the crowbar and wedged it between the door and the wooden frame. After several attempts, he freed the door, which released with a loud creak. The boys opened it wide, feeling cool air gush from the tunnel.

"Whoa!" Denzel exclaimed as he ran inside. The tunnel was tall enough to enter standing up, and he quickly disappeared into its looming darkness.

John walked back to his horse, retrieved a flashlight from his saddlebag, and followed Denzel into the tunnel. It was cool inside, and John pointed the light around studying the wood shoring, pieces of junk here and there and a small ore-car track down the middle of the dirt floor.

"Let's see how far back it goes," Denzel said.

"Okay," said John with some apprehension.

They followed the shaft back for about ten minutes, finding nothing of interest except bare walls, until the tunnel came to an abrupt end.

As they returned to the front entrance, John sighed in relief. He had felt a little claustrophobic in that shaft.

Denzel walked away from the mine entrance and looked around, still looking for excitement. Turning around, he noticed John's relief.

"What's the matter, Tonto, you get scared in there? Nothing is going to happen to us. Be cool."

John smiled and turned back to look at the tunnel's entrance. *Yeah, what do I have to be afraid of,* he thought.

John heard what sounded like wood cracking, and then a crash. He looked back to where Denzel had been standing. He was nowhere in sight. He had disappeared.

John ran toward the spot but stopped suddenly, feeling the

ground shift under his feet. A hole gaped about ten feet in front of him. Splintered wood planks jutted out from beneath the surface. He back-pedaled on the balls of his feet as he watched dirt flow into the hole from the edges of the pit like sand draining in an hourglass. Denzel had fallen into a deep hole that had been covered with wood and hidden by blowing sand.

"Help me! John, help me."

Buzzzzzzzzzzzzzzzzzz ... Coming from the hole.

Rattlesnakes. Lots of them, from the sound of it.

Denzel had fallen into a rattlesnake den.

John took a few hesitant steps closer to the hole, but couldn't get close enough without making more of the wood collapse. The sand had stopped flowing from the edges of the pit.

"Denzel, where are you? I can't see you."

"I'm hanging onto a wood beam on the side of what looks like a mine shaft. There's nothing above me to grab onto to climb out. John, there's dozens of rattlesnakes about fifteen feet below me, on the floor of the shaft."

"Hang on, Denzel, I'll get you out!"

He ran to his horse, led him near the hole and turned his rear to the shaft's opening. He took his rope and formed a loop at one end.

"I'm going to throw you a rope. Put the lasso around your chest under your arms, okay?"

"Hurry up," shouted Denzel. "My arms are getting tired."

"How far down are you?"

"About ten feet."

John threw the lasso into the hole. It disappeared into blackness.

"Can you reach it?"

"I can't, I can't reach it! It's out in the middle of the shaft. Oh," he cursed. "Help me, John!"

John pulled the rope out and ran for the crowbar. He scrambled back as close to the hole as he dared, the rotten wood creaking under his weight. He brushed away the sand from a plank directly over where he hoped Denzel clung. He found the end of the wood and with the crowbar pried it up slowly, the rusty nails screeching in protest. As it began to break off into the hole, he yelled, "Look out Denzel, a piece of wood is going to fall past you." *I hope*, he said to himself.

The wood cracked and broke off, disappearing into the blackness. John heard it crash to the bottom disturbing the rattlesnakes again.

Buzzzzzzzzzzzzzzzzzzz

He threw the lasso into the vacancy, closer to the edge of the shaft.

"I got it."

"Put it around you, quick!" John shouted. He pulled the rope taut and tied it around the saddlehorn. *Just like that guy in the movies*, he thought to himself, *Jeff, what's his name?* "I'm going to pull you up now. Ya ready?"

"Okay, I'm ready."

John eased his horse forward. Its eyes widened and it leaped slightly under the rope's pressure, skittish from the snakes it heard but couldn't see.

"Whoa, boy, easy, come on now. We gotta pull Denzel out of that snake pit." The horse calmed and moved forward steadily under John's guidance.

*Chandler*, remembered John. *Just like Jeff Chandler would have done it!*

Denzel's hands first appeared at the edge of the hole. He lifted himself up and over, crawled a few feet and collapsed.

John ran to him and took the rope off his sand-covered body. "You okay?" he asked, sitting next to him.

"Yes, you saved my life, John," Denzel gasped, his chest heaving. "I'd be dead, if it weren't for you." He looked at John, his eyes narrowed. "I'll never forget what you did for me, for the rest of my life."

John shrugged his shoulders and grinned, not considering it a big deal. He couldn't suspect the great impact today's events would have on his distant future.

The two boys sat together on the ground for a few minutes, steeped in the sensation of brushing past the shadow of death. From a distance, they appeared as tiny black specs against the rocky mountain hillside — two dots on the wide-open desert.

*And the beast which I saw was like a leopard and his feet were like the feet of a bear, and his mouth like the mouth of a lion; And the dragon gave him his power, and his throne, and great authority.*

— Revelation 13:2

# Chapter 4

**July 20, 1981**
Estate outside Cordoba, Arizona

.............................................

FRANK SAT ON THE BALCONY of the main house overlooking the riding arena. Yellow-tinted sun glasses transformed his green eyes to the color of aqua, and they were now focused on something deep in his mind.

A noise from the hallway brought him out of his concentration and he looked around to see Denzel, now eighteen, ramble onto the balcony. The boy had grown tall and, to Frank, seemed too thin. However, he was healthy and active — too much of the latter sometimes, Frank occasionally thought, but then that was youth.

Denzel wore tight riding pants, a polo shirt, and high-top riding boots. His short black curls glistened with perspiration, and his tanned, handsome face framed the ever-present sneer.

He flopped into a chair and poured a glass of water from a pitcher on a nearby table. *He's a ball of energy,* thought Frank. *He never sits still for a moment.*

"How was your riding today?" Frank asked.

"Good, very good. I will win the jumping finals in Scottsdale tomorrow." He toasted himself in a victory salute. "No one can beat me!"

"The day after your competition, we're going to take a little trip into the desert," Frank said.

Denzel stopped drinking. "What desert?"

"That one," Frank said, nodding to the open stretch of sand south of the ranch.

"There's nothing out that way for hundreds of miles. Why are we going out there, Uncle Frank?"

The green eyes behind the sunglasses narrowed. "You'll see when we get there."

**Four days later …**
Two hundred miles south of Cordoba in what is known as the great sand sea of Arizona

The desert stretched in all directions, an uninhabited wilderness laced with mountains, rugged and forbidding, rising out of the dry and barren earth. They soared into the cloudless blue sky with jagged points, like giant stone stalagmites. Blazing sun tortured hot sand on rough ground that had never felt the imprint of human feet. There was no wind to carry away the oppressive heat, and it stagnated on the surface like liquid gravity..

The ominous quiet was broken by the whirling blades of a helicopter, coming from the north. The aircraft suddenly burst into sight over a ridge, flying close to the ground. Of the new French design, the jet-powered copter had a sleek body painted in several hues of purple. Except for identification numbers on the tail, it had no other markings.

The pilot was Frank Pettinati, and the only passenger Denzel. The aircraft swung around twice in a circle, then landed slowly, whipping up sand in giant swirls.

After letting the jet cool for several minutes, Frank cut the engine and stepped out onto the rocky ground. He wore khaki desert fatigues, brown hiking boots, and a bush hat, with one side pinned up Australian style. Green aviator sunglasses tinted his eyes and an unlit cigar jutted from his mouth.

Denzel came around from the other side of the helicopter, dressed in sand-colored military fatigues, hiking boots, and a cap.

The rotor blades came to a stop. Twin sets of boots crunched the hot gravel as the two men walked away from the aircraft.

"I don't understand, Uncle Frank. What are we doing out here in this hell hole?"

"Well, for one thing," Frank said as he came to a halt, sliding his cigar to the other side of his mouth and looking inquisitively around the area, "you might as well get used to not calling me uncle any more."

Denzel slowly turned to Frank with a confused frown. He could not read the big man's eyes because of the dark glasses.

"I've brought you here to meet your father," Frank announced matter-of-factly, turning to Denzel with a sly grin.

"My father? You told me my parents were dead."

"Your mother is," Frank said, "but your father is very much alive."

Frank patted Denzel on the shoulder and started walking back to the helicopter. "Wait here," he said over his shoulder. "He'll be along soon. I'll come back for you in forty days."

"Forty days!" Denzel's mouth dropped open. Confused and bewildered, he looked around at the barren desert as if the answer to his questions might suddenly appear on one of the boulders. "You're just going to leave me here?" he shouted after Frank, his hands held out in disbelief.

Frank stopped and turned, an all knowing look on his tanned face. "You'll be fine, Denzel." He removed the cigar from his mouth and studied it for a second. His eyes then slowly rose to stare at Denzel. "You're about to learn who and what you really are."

Denzel stood like a statue, eyes widening in surprise.

Frank climbed into the helicopter. The rotor blades began to turn with a high-pitched whine, building quickly into a powerful whirling fan. The aircraft rose and circled around Denzel once, as the young man held his arms over his eyes to fend off the blowing sand, then flew away and out of sight. Inside the cockpit Frank, chuckled at his inner thoughts. His cigar magically lit by itself.

Denzel stared off at the horizon long after the sound of the aircraft died away. As if coming out of a trance, his eyes fluttered and his shoulders slumped. Shoving his hands into his pockets, he turned around, slowly searching the open desert.

Suddenly he froze. He gulped a lump of fear. Something moved behind him, like a heat wave from a blast furnace assaulting his back. Denzel felt as if his heart had stopped, he couldn't breathe. His eyes widened with terror. Whatever loomed behind him was real, and terrible — and huge.

**August 31, 1981**
Desert rock hills,
30 miles south of Cordoba, Arizona

DRESSED IN LEVI'S AND A T-SHIRT, John Allen sat crossed-legged on the hard ground watching his grandfather start a campfire. The eighteen-year-old was quickly becoming a man. His once tall and skinny body was filling out, and the sharply chiseled Cherokee lines in his face grew ever more prominent.

Grandpa Allen kneeled on the ground near a small pile of sticks, his white hair flowed down to his shoulders, his face old and wrinkled. He was skinny as a rail and moved slowly, but his eyes gleamed and his mind was sharp and full of wit. He was trying to light a fire with a cigarette lighter.

"Hey, grandpa, aren't Indians supposed to light a fire with a string and sticks?"

"You know, you're not so big that I can't whip you for sassing yer elders."

John nodded, figuring if the old man had a mind to, he probably could.

He knew his grandpa had been quite a whirlwind in his youth. He'd heard all the stories about fighting the Japanese in the South Pacific. He knew the meaning of every medal of Grandpa's that hung in the glass cases in their living room.

As the campfire finally began to burn, the old man sat on his haunches and lit a cigarette. John could never figure out how his grandpa could squat like that for long periods of time.

They were camping out tonight for the last time, for probably a very long time. John would leave for boot camp tomorrow.

Grandpa Allen, lost in thought, held the cigarette in his mouth until a long ash formed at its end. Smoke curled from his nose as he stared at the sunset of molted red clouds on the far desert horizon.

After a period of silence, he spoke. "Only make friends in the military with men who have honor," he seemed to say to the setting sun. "And when things get tough, those will be the ones who stick with you," he said as if recalling a long ago memory. "Don't act like you know it all, boy. Learn what they have to teach you. Then practice it with shrewdness and cunning, and you'll do well." Turning to John, he added, "Since your grandma died, you are all I've had, son. I'm going to miss you."

"I'll miss you, too," John said. "I'll keep in touch."

"Oh, I know you will, John. This ain't the end of things. It's just your beginning."

The old man turned away and watched the last vibrant rays of the sun sink behind the mountains. He did not want John to see the tears forming in his eyes.

He thought about his grandson. The boy had always seemed so solemn. The old man wondered if it was just his nature or had he failed somehow in raising him.

"I had a dream about you the other night," the old man said. "You were in a strange place, a camp surrounded by rock, like a city carved out of stone. In my dream you were leading men into battle for a righteous cause."

John looked at his grandpa, not knowing what to say. He had never heard his grandfather talk this way before.

The old man stared at the night sky and took a last drag on the cigarette before flicking it into the campfire.

"I know you haven't been interested in the things of God," he said. "And I've tried not to preach to you because the Lord knows I'm not much good at it. But a man isn't complete without that spiritual void inside him getting filled with God. He will give you purpose for your life, if you let Him."

The old man looked at John and spoke as if from experience. "When you're young, you set the course of your heart that can lead you for the rest of your life. Consider carefully which direction you choose. With God, it will always be complete. Without Him, you wander, without direction. I heard a preacher say once that heaven is a prepared place for a prepared people. Think about it, son. That is all I ask."

John had been staring at the ground. After a few moments he looked up, the fire reflecting on his impassive face.

"I'll remember what you've said, Grandpa."

He left for boot camp on the East Coast the next day.

**September 1, 1981**
Two hundred miles south
of Cordoba, Arizona,
in what is known as the great sand sea

THE RUGGED DESERT landscape hadn't changed in forty

days. The jagged mountains were still forbidding and desolate. Across the wilderness the air continued to ripple like wind-blown water, oppressively hot

But Denzel was different.

Older. And meaner. His face covered with a ragged beard, and his hair long and matted. His clothes were soiled and torn, his body dirty. He looked like a wild beast.

He sat, waiting, with his head in his hands.

Suddenly he looked up, listening intently. Under a darkened brow, eyes the color of the sun gazed out. Off in the distance, from what direction Denzel could not perceive, the whirling sound of a helicopter cut through the desert stillness.

He rose from his sitting position like a powerful monarch, tall, confident, and threatening. Motionless, he waited, eyes like twin burning suns radiating from under heavy lids.

With a burst of noise, the purple aircraft popped over a crest and circled Denzel. He could see Frank was the pilot, dressed exactly as he had been forty days ago, as if it had been only yesterday.

*Had it been only yesterday?* thought Denzel, crazed with exhaustion. *No,* clearing his head, *I'll never forget the last forty days, not ever.*

Frank had been right. Denzel had learned who he was and who his father was. When his father appeared behind him on that first day, forty days ago, he'd been shocked and terrified. Anyone would be if they suddenly discovered their father was Satan, the devil himself.

But over the next forty days, Denzel learned his father's purpose and plans for him. He learned his destiny, and the power he would have, and he became pleased with the idea. Satan taught him many things to prepare him for his future, for the day he would become ruler of the Earth.

The helicopter landed. Denzel walked over and climbed in.

Frank pulled a silver flask of whiskey from behind the seat and handed it to him.

The young man tipped the flask to his eager mouth and in

several gulps emptied it. Wiping his mouth with the back of his hand, he gazed at Frank sternly, the changed relationship visibly apparent in his eyes.

"Get me out of here."

Frank lifted the copter in a swirl of sand and wind.

**September 2, 1981**
City cemetery
Red Bluff, Oklahoma

THE BRIGHT YELLOW AND CRIMSON streaks of the sunset melted into the horizon, thrusting their last rays onto the cemetery's red earth. The cutting wind blew unopposed across open ground, and whistled longingly in a continuous chilling shrill. The moaning current stirred rapidly around a lone dark figure silhouetted against the red sky. The wind wildly whipped the tails of his long coat.

The tall form stood quite still before a gravestone bathed in the red glow of the fading sun. Tear-filled eyes read its inscription, over and over again.

JIM R. ALLEN
Dec. 4, 1943 - June 10, 1967

LINDA M. ALLEN
April 10, 1944 - June 10, 1967

*How could you possibly give your heart to a God,* the lone figure thought to himself, *when it has been shattered and broken your whole life? Never experiencing the love or the touch of a mother or the embrace of a father.*

*How can you love a God who took away your parents before you ever had the chance to know them?*

The figure decided he would not change the course of his heart. Not now, not ever.

# PART II

# The Stage Is Set

*For we wrestle not against flesh and blood, but against principalities, against powers, against the rulers of darkness of this world, against spiritual wickedness in high places.*

— Ephesians 6:12

# Chapter 5

**Present day,**
Wednesday, September 8, 11:27 a.m.
Oak Hill, California,
180 miles from Los Angeles
in the Mojave Desert

.............................................

SEEN FROM A DISTANCE, Oak Hill, California, bakes in the hot desert sun. Nestled in a valley surrounded by barren brown hills and mountains, and seemingly forgotten by the modern world of the early twenty-first century, Oak Hill sits forlorn in the vast desert, lost in time. Drivers passing on the main highway nearby wonder why anyone in his or her right mind would ever choose to live there.

Oak Hill got its name from a grove of oak trees in what is now the downtown park. The story goes that, in the 1850s a farmer from Illinois, on his way in a covered wagon to settle in Los Angeles, broke down there. Unable to journey on, and with a wagon full of oak-tree seedlings, he decided to put down roots, literally. The town began to grow from that first settler.

Oak Hill's only claim to fame came during World War II, when an army base was built there. The base, closed in military cutbacks in the early 1980s, was now abandoned.

The surrounding desert sweeps up and down in expanses of brush-covered sand and rock. Together with the jagged, barren mountains, the region appears to be the landscape of some dead planet. It is a solitary, mostly uninhabited wasteland. The temperature is always high, the air is always still. This is a mysterious place, filled with an abundance of strange, spooky stories and unexplained happenings: Strange lights in the mountains, secret military bases, UFOs in the sky.

People in Oak Hill do not talk about such matters to strangers, but unusual and unseen things happen out there.

The noonday sky is filled with the sun's bright brilliance; it is the hottest time of the day. There was no movement on the desert expanse from anything in nature.

About ten miles from Oak Hill, on a high open plateau, a figure appeared on the horizon, moving slowly through the rippling, hazy heat waves. As the image moved closer, it seemed to hover just above the ground. It finally came to a stop on a ridge overlooking the town of Oak Hill in the distant valley.

The creature's features became clear as it stood majestically in the sun's bright light. It was tall, over ten feet in height, human in form, with a wide powerful chest, and thick arms and legs that ended in dreadful looking claws.

His head resembled that of an eagle and twisted with strong jerking motions when it moved. The monster had huge, massive wings that flowed out of his back. They were now folded and drawn together, sitting high behind him. His entire body, head, and wings were covered with slick brown scales that gleamed in the noonday sun.

Around his waist hung a brown leather belt. On the left side was a gold scabbard that held a massive sword, the handle encrusted with precious stones. A wide sash hung from one shoulder across his powerful chest to his belt; it was filled with rubies, emeralds, diamonds, and strange-looking emblems.

The triangular, hooded yellow eyes of the creature looked out over the vast stretch of desert toward the town of Oak Hill, like a wild beast contemplating its kill.

No human had ever seen this abnormal spirit, even though he had lived on earth for more than 6,000 years. His name was Legion and he was high prince of this part of the world, now called America. He was one of the most powerful generals in Satan's high command of fallen angels.

Legion's eyes scanned the wide-open vistas of the desert then looked beyond it. This land, this country, was his domain. He had grown powerful, perhaps the most powerful of all of Satan's princes, because of the evil he had helped prevail in this land. It had not always been like this. There was a time, he could still painfully remember, his eagle eyes lifting upward to the sky in recollection, when he had been a mere lieutenant in a place far away two thousand years ago.

Together with the demons under his command, Legion had been summoned to the land of Israel. Jesus had come to earth and was now walking that land around the shores of Galilee, teaching the hu-mans about the most-high God.

In the place called Gerasene, Legion and his group had dwelled in a man. They had done well, causing much confusion and showing their power to the hu-mans there. Suddenly one terrible day, the Holy One, the Son of the most-high God, Jesus, stepped out of a boat near to where they were. He had caught them unaware, and they sensed his overwhelming power immediately. They cried out to Jesus to let them escape from his presence. Legion beseeched Jesus, asking him to let them leave the hu-man they had tormented and to dwell in some swine nearby.

Jesus let them go, and they went into the swine. The pigs then rushed over a cliff and killed themselves, leaving Legion and his followers with nowhere to dwell or no ability to cause any more trouble in that land.

Ever since, Legion had lived with the humiliation of Gerasene. Legion and his followers were punished. Banished to a new land, a place inhabited by none of the hu-mans they were accustomed to. In this land, this America, the new race lived close to the earth. Their values differed greatly. Greed did not eat at their hearts, nor did they strive to amass wealth or position. Legion and his demons wandered among them across wide expanses, helpless at first to gain power and control. While they whispered deceit and darkness into these new souls, they longed still for the old ways, familiar ways.

After a long time Old World hu-mans started to come and live in this land. Fleeing the oppression of other princes, they created a country based on the laws of the Most High God. Legion came to believe he was doomed forever.

Despite the difficulty of fighting against such a powerful faith in God, Legion and his followers persevered. Over the following centuries, the hu-mans became complacent. They grew rich and powerful. They began to lose sight of what had made their country good and strong. Many decided God was dead, and that they could forge their own destinies without Him.

Legion had pumped the evils of hate, crime, and promiscuity into those first cracks in the nation's faith. That led slowly to widespread violations of all of God's laws. It soon became fashionable not to worship God, much less to keep his commandments. The land was now filled with the odor of murder, pornography, child abuse, homosexuality, abortion, the love of money, and the worship of Satan through many different idols.

Many still believed in the Most High God, but they did not stand together as a whole to generate the power needed to combat

Legion's ever-growing influence on society. The few groups that did were labeled old-fashioned and scorned by the worldly as "lost in the darkness of the faith in God."

Legion had finally recovered from that dark day in Gerasene, two thousand years ago. He had made his amends. He was now powerful enough to be leader of all of Satan's princes, his uttermost desire. His plan was to rule over all of them in Satan's coming kingdom, a domain whose time on earth was quickly approaching.

Legion's reminisces were suddenly interrupted by another figure that materialized out of thin air nearby. This creature was smaller than Legion. He stood about four feet tall and was solid black. The demon had wings and a tail, and his body was thin and wiry, with vertebrae-looking bumps covering most of it. He wore a belt around his waist with a dagger on one side. The scabbard held a single red ruby, which matched the dark spirit's fiery eyes. His name was Executor, and he was second in command over the millions of demons under Legion's control.

Executor waited impatiently to speak, red-hot piercing eyes watching his lord until Legion jerked his head to him in acknowledgment. The foul spirit respectfully moved closer, a limp in his walk. Battle scars marked his loathsome body. The vile supernatural being did not have the power to change his appearance as Legion did.

Executor stopped well outside of Legion's arm length, bowing as he carefully eyed the large sword at his master's side. Many times he had seen Legion draw that sword and destroy, like lightning, anything that dared to oppose him. Over the centuries Executor had kept his position of authority, not to mention his life, by always maintaining a safe distance from that terrible sword, especially when Legion was in one of his rages.

"You summoned me, my lord," hissed Executor. When he spoke, a viper-shaped, purple tongue zipped in and out between his lips as reddish hot air curled from his nostrils. Drips of green slime drooled from his mouth in anticipation of a lustfully satisfying assignment from his sinister lord.

Legion regally turned his eagle-shaped head and looked toward the town of Oak Hill.

"I have decided to make this area our Base Command Center for the coming conflict. Start bringing in those of our number that we will require."

Executor's red eyes surveyed the empty desert, giving the small town a quick glance before he stared upward to Legion with a furrowed brow.

"My lord cannot be serious," he said. "Why make this wasteland and puny village our base? Why not use one of our strongholds of iniquity like San Francisco?"

Legion swung around like a coiled cobra, glossy yellow eyes blazing in anger, his claw on the hilt of his sword.

"Do not question my commands, Executor," he said, nostrils flaring, "or I will replace you with someone who will follow. I have my reasons, and I need not explain them to you."

A visibly shaken Executor felt a gulp of fear draining down his thin neck as he stepped backward at the outburst, knowing he had acted foolishly.

"Yes, my lord," he answered rapidly, his posture held rigid as he tried to retain some dignity to cover his fear. "At your command," he said. "I will start preparing immediately."

Legion nodded curt dismissal.

With a loud pop Executor disappeared in a wisp of gray smoke.

Legion swiveled his head to gaze at Oak Hill, his evil eyes searching out the town's single church. It was a small, white wood building on the outskirts. Legion had decided he wanted to command from a place where little power would be generated for the heavenly host. He felt sure that not much would emanate from this unpretentious building to oppose him.

His eagle eyes then traveled across town to a middle school, near an abandoned military base. He could see many hu-man children in the schoolyard. *Yes,* he thought. He would start something there right away in his plans for the future. He had a special dark angel named Og he would call in for that job. Og would be perfect for starting confusion in the town.

MISS BILLIE ANDERSON watched members of the eighth-grade class of Oak Hill middle school eating their lunch. *Well,* she reasoned at second thought, *some of them were eating.* Others were running around cutting up, or in cliques whispering terribly important things to one another.

It was Billie's day to monitor the second lunch period, a thankless, dull task. With arms crossed, she leaned against one of the school's stucco walls in the shade, wearing a white cotton dress with a print of violet flowers. Standing there in deep thought concerning her life, Billie presented the picture of a conventional eighth-grade English teacher. She knew she wasn't a raving beauty, with her mousy brown hair and average figure. Now, at the age of twenty-seven, she no longer believed that was really the reason she wasn't married, as she had sometimes thought when she was younger. The true reason was that the Lord had not brought the right man into her life yet. To Billie, these days, love was just a dream.

Her thoughts were interrupted by a commotion she caught out of the corner of her eye. She turned her head in the direction of the ruckus and with a sigh unfolded her arms and slipped away from the wall.

Donny Mathews and a boy named Chuck were in a shouting match at one of the lunch tables. *Time to settle down the natives,* she thought as she moved in their direction. As she approached the two boys, she frowned. That Donny was cursing again.

"All right," Billie said, going into drill-sergeant mode. "That's enough. Chuck, you get to your next class." She nodded her head toward the door. "Donny, I'm putting you on report for swearing. Now sit down and finish your lunch, and then you head for class."

For a moment, Billie silently studied the dark-headed Donny as he sat glowering at his lunch. She could not help but stare at the picture of a hellish looking dragon advertising a video game, silk-screened on the black T-shirt that clung to his skinny body. Shaking her head in amazement, she wondered why so many kids liked the idea of identifying with evil. She turned and walked toward her post against the wall.

Donny silently cursed as he stared at "Miss Goody-Goody Anderson" as she walked away. Great, that was his third time on report. That meant the school would call his parents, and they would have to have a special meeting with the principal.

"Well, I guess you showed her, Spell Wizard," said Donny's friend Bobby, plunking down next to him.

"Yea, why didn't you just cast a spell on her and send her to your dungeon," teased another boy, David, across the table.

"Why don't you two gnomes eat a bug!" Donny said angrily to his two closest friends. That brought on laughs from both boys, until, finally, Donny had to laugh, too.

"Hey Donny, what is it with you and Chuck," David asked. "Why is he picking a fight with you?"

"Oh well, super jock doesn't like me talking to Kathy Polk. He says she's his girl. But she told me he's full of it."

This revelation brought surprised looks from Donny's buddies. Both found it hard to believe that their friend had a speaking relationship with the most popular girl in school.

"Uh huh," Bobby said. "When do you do all of this talking with Kathy Polk?"

"Yeah," David said. "I ain't never seen you talking to her."

"Well, we've been talking between classes the last couple of days. You know, I do have a life outside of you two nerds."

Donny's friends just grinned at each other, nodding in silent assessment of their friend.

"What?" Donny asked, looking back and forth at them both.

Donny caught sight of Kathy sitting with a group of girls at a table a few aisles away. She was beautiful, blonde, and tanned, with a happy smile. He started to fantasize about how she might look dressed up like a sexy woman witch or a near-naked female warrior, like those pictured in the role-playing books of the games he and his friends enjoyed.

Kathy turned her eyes and caught him staring at her, and he quickly looked down, feeling embarrassed. If only she would come over and say hi to him in front of his buddies. Man, that would put their heads in the dirt.

As if she had heard his silent command, she said good-bye to her friends, picked up her books, and started to walk his way.

*Whoa,* thought Donny his eyes growing wide and echoing his smile. *Maybe my power of casting spells is becoming real.*

Kathy stopped next to Donny, holding her books against her chest.

"Hi, Donny," she said sweetly.

"Oh, hi," he replied in his most manly voice, feigning surprise, knowing his friends were watching.

"I wanted to invite you to a Bible study some of my friends are starting after school on Tuesdays in the cafeteria," she said. "I thought you might like to come."

Donny stared at Kathy for a moment in agony. It was impossible to visualize her dressed up sexy any more, much less believe his ears. Bible study! What kind of a geek did she think he was? That was that Jesus stuff. Everybody knew Christians were wimps. He'd never be like that. Donny's mind raced for several seconds as he thought of a quick lie.

"Oh … well … I gotta do some stuff for my dad on Tuesdays, but, ah, thanks for inviting me."

"Oh," Kathy said. "Come sometime if you can, okay. See ya." She walked away, ponytail swaying.

"Bible study!" David exclaimed. "My ol' man says that Bible stuff is for people who need a crutch in life."

"Tooooooo baaaaaaad you can't go with Kathy," Bobby said with fake remorse. "The Spell Wizard strikes out again."

"Well, at least she asked me. I didn't hear her ask either of you two gnomes."

The bell rang, and everybody scrambled to class while Donny lagged behind just enough to look cool.

An old man, dressed in Levi's, a denim shirt, and a cowboy hat stood across the street from the school and watched the children file into the building. As the last few rushed inside and the doors closed, he focused his attention on the surrounding desert and the jagged mountains on the horizon. He slowly turned his head, his face, with its many age lines, becoming visible under the shadow of the hat's brim. His piercing blue eyes scanned the horizon, filled with deep thought and concern.

The Messenger sighed heavily, shoving his hands into the pockets of his jeans, and looking down in contemplation at the pavement. He had been drawn to this town and the surrounding area, alarmed by signs of growing satanic power. Whenever the forces of evil massed in a new area on earth, the concentration of energy acted like a beacon drawing him to investigate.

The old man's head tilted upward, his brilliant blue eyes focusing not on the solid things of earth but upon wicked vibrations in the air. The dark power emanating from the desert expanded and grew, devouring the life force as a flame eats oxygen, signaling the approach of calamity. Something of enormous, disastrous proportion was coming

The Messenger glanced one final time at the school and the little town around it. Resigned, he turned and walked down the sidewalk, eyes searching the horizon.

*Bless the Lord, ye his angels, that excel in strength, that do his commandments, hearkening unto the voice of his word.*

— Psalms 103:20

# Chapter 6

GARRETT AND CALEB WERE IN HEAVEN. This was not really unusual, since they were angels and members of the heavenly host. However, since they worked on earth most of the time, it was nice to be in heaven for a while. They had just returned from finishing their most recent assignment, helping an American church in Tennessee that had been fighting persecution from a neighboring whiskey distillery.

Garrett, the more experienced of the two, was tall, with blond hair and soft blue eyes. Caleb, who had transferred over a couple thousand years ago from child-care, had dark hair and deep brown eyes.

Their specialty was churches. Although each Christian church had its own guardian angel to watch over it, Garrett and Caleb were sent in when a church needed extra help.

The two angels made a good team, because, besides the attributes of strength and wisdom, the Lord had made them both with a touch of good humor included in their nature.

Their boss was the archangel Gabriel, one of the most powerful angels in all of heaven. His victories and accomplishments were legendary among all the angels. For instance, he defeated the princes of Persia and Greece, several of Satan's strongest generals. Gabriel had been the envoy to Daniel in the Old Testament and also told Mary about her part in the birth of the Son of God.

Although Garrett and Caleb were very happy to be on "Team Gabriel," as they called it, they had often wondered if their prudent boss thought them not conservative enough at times.

As Garrett and Caleb reported to headquarters, they noticed a lot of activity, much more than normal. Every angel was moving around quickly with heightened determination.

"I wonder what's up?" asked Caleb.

"I'm sure we'll find out soon enough," said Garrett as they walked into their department. Once inside they saw Gabriel talking to another angel outside of his office.

" … And tell Michael I need to talk to him when he has a minute," Gabriel said, dismissing the angel. He noticed Garrett and Caleb and motioned them into his office.

"Well, I see you two are back." Gabriel sat behind his desk and motioned the two angels to chairs in front of him.

"Say, boss — what's going on around here?" Caleb asked.

"The Lord God has instructed me to prepare. It is the season for His removal of the saved ones on earth," the archangel announced slowly and deliberately. "And the enemy knows it."

His words hung in the air as Caleb and Garrett looked at each other. Gabriel then picked up several papers on his desk and studied them briefly. "I have a report here about your last assignment," he said.

Garrett and Caleb looked at each other out of the corner of their eyes. Had they done something to displease Gabriel? they both wondered.

When they had left earth, the people's faith in the church to which they had been assigned had grown considerably compared to when they had first arrived. That had been in the face of strong persecution from a whiskey distillery.

"It seems," said Gabriel in a stern tone, "that the distillery across the street from the church burned down last night."

"It did?" Caleb exclaimed. "That's great!" he said. He grinned, but his smile soon faded under the archangel's stare. "Do you think we did it?" he said, his eyes wide and looking at Garrett in alarm and then back at Gabriel. "Because we didn't."

Which was true. Everyone knows an angel cannot lie.

"No," Gabriel answered. "I know you did not do it. I just wanted you to know, because you had been working on the case. I believe the Christians there will not have any more trouble with the atheist owners of the distillery," Gabriel said, reading the report in his hand. "I do find it interesting that the owners have filled out an insurance claim stating the cause of the fire to be an act of God."

Garrett and Caleb both grinned at that because, well … it was funny. Gabriel could have thought it funny, too, they reasoned, but he did not show it. He just lifted one eyebrow at them in silence.

"Do either of you have anything else to report?"

"Yes, sir," announced Caleb. "Have you heard that the military in Israel has created a new missile that is more accurate and can travel farther than any other missile on earth. Did you know that they named it 'Gabriel'!"

Gabriel looked at Caleb for a moment in silent contemplation. "I meant about your last assignment," he said.

"Oh … well, no, sir," said Caleb.

Garrett shook his head, "No, sir."

Gabriel sat back and folded his arms as he studied the two angels. More than once he'd questioned their unconventional ways and peculiar mannerisms. Yet they always managed to succeed at whatever he asked of them. He had to admit they made a good team. Should he entrust this new assignment to them?

Since his return from Oak Hill, the situation there had been on his mind constantly. Adversity could so quickly become tragedy where the forces of evil gathered. He needed a team he could trust, one to adapt quickly should the situation escalate. It was of the utmost importance.

Yes, he would send Garrett and Caleb. They would be best for the task.

Gabriel leaned forward. "There is an unusual enemy buildup around a town in California called Oak Hill," he said. "I want you two to go down there and report to me everything you can find out. I will reassign the angel working there now. You will take over the watch on the town's only church and its minister, a Rev. Will Thompson.

"I also want you to stay near a Major John Allen, who will arrive shortly. Report directly to me, Garrett. If you need more help, I will send it."

"We will leave right away, sir," Garrett said.

As they turned to leave, Gabriel said, "I have a bad feeling about this buildup of evil in Oak Hill, right there, right now. If you run into strong opposition, be very careful."

The two angels saw a concern in their boss they had never seen before.

"Yes, sir, we will," said Garrett.

The two left heaven.

*I considered the horns, and, behold, there came up among them another little horn, before which there were three of the first horns plucked up by the roots; and, behold, in this horn were eyes like the eyes of a man, and a mouth speaking great things.*

— Daniel 7; 8

# Chapter 7

**Thursday, November 9**
Estate of German industrialist
Enrich Bremner
Ardennes Forest, West Germany

........................................

THE LARGE TRACT OF LAND was thick with trees, overwhelming the buildings on the estate. A blustery cold wind was blowing through the entwined branches of the dark trees, a prelude to the coming winter.

The Messenger stood silently in the forest, wearing his long coat and wide-brimmed hat. His brilliant blue eyes were fixed on the main house.

The men of the Circle were all present, including Denzel Marduk, that seed of Lucifer, and his adjunct, Frank Pettinati.

For many years now Frank had been preparing Denzel. He had taught the young man all about his business ventures and had virtually turned over the management of his worldwide empire to Denzel. Now, they were also setting the stage for Denzel to become the youngest Secretary General of the United Nations. It would be accomplished easily with the help and influence of the Circle.

Denzel had also grown in supernatural powers, evil abilities placed in him by his father. He had a wicked force and energy unlike any man on earth had ever possessed. Over the years, the men of the Circle had watched Denzel. They had always known that someday he would become one of them.

The Messenger's eyes narrowed as if seeing inside the mansion.

**The men of the Circle do not realize it quite yet, but that someday is now.**

The ten men had gathered for their semi-annual meeting at the estate owned by Bremer. Over several days, the members each arrived with their entourages. They socialized informally, and used the many facilities of the vast estate.

Today the CIRCLE met privately for their first joint meeting. In a large room with a long dining table, five men sat on one side of the table, five on the other.

The meeting had just begun when a pair of large double doors flew open and Denzel entered the room unannounced. Dressed in a black suit and red tie, he looked and acted jovial. Sitting with the men, Frank watched him swagger up to the head of the table. Anyone who did not know Denzel would have thought he was drunk. Frank knew differently and was not surprised to see Denzel acting jovial, for the meaning of the word *jovial* came from an astrological notion of the planet Jupiter's influence on people. Frank knew that

Jupiter was, at present, in its closest point to the earth in their orbits around the sun. From a satanic view, the planets' close proximity always had an influence on Denzel. As he watched Denzel closely, Frank also knew that when the volatile young man was feeling this way, he could be explosive in rage and dangerously wicked.

Erich, the German host, stood up and shouted, "What is the meaning of this? You know this meeting is private. Marduk, what is it we can do for you?"

"It's not what you can do for me," Denzel said. He focused his eyes intently on a pencil lying toward the middle of the table, which suddenly started skimming by itself down the glossy wood surface and into his hand. "What it *is*," he said, as he ground the pencil into the table's surface and leaned on it, glaring at each man individually, "is what *I* can do for *you*, gentlemen.

"I believe it is time you had a leader." He paused dramatically. "And *I* am that leader."

"Get out," the German said. "No one dares to leads us. The Circle through the centuries has never had anyone lead it." Erich looked around at the other men, gathering support from some of their angry nods. Then he glared at Denzel. "You think yourself great enough to propose such a thing to us, much less expect to lead us? You forget, Marduk, to whom you speak. We neither need nor want a leader. You are treading on thin ice by challenging us in this manner. And let me add, you do not decide if you ever become one of us," Erich said. "We decide! Do not come in here and try to impress us with your cheap parlor tricks." His German accent lay thick on his words as his anger boiled. "You do not have the political power or money to be the equal of the least of us," shouted Erich. His eyes burned like hot coals as he stared at Denzel.

Denzel stood quietly for an uncomfortably long pause, studying each man around the table. His eyes then locked on the enraged German. "You are wrong, my dear Erich," Denzel said in a deep and dangerous tone. "For, you see, Mr. Vincenzoni"—Denzel's eyes quickly shot over to the man named—"and Mr. Giuffre"—he quickly turned and stared at that man—"are both retiring, and they have no families. So, they have already signed most of their holdings"—Denzel placed his hand on his chest in mock astonishment—"to me."

Everyone at the table turned in startled disbelief at the two men just named. To their utter astonishment both men bowed their heads in silent acknowledgment of Denzel's claim. The other men around the table sat motionless, a dreadful realization beginning to engulf these exceedingly powerful men.

Then Frank spoke, signaling the *coup de grace*, "And I have turned over all of my resources to Denzel as well."

The remaining men appeared stunned.

"So you see," Denzel said, impervious to Erich's hateful stare. "I am already in control of three of you."

"What kind of an ambush is this?" said Erich, growling like a German Shepherd attack dog. "You can't just waltz in here and think you can take control of all of us."

Marduk turned to him, his body moving like a predatory killing machine, his insane anger fueling a glowing neon yellow in his eyes. Denzel's right arm suddenly shot out, the hand outstretched like a weapon at Erich. An explosion of searing, electrical current echoed through the room as red bolts of lightning shot out of his fingertips. Fire engulfed the German, extending all around him like a visible aura. Erich stood there, his body vibrating with pain, his mouth open in a silent scream of agony.

Frank sat close to where Denzel stood, and after a moment he looked up at him and spoke softly.

"Denzel ..."

The yellow eyes narrowed in hate.

"Denzel ..."

The lightning bolts ceased. Erich slumped into his chair unconscious, his suit smoldering and giving off wisps of smoke.

The fires of hate continued to lick at Denzel. He stood transfixed in anger for several moments, a deranged expression on his face as he looked around the table at the frightened men staring back at him.

Inhaling deeply, as if recovering from a long race, Denzel began to compose himself. He shot the cuffs of his shirt sleeves to the precise half-inch below the jacket, adjusted the knot of his crimson silk tie to lie exactly between the points of the collar, gave a slight tug to the hem of his jacket so it hung correctly on his lithe body. A sneer of arrogance informing his handsome face, he surveyed first Erich, slumped like a rag doll in his chair, then each of the others stunned into silence.

"Now," Denzel said, "does anybody else object to my becoming your leader."

No one spoke.

THAT EVENING, YELLOW LIGHT streamed from the windows of the main house and into the black night. The sounds of music and people laughing drifted out of the mansion.

The window to Denzel's third-floor suite was dark. Inside the spacious rooms eerie shadows hung across the walls. The main sitting room was quiet and gloomy.

Denzel sat in a leather chair facing the window, light from the full moon slanting across the floor around him. He had shed his suit jacket and tie, and his shirt was open at the collar. His hair was ruffled and he was slouched in the chair drinking whiskey from a crystal decanter. His brow arched hatefully; his eyes narrowed in thought.

A knock sounded at the door.

"Come in!" he said.

A tuxedo-clad Frank walked into the room. He looked around in the darkness until he spotted the figure slouched in the chair. "Denzel," he said, "people at the party are asking for you."

"I don't give a … "

"You should at least make an appearance," Frank suggested. "It's cold in here," he said as his gaze stopped at the wood in the fireplace. It suddenly burst into flames.

Denzel jumped up from his chair. "I don't do everything you think I should, Frank. And don't forget who gave you that power," he said, pointing to the blaze in the fireplace. With a loud whoosh, the flames went out completely.

Frank gazed into Denzel's yellow eyes and deduced that Denzel was upset for his restraining him earlier with Erich. He also realized he was not just talking to Denzel right now. Satan dwelled in the handsome young man at the moment — an occurrence that manifested more and more frequently of late.

Frank had not achieved his position in life without an incredibly intelligent mind. He skillfully shifted his thinking to speak not only to Denzel, but also to the one inside him at this moment.

"There is no reason for us to spar," the big man said. He shoved his hands into his pockets and tilted his head. "Tell me, what is wrong?" he asked, already knowing the answer.

"I should have killed that German pig today" The deep sounds that came out of his mouth were not Denzel's. "How dare he try to stand against me." The possessed young man stalked around the room in a rage.

Frank listened, burying his chin into his neck as he watched through the tops of his eyes as Denzel ranted and raved. It was part of Frank's job to handle the human aspects of their plan, and he reminded the one inside Denzel of that now.

"Denzel cannot come across like some gangster," he began. "The world is looking for a messiah, not a Hitler. When he has gained their trust as a 'man of peace,' when they believe he is unlike any leader who has ever been, then they will give you the world on a silver platter. Then you can crush any opposition to your kingdom, forcefully and decisively. For now, however, Denzel must be a man of peace, in every way. It would have accomplished nothing to kill Erich," Frank assured. "You made your point."

Denzel stopped pacing and looked out the window. After a few moments, with a whoop, the fire resumed in the fireplace. Denzel's anger was now only a simmer, but all the haughtiness remained.

"You are right, my friend," he said, his body visibly relaxing.

Frank stepped to the wet bar and poured two drinks. He walked over and gave one to Denzel. As he took the glass, Denzel gave Frank an evil smirk."I will go down to the party with you."

The light of the fire glowed against the silhouetted figures of the two men as they stood for a moment in silence in the dark room and sipped their drinks. Frank looked at Denzel for a moment in contemplation, as if deciding on something in his mind.

"Before we go," Frank said, "I've been saving a gift for you. I think it's time." He pulled a paper from inside his suit coat and handed it to Denzel.

It was a press release, dated October 20, 1989.

**Space Craft Galileo on Its Way to Jupiter**

*Successful Launch from Shuttle Atlantis*

"You're giving me a space ship?"

Frank chuckled and sat down in the leather chair, his green eyes full of deviltry. "No. Let me give a little background first. The spacecraft Galileo is actually a probe to the planet Jupiter — your planet, Marduk," Frank said with emphasis, as he searched deep into Denzel's yellow eyes, then past those twin burning suns to the entity behind them. "The most brilliant light of all the planets."

"Yes," Denzel said, his eyes growing narrow, the internal deep voice inside of him intersecting. "Many men through the ages have worshiped me through that light."

"Yes, exactly," Frank agreed. "Well," he continued, "the probe arrived at Jupiter in 1995, and it has been in orbit around it or its moons ever since.

"In September 2003, it was reported that Galileo was directed into the planet and destroyed, although no proof was ever shown that it actually happened. In truth, it was just a cover story to conceal a future purpose. As far as most anyone knows, Galileo is gone, destroyed, but in fact it is still in orbit around Jupiter, waiting to complete a secret mission.

"The spacecraft needed about five pounds of plutonium to power it for almost eternity, and that is what the public was told it contained. But, the fact is, it has almost fifty pounds on board," Frank revealed, eyeing Denzel with a conspiratory smirk.

Denzel studied him, pausing before he said, "Why do I get the feeling you had something to do with that?"

Frank shaped the fingers of his hands into a pyramid and smiled with amusement, not offering the obvious answer. "Well, the point is," he resumed, "certain people under my control at NASA can secretly make Galileo do anything I want for as long a period as I wish—as long as the money to keep up communications with it keeps these people hiding the secret," Frank said, smiling, his green eyes speaking volumes to the fact that clearly the funding was coming from him.

"Anyhow," continued Frank, talking as if he were relaying a parable, "Galileo can circle Jupiter for years and years. Or at some time I may decide to cause it to slam into the planet Jupiter, which really isn't a planet in the real sense of the word. It isn't a solid mass. Jupiter is made up mostly of a mixture of hydrogen and nitrogen gasses. It is actually a baby star."

"And what would happen if Galileo crashes into Jupiter?"

"The pressure it will encounter will cause a reaction similar to that of an atomic bomb," Frank said, his words tumbling out.

"It will cause the birth of a star, a brilliant light that will be seen from earth both day and night. It will be like the mythical star of Bethlehem."

Denzel's eyes grew wide.

"People on earth will interpret it as a sign of religious significance! To many it will herald the coming of the messiah," Frank said.

Denzel pointed a finger at Frank. "You will tell them when to explode the probe?"

"Yes," nodded Frank. "When the time is right. When you are ready to take control of the world."

"Yes," repeated Denzel as he looked away and stared into the fire, his countenance taking on a truly devilish grin. "When the time is right."

"By the way," Frank said as he got up and started for the door. "The people at NASA have already named the new star." He turned back and grinned, his green eyes burning with mischief. Frank looked deep into Denzel's yellow eyes. "They are going to call it Lucifer."

# Chapter 8

**10:37 a.m., Friday, September 10**
U.S. Army base,
Fort Chapin, California

THE SPRAWLING MILITARY COMPLEX, stretching over a flat openness covering over 1,000 square miles of the Mojave Desert, was considered the Army's top national training center. Military vehicles swarmed back and forth on its many roads in columns like drab green worker ants, and thousands of military troops could be seen moving around the desert garrison.

Major John Allen, U.S. Army Intelligence, stood at his office window and watched as a group of soldiers marched on a nearby parade ground.

The skinny Indian boy of the Arizona desert had grown into a man. More than six feet tall, the body under his uniform was muscled and toned through military training. John looked and acted every bit Army. His once-long black hair was now cut military short, and the handsome face resembled, to many, a Hollywood actor of the 50's. The chiseled features seemed almost threatening, characteristic of the warriors of his forefathers. His eyes, always brimming with intent, were the color of the clear sky. His mouth was almost always firm and straight with determination but could break into a smile capable of disarming friend or foe.

As John stood by the window, his arms crossed, he watched the men drilling. The activity reminded him of when he first enlisted at the age of eighteen and the early days of his training. *It seems so long ago,* he mused, his gaze turning inward from the marching men to somewhere else inside his mind.

A lot had happened since he joined the military. He rose through the ranks, with many action stops along the way — Grenada, Panama, the Gulf War, Bosnia, Iraq. He had been involved in all of them. All he had ever wanted in life was here in the Army. But now, at the height of his career, and on the fast track forward in his chosen career, he felt something missing.

"What's your trouble?" he chided himself. He had everything he ever wanted in the military. Was he feeling a loss because he had no family? His grandfather had died ten years ago, the only relative he had ever known. "Is this inner void the lack of a wife and family?" he taunted himself. He had dated women through the years, of course, but the Army seemed to always thwart any lasting relationship.

"Is that your trouble?" he wondered, his mind wandering.

No, he decided, looking off in to the distant skyline. It wasn't any of those things.

What was this mysterious emptiness that was bothering him?

What was missing in his life?

"Major," came the voice of his secretary over the intercom on his desk, "Sergeant Donavin is here to see you. He says he knows you."

*Donavin, Donavin?* John's eyes slipped from the horizon and flipped through the card file in his brain. *Oh shoot, how could I have forgotten Sam Donavin, my driver in Saudi Arabia during the first Gulf war?* They had become close friends during that time, but had been out of touch since. *What's he doing here at Fort Chapin?* John wondered as he pushed the intercom's button.

"Thank you, Judy. Please send him in."

The door opened and Sam Donavin walked in. He was a burly man with dark curly hair, rugged face, and a puffy body that seemed to stretch his Sergeant's uniform to the limit.

The Sergeant smiled broadly when he saw John and they shook hands. "How ya doing, Major?" he bellowed.

"Just fine, Sam." John said, remembering just how robust his old friend could be. "You old war dog, where've you been keeping yourself?"

"Oh, here and there," Sam said as he sat down in the chair John offered him. "You know the Army, Major."

"Yes, I know," John said, recalling his earlier thoughts.

"So what brings you to Fort Chapin?"

"Oh, just passin' through — you know, just passin' through." The Sergeant's jolly demeanor faded to a sudden serious look. "I've been assigned to a special transport group working three states here."

"Transport?" John asked, his stern eyes narrowing. "You mean, trucks?"

"Yes, sir," Sam said, his face carrying a hint of secretiveness. "We've been delivering a lot of material to bases all over California, Nevada, and Arizona."

The sixth sense that John had developed as an intelligence officer suddenly set off alarm bells. A frown accentuated his rugged features. He was not aware of any major logistics operations at this time to any bases in the area. As he studied Sam, whose eyes darted around the room, he knew his old friend had not just stopped by to see him for old time's sake.

Something was wrong.

"You didn't just come to see me," John said, eyeing his friend.

Sam returned his look with hope-filled eyes. "No, sir, I didn't." His words ended with his mouth tightly compressed.

"Well, Sergeant," John asked, "what's up?"

Sam looked down at the floor for a moment and then back up. John could tell he was wrestling with a difficult decision.

"You remember in Saudi Arabia, sir," he spat out, "how they wanted us to wear those U.N. patches, and many of us didn't like it?"

"Yes," John said. He had seen the same thing in Bosnia. Many U.S. servicemen viewed the U.N. peacekeeping idea as foreign to their understanding of belonging to and fighting for the U.S. military. It was an opinion he personally felt very strongly about. He had refused ever to wear the U.N. ensignia, to the consternation of some of his superiors.

"Well," Sam continued, looking around as if someone might hear him. "After all the conversations we had in Saudi Arabia, I know how you feel about these 'New World Order' folks in regards to these United States of America."

John sat back in his chair, remembering the many sleepless nights in the Arabian Desert, when he and Sam had talked about the U.N. and its objectives.

"Go on," John said, feeling he was about to hear something he was not going to like. He hated the idea of the U.S. military working as mercenaries for the United Nations.

Sam leaned closer to John's desk. "I've been seeing strange things on this assignment. Things I do not understand and I don't like, and I don't think most Americans would approve of either," he added dramatically. "Maybe you know all about it, Major." He leaned back. "Maybe I shouldn't be blabbing about it and just mind my own business."

John could see his old friend was becoming nervous, and having second thoughts in talking about what was bothering him.

"Sam, tell me what you've seen," John said. "I think you need to get it off your chest. If I don't know about it, I have the feeling I would want to. You know I wouldn't tell anyone where I heard it, if that's what you're worried about."

Sam looked relieved and resumed, this time more at ease.

"There are lots of old bases out there in the desert, as you know Major, most of them built during World War II. Many are closed and have been vacant for decades."

Sam leaned closer once again and spoke softly. "We've been delivering tons of supplies to many of those camps for six months now. There are hundreds of thousands of Russian troops out there, Major. Russians — with U.N. markings!"

John felt a knot tighten in his chest. He wasn't aware of any major buildup of foreign troops in the United States, and yet he did not doubt what Sam was telling him.

"You've seen these troops yourself, Sam?" he asked.

"Oh yeah. They keep most of them hidden, but we go right into their bivouacs in dozens of camps in California, Nevada, and Arizona."

"And I presume they're armed?"

Sam let out a long soft whistle. "You bet, sir. They're up to division strength. Even tanks."

"Tanks? You mean Russian tanks?"

"Yes. I've even seen several T-72s with missiles."

John was stunned. The United States had been invaded without anyone firing a single shot. He glanced out the window at the blue sky he'd been looking at only minutes before. The world was suddenly a diabolically different place under that same sky. The surrounding desert held a terrible secret threatening his country. This number of foreign troops on United States soil, U.N. or not, was a military invasion. The situation — no, conspiracy — was apparently a tightly-held secret, probably organized by that inner power circle within the government he'd only glimpsed now and then through his intelligence work. It was the real power that ran the country, hidden deeper than any agency like the FBI or CIA, or even the President. John was certain the presence of Russian soldiers in the United States was something few people were aware of.

"What's the nearest base where you've seen these troops?"

The sergeant pondered for a moment. "Probably Oak Hill. It's an old Army base that's been closed since the early 80s. It's up Highway 96, about 220 miles from here."

"Has anyone told you to keep quiet about the Russians, Sam?"

"No. The few people I know who are involved seem to act like it's all normal. You didn't know about it, though. Am I right?"

"No, I did not," John said. "But believe me, I'm going to find out about it." The Cherokee lines in his face projected prominently — a sign of oncoming wrath to those who knew him well.

Sam nodded. "Major, I wouldn't care to be in those Russian's shoes, when you count coup on those boys."

Later, after Sam had left, John sat at his desk and stared out the window. *Why are so many foreign troops being stationed here in the U.S.?* he wondered.

Something was happening. He needed to investigate it, not only for the security of his country, but also for his own sake. There was no use going to his superiors about it just yet, he reasoned. They would just deny it, if they knew about it, try to throw him off track. He needed positive, substantial proof.

John decided he'd run up to Oak Hill over the weekend. His position allowed him considerable autonomy. He could do some quick investigating without his superiors noticing. But that was not what worried him as he got up and walked over to the window, looking toward the desert's far horizon. What suddenly tormented his heart and made him pause was — what he was going to do once he found what he was searching for?

*And I saw one of his heads as though it were wounded to death; and his deadly wound was healed, and all the world wondered after the beast.*

— Revelation 13:3

# Chapter 9

**9:34 a.m., Saturday, September 11**
United Nations Building, New York City

.........................................

THE COURTYARD IN front of the tall building was a mass of people rushing to and fro in every direction. No one paid any attention to the old man, dressed in a long dark coat and black Fedora, who stood near the front entrance directing his blue eyes upward in deep contemplation of the glass skyscraper.

Like a stranger in a foreign land, the Messenger slowly looked around the surrounding area and surveyed the harried people rushing by him. His eyes sought the building's front entrance. After careful consideration, he proceeded through the main doors and stopped inside the large foyer to continue observing.

**When you walk around the United Nations building, there is a feeling that you are in a different world. It is a strange sensation if you are a citizen of a country that you love. It is an eerie fear, for the future of your own country, and for the world.**

**The Ambassadors in this building who represent the many countries of this earth have a goal, a common standard in mind. The end, of which, they are striving to attain — a 'one-world government' — is already very real to them. They are working at, and succeeding in, making it a reality outside these glass walls.**

**Today the nation members of the General Assembly are celebrating the induction of the new Secretary General of the UN. He is a man relatively unknown to the world, but the perfect man to understand the objectives of this organization.**

**His name is Marduk, Denzel Marduk. He will soon not only lead the nations of the world into a new age of one-world government, but he will also demand to be their king.**

The Messenger walked down a hallway, becoming one of the many people in the crowd.

FRANK PETTINATI SAT AT HIS DESK in his new office, adjoining Denzel's office in the United Nations building. It was almost time to join Denzel for his first press conference as the new Secretary General of the United Nations.

Frank clicked on his e-mail on the computer at his side to see if he had any important messages before he left. Only one appeared, sender unknown — which was unusual, thought Frank, especially when only a few close business associates knew his e-mail address. Frank clicked on the message; the words seemed to scream off the screen at him.

"HELLO SERGIO" was all it read.

Frank stared at the words in surreal unbelief. His blood ran cold. No one knew him by that name; it had been buried six decades ago. Who could possibly be e-mailing him as Sergio? And if they knew his real name, what else did they know about his past?

"H E L L O  S E R G I O"

Frank could not tear his blazing green eyes from the screen; he felt like he was having a bad dream. For the first time in many decades, the big man felt a little unnerved. This could cause a problem. He did not like surprises, and he hated the possibility of being out of control on something this important, especially now with Denzel just becoming Secretary of the U.N.

"H E L L O  S E R G I O"

The name Sergio brought back a flood of long-suppressed memories of his Nazi past. Foremost, he was the father of the formula of the poison gas used in the gas chambers of such infamous places as Auschwitz and Triblinka. What's more, for the last years of the war he had been an eager participant in the use of his insidious new gas in the mass killings in the death camps. He had never tired of watching Jews die horribly from his invention in the specially constructed chambers, and then watching the disposal of their bodies in the huge ovens. Someday he would help Denzel eradicate the Jews from the face of the earth, once and for all, completing the job he had started so long ago.

But for now, his wartime past was something Frank could not allow to become international news. Too many fools would consider his actions reprehensible, even terrible. Worse, his exposure could rebound on Denzel, possibly reduce his effectiveness in the weeks ahead. That threat, more than any personal risk to himself, caused anger to erupt through his momentary fear.

Frank's stormy green eyes studied the words on the screen. Who sent them? What was their reason for threatening to expose him at this moment and time? *It's most assuredly blackmail,* he decided. Of course, that was a ploy he had engaged in a hundred times, so at least he could identify with the notion. Yes, he had been skilled in extortion far too long not to recognize it when he saw it.

Frank let out a long audible breath that ended with a savage hiss. Well, whoever it was would show his hand for the payoff, he surmised, feeling in control of things once again. He would learn who his electronic tormentor was.

And then … he would kill him.

*As simple as that,* Frank reasoned. He erased the message, dismissing the aggravation for now. He stood and walked out of the office to join Denzel.

There is a pyramid-shaped meditation chamber in the U.N. building. Centered in the room is a large black stone called "the altar." Marduk stood, eyes closed as if in a trance, before the ominous stone as Frank slipped in quietly through the back door and stopped to watch him. It had taken several years of hard work for Denzel to be named Secretary General. Nevertheless, with the power and influence of The Circle, Marduk had finally achieved this important step in Satan's plan to rule the earth.

Frank felt proud of Denzel. He had raised and watched the boy grow into a mature man and now a powerful leader. Marduk was handsome, intelligent, cunning, and, most of all, empowered by his father Satan. He was ready to step into his predetermined ascension to rule the world, a destiny in which Frank would play an integral part. Everything was going as planned.

Denzel opened his eyes and turned toward Frank. His presence radiated a malignant force that engulfed the atmosphere around him infusing it with wanton evil. The physical manifestation bombarded even Frank's hardened senses, making him pause in awe.

"I am ready to go to the press conference," Denzel said.

Wearing a cunning grin on his face, Frank respectfully opened the door to the main hallway. They both walked out and started toward the pressroom. Two U.N. armed guards, dressed in black suits, fell in step on either side of Marduk. Each bodyguard had an ear microphone, and was in continuous communication with the building security network.

Ann Stefannelli watched the pair come down the hallway toward her. The retired mother superior had aged gracefully, and her blue eyes still gleamed intently. She could not help but notice that Mr. Pettinati seemed not to have grown any older since that day many years ago when he had come to get that baby boy.

That mysterious baby boy.

The unexplained events of that birth had haunted her all these years. It had become an obsession that preoccupied her later life. She had tried to forget about that day, so many years ago, and the impossible circumstances surrounding it. Her mind had told her to forget it, but her heart had always seemed to know the truth. A truth that, at first, had been too horrible even to contemplate. It had taken her years finally to let her mind encompass it.

She knew who Marduk was.

Moreover, it had happened in her convent, under her authority. It was true she had not seen it coming nor understood the diabolical events as they happened. But if only ... if only ... she had done something at the time — anything — to forestall the outcome. She had been tricked like a naïve schoolgirl; they had used her and then they had vanished for years. She had prayed to the Lord for forgiveness, and she knew He had forgiven her. But she kept living year after year with the knowledge of who that baby was.

Yes, she knew who he was, and what he soon would do. She had read her Bible, especially the passages in Daniel and Revelation that told about him, described him, and foretold his terrible mission. That was how she had come to understand the only way that baby could have been conceived. The only possible father he could have had. Satan would have had the supernatural power to make Mary Giuffre pregnant. Therefore, with that knowledge, she waited, watching for the other parts of the puzzle to fall into place. When Denzel Marduk had come into the public arena, she knew.

Marduk was the man of perdition — the ANTICHRIST! — and she had had a part in his beginning.

But after all these years, what could she do about it?

People would think her just a crazy old woman if she tried

to explain it to anyone. They would not listen to her story about what she had witnessed, nor would they agree with her that what she knew in her heart: Marduk was the spearhead of a terrible conspiracy. She was just an old woman now, what could she do?

Then an idea started to form in her mind. With the Lord's help, maybe she could do something. She had been there at Denzel's terrible birth, when his coming had ended a young girl's life in agony and terror. Maybe she could also be a part of his death. With God's help anything was possible, especially to right a wrong, a wrong so much against the Lord himself. Her life was finished. It did not matter if she lived any longer. But if she could make a difference now, redeem her awful failure of trust, she could stand before her Lord without trepidation.

The men were closer to her now, pressing through the crowd of people. Ann's blue eyes widened and her heart shrank with fear at the overwhelming presence of Marduk. The Spirit inside of her recognized the evil vibrating from this antagonist of Christ. And then the Spirit gave her courage, a quality of power she had never before experienced in her soul.

Her hand held the .38-caliber pistol firmly under the folds of her habit. She quickly scanned the hallway to see if anyone was watching her. No one except, her head stopped suddenly, except that old man in a dark overcoat and hat standing over in a far corner. His piercing blue eyes seemed to look right at her, to radiate calm and purpose. She suddenly felt an inner peace and strength flow into her from the old man.

Ann's eyes darted for a second to Marduk as he came closer, then glanced back at the old man. She blinked several times in astonishment, her eyes widening in disbelief. He was gone, disappearing as if by magic. She quickly looked back at Denzel, who was almost in front of her now. She sighed, straightened her spine in determination.

Frank noticed the old woman watching them so intently as they moved through the crowd. For a surreal moment he thought he recognized her from somewhere.

The two guards also noticed the woman, but they had dismissed her as nothing but an old nun come to watch history being made. They looked beyond as they approached her.

Ann lunged into Marduk. Frank's eyes went wide with horror as he saw the pistol shoved into Denzel's temple. The gunshot was deafening. The blast stunned everyone around, its echoes reverberating down the hallway. Smoke hid Denzel's head for a moment, and then he fell sideways.

The two security men had been caught off guard, but they quickly drew their automatic pistols and fired several times into the woman assassin. As the bullets ripped through her body, Ann's face lifted up to heaven and seemed to radiate a glow. She smiled. As she slumped in a death throe, her clear blue eyes fell on Denzel lying on the floor. Her eyelids closed slowly, her face content. She had most certainly inflicted a deadly wound.

"THIS IS A SPECIAL BULLETIN from CBS News."

The newsman appeared on the TV screen interrupting the morning soap opera. He looked harried, struggling to sound calm and controlled. "We have just learned," he said in a rush of words, "that the newly installed Secretary General of the United Nations," he had to look down then to a sheet of paper he held to remember the name, "Denzel ... Marduk ... has been shot on his way to a press conference at the U.N. building in New York. We switch you now to our correspondent, Jack Carter, who is on the scene."

An image of a newsman appeared. He was standing in a hallway, and people were moving quickly back and forth behind him in pandemonium. Shouts and signs of general confusion came from everywhere. As the newsman held a hand to one ear, he spoke into the camera.

"We are at the scene of what appears to be an assassination attempt on the new Secretary General, Denzel Marduk," the newsman shouted. The camera panned off the reporter and focused down the hallway to where paramedics and a group of people were huddled around a man on the floor. The newsman kept talking.

"We have unconfirmed reports that the assassin was a woman, dressed as a nun, and that she was shot by security men guarding Mr. Marduk."

The newsman continued to report the scant details of the shooting. News media would focus on nothing else for the rest of the day.

Scenes of Marduk lying on the floor would be repeated over and over on national television and around the world. People of the 60's generation would compare them to the pictures that had been taken at the Bobby Kennedy assassination. And like Kennedy had lain in the hospital for two days before he died, most people suspected the same fate awaited Marduk. For, even though he was not dead, early medical reports described too much damage for any man to sustain and live.

**11:34 a.m.**
Highway 95 north out of Los Angeles

WILL THOMPSON WAS GETTING nowhere fast, driving his desert-camouflaged 1949 Dodge Power-Wagon pickup in heavy traffic. It was Saturday, and the entire population of Los Angeles appeared to be trying to leave the city.

As pastor of a church in a small desert town north of Los Angeles, Will had gone to the city to visit one of his congregation who was in the hospital. His mistake had been to choose Saturday instead of a weekday to make the journey. Will didn't come to the big city much and had forgotten what traffic could be like on the weekend.

To anyone who didn't know him, Will's appearance did not fit his job description. He was a big man, over six feet four with fiery red, unruly hair and a wiry red full beard. Under bushy eyebrows the same color as his hair, dark opal eyes reflected the light with an iridescent gleam. His face was framed with roughened features, but a smile always seemed to be present above the square lantern jaw. His muscled tall frame and ruddy complexion, along with his wild red hair, made him appear more like a Viking warrior than a Christian minister.

As Will sat in the bumper-to-bumper traffic, he thought about how glad he would be to get out of the city and back to his home in the wide-open desert. He hadn't always felt that way. As he glanced at a large church building next to the freeway, his mind drifted to his graduation from divinity school, ten years ago. He'd been sure then that he was meant to be in a large church, doing great things. However, the Lord had compelled him instead to a small church, way out in the middle of the desert.

At first, he had felt he was living at the end of the world, until he grew to love the people of his little church. Now he would not trade it for the largest church in the land. He was happy to be where the Lord had placed him. He knew his church in the desert would never do anything earth-shaking, but he was sure that he was doing the work the Lord wanted him to do. "Feeding his sheep."

As the traffic began to move toward a normal pace, Will watched a 4x4 pickup with a trailer filled with dirt bikes speed up dangerously and swerve around a van towing a ski boat. The four-lane highway was filled with harried people, many with short tempers and unrelenting bad manners, dragging their gods out to the desert to worship them this weekend. *Instead, they should be going to church, and worshipping the true God,* thought Will, shaking his head.

Saddened by the craziness around him, Will turned on his car radio to look for a Christian station just as a news flash began. He listened to the newscaster tell about the assassination attempt on Denzel Marduk. They were saying Marduk would probably not live.

Will's jaw slid sideways slightly. "Umph," he said to himself, "well, what do you know about that. I believe things are starting to happen." He spoke softly glancing down at a spiral notebook sitting on top of his Bible on the seat next to him. "If I were a betting man," he said to his steering wheel, "I would bet Marduk lives." Will gazed out his windshield with a new perspective as his old pickup, engulfed in a thousand other vehicles, crawled en masse down the California freeway.

MAJOR JOHN ALLEN LEANED BACK in the driver's seat of his military-issue gray Ford and watched the open desert pass by as he also drove along Highway 95 a hour north of Will. His experience was quite different. He was enjoying the drive on the open highway, especially since there was hardly any traffic. John had left Fort Chapin at noon, and figured he would make it to Oak Hill in less than two hours. Maybe, he thought, he would have a chance today to start reconnoitering the base for the U.N. troops Sam had told him about.

Five hundred feet above John's car, silhouetted like a hawk against the sun, a black-bodied demon circled lazily on the hot desert wind currents. The dark creature's red eyes locked on the gray automobile moving down the highway, and he sloped laterally in a slow and heavy turn to follow. The demon's name was Falser, and he was part of the outer perimeter guard posted around Oak Hill when Legion made it his base of operation. The black spirit knew the driver in the car below him was from the military, even though hu-man was not wearing a uniform. A dark instinct incited Falser, and the demon decided to keep a close eye on the hu-man.

Falser lazily stretched out his long wings and flew along in a slow glide, matching the speed of the car below him. The gray Ford zoomed down the blacktop highway unfolding off into the wide expanse of the desert.

Two bright lights suddenly thundered past the unwary Falser, one on either side of the startled demon. The resulting blast of air sent the dark spirit tumbling out of control. The demon uttered a high-pitched scream as he plummeted like a rock to the desert floor. With a thud, Falser slammed into the desert floor, throwing up a rooster-tail plume of sand.

Painfully raising his head out of the sand, Falser searched the sky as he hacked harsh, dry coughs and spat sand out of his mouth. The two bright lights banked, one to the left, the other to the right, soaring like a pair of jet fighters straight up and then around back toward him.

The demon's red eyes narrowed into neon slits under an arched brow, and his mouth formed a snarl. The black spirit sensed — and then, as the lights charged closer — he knew what they were. And he knew they were coming back for him. Falser raised his knobby black fist in defiance and cursed at the two lights. "Next time," he snarled. He needed to report this to Executor. Right now.

With a sudden loud pop and a wisp of gray smoke, Falser disappeared.

Flying closely together, the two lights that were Garrett and Caleb made a U turn in the air over the spot where the demon had disappeared. After a pause, the two heavenly angels flew off in close formation until they were directly over John's car.

The engine in the gray Ford beneath the angels suddenly stopped running. John steered the car to the side of the road and rolled to a stop, tires crunching on the roadside gravel. He tried several times to restart the engine but didn't succeed. John could not believe his bad luck. The car had plenty of gas — what could be wrong? Opening the door, he stepped into the oppressive heat and stood looking around at the empty desert. The flat wasteland seemed to extend forever in every direction without a structure in sight.

Overhead the blue sky was clear, and brilliant rays of the sun bore down on him. John stared at the car as he walked around to the front and raised the hood. He began checking for loose wires, or anything he could see wrong. After fifteen minutes of struggling with the problem, he slammed the hood in disgust. His blue eyes slowly searched the barren desert. *Well,* he thought, *what now?* He didn't carry a cell phone so he had no way of contacting the outside world. John loosened his tie and unbuttoned the collar of his shirt as he considered his options. The blacktop highway stretched for miles in both directions, with not a car in sight. Even if someone did come along, they probably won't stop. This was, after all, California.

John turned, and out of frustration he kicked the front tire, just because it felt good.

Will had finally escaped the heavy traffic and was cruising freely along the deserted highway. The red-bearded preacher felt good to be out in the open desert and on his way home. The large knobby tires of the Power-Wagon hummed a continuous staccato on the asphalt as the powerful six-cylinder L-head engine ticked like a well-oiled machine under the hood.

As Will crested a hill, in the distance he spotted a man kicking the tire of a car stalled on the side of the road. Will could not help chuckling to himself ... he knew the feeling.

John heard the whine of the tires of the 4x4, and he turned to look. A bleary mirage was coming toward him through the wavering heat waves. While the pickup rumbled closer he held out a hand wondering if the driver would stop. As the truck slowed and rolled toward him, he couldn't help admiring the nicely restored old vehicle. It was a late-40s Dodge pickup with sixteen-inch tires that made the camouflage-painted body sit high. The truck was built out of heavy metal that caused the body to look chunky and strong like a tank.

The pickup came to a stop. The passenger window was directly in front of John so he had a clear view of the driver. If he had thought the vehicle imposing, the owner behind the wheel was even more so. The red-bearded man looked like he had just stepped off a Viking war ship from the tenth century. For a moment John's eyes unconsciously searched the truck's interior for a sword or battle-ax. Then the huge red-haired man smiled.

"Can I help you?" Will asked, leaning over and studying the stranger. The man's face had a strangely familiar likeness Will could not put a name to. Although he had Caucasian tanned skin, he looked Native American, and the harsh sharp lines of his face made him look vaguely threatening.

John looked at Will and shrugged his shoulders."My car just quit on me. I can't figure out what's wrong. Could you give me a lift?"

Will studied the guy. He seemed normal, but you had to be careful these days. Then that quiet voice, a voice that had taken him years to pay attention to, said simply, "He's okay."

"Sure. Hop in."

John grabbed his suitcase, locked his car, and climbed in next to Will. "Thank you," he said, "I didn't know what I was going to do there for a while."

Will studied his new passenger. The man was tall and well-built, he wore comfortable-looking dress slacks, a shirt and tie, but it was his handsome face that Will kept looking at. Then he realized the guy looked just like an old movie star, what was his name? … Chandler, yeah, Jeff Chandler. Will shifted into first gear, pulled away, and asked, "Has anyone ever told you that you look like … ?"

"Yes," interrupted John dryly.

Garrett and Caleb sat together on the roof of John's car and watched him and Will drive away.

"How did you make his car stop running?" Caleb asked.

"Just a little vapor lock in the fuel line," Garrett answered matter-of-factly, looking upward at the sky. He then aimed his eyes at Caleb. "It's all right now."

"Well," asked Caleb in his best Laurel-and-Hardy voice, "why did you do it?"

"Because," Garrett answered slowly, watching the pickup drive out of sight, "John needed to meet our friend Will, and this way they have about an hour to get acquainted."

"I see," nodded Caleb, his eyes drifting to the nameplate on the car. "F … O… R … D … what does that stand for?"

"Fix … Or … Repair … Daily."

"Really?"

"No, actually, it means Flimsy … Old … Rebuilt … Dodge."

Caleb was beginning to catch on now. "Or," he said, lifting up one finger in thought while looking over to the mound of sand the demon had plunged into.

"How 'bout … Fight … Or … Run … Demon?"

Garrett paused in deep thought for a moment and then, nodding his head, he grinned,

"I like that."

JOHN ALLEN," John said, introducing himself. He extended his hand for a shake in between Will's shifting of gears as the Power-Wagon picked up speed.

"Will Thompson," Will responded as he shook John's hand, "Do you love Jesus?"

"What?" John asked. He was taken aback, his eyelids fluttering as his brain seemed to short circuit. It had been a long time since he'd heard the name Jesus. Suddenly something in his mind seemed to let loose … *That's your trouble.*

"Oh, it's a habit I have when I meet someone new," Will said as he eased into fourth gear.

John stared at him impassively, wondering if he'd gotten into a truck with a "nut case."

"I asked you if you love Jesus to find out if you're Christian."

"Well, I'm not," John said. "I've never had a lot of time for religion."

"Religion is a word made up by man," Will said. "It has nothing to do with whether you're a born-again believer in Jesus Christ."

"You sound like a preacher."

"I am," Will admitted with a grin. "I have the one and only church in Oak Hill, California."

"Well, that explains the short sermon." John studied the bearded man out of the corner of his eye. It was strange, but he had to admit to himself that he was beginning to like this guy. John did not make friends easily. In fact, he had never had a really close friend except maybe Sam. But wartime friendships were in a whole different category. The warm emotion he suddenly felt from this friendly giant inclined him to want to reciprocate.

"Where ya headed?" Will asked, bringing John out of his revery.

John shot him a look that could have been construed as a smile "Oak Hill."

"Cool," Will said. "I'll take you there. You in the military? I saw the ID sticker on the car bumper."

"Yes, I am," John answered hesitantly, his normal, cautious demeanor slipping back.

"What do you do?" Will asked, bending over slightly in John's direction and wiggling a bushy red eyebrow. "Or is it a secret?"

John couldn't help but finally produce one of his rare smiles at the big guy; he sure was a happy fellow. "I'm a Major in Army Intelligence, and please," he cautioned dramatically, "no jokes about the contradiction in terms."

"Oh, I wouldn't," Will said, suddenly serious. "My father was in Army Intelligence during World War II."

"Really, was he a spy?"

"No. Actually, he was a lawyer. He was one of the prosecutors at Nuremberg.

"Really," John said, "I like talking with the old intelligence men. I'd love to meet him someday."

Will shook his head slowly. "My folks died in an auto accident when I was young."

John was stunned. He looked at Will as if he'd just landed from Mars. John had never known anyone who had grown up without parents, someone like himself. And suddenly here was somebody now, someone so happy and full of life. The paradox was troubling to him. He had grown used to feeling he was justified in his wallowing over not ever knowing his mother and father. He had lived with it like a facial scar as a child, and as an adult he'd worn their deaths and absence like a badge next to the other ribbons on his uniform.

The two men rode in silence for a few minutes when Will finally spoke. "Did you hear someone shot Denzel Marduk this morning?"

John looked blank for a moment. This free ride was becoming more troubling by the minute. It had been a long time since he'd heard anything about Denzel. He should have had the radio on while he drove. It wasn't good to get so out of touch. Not in his job. "Really? Is he going to live?"

"The news says he probably won't. He was shot in the head."

The picture of Denzel that surfaced in John's mind was when they'd been teenagers. He hadn't seen or heard from him since he left for the Army. John stared out the window at the passing desert, the vibrations of the 4x4 rocking him in thought. Denzel was dying. It seemed like another lifetime ago when he had known him.

After a few moments, John spoke as he continued to look out the window. "I grew up with him."

"You mean Marduk? You're kidding?"

"No, I'm not kidding. We grew up as teenagers on a ranch in Arizona."

Suddenly, miraculously, Will felt the spirit of the Lord come over him. He now understood, without a doubt, that it was no accident he had picked up this man. Will's spiritual discernment told him there was a reason. God was working here.

Stunned, Will looked ahead at the road. He knew something was happening here but not just yet what it might be. *Oh, Lord, what have you got planned for me?* he wondered as he glanced at John, who was still looking out his side window.

After a few minutes of careful thought and prayer, Will spoke, "Do you know what the term 'Eschatology means'?"

"No, I can't say I do."

"It's the study of end-time events of the world, according to the Bible," Will explained. "I believe, according to what the Bible says, that we are living in those last days. I also have come to believe your friend Denzel will play a big part in it. Have you ever heard the term, 'Antichrist'?"

John looked strangely at Will. He could not help but think this conversation was turning weird. "You're not going to tell me Denzel Marduk is the Antichrist now, are you?" he said. "I knew him for many years. He was a snooty brat and pretty full of himself, but he wasn't the Devil incarnate."

"So you do know something about what the Bible says about the Antichrist?" Will asked.

"Well, yes," John said. He was a little uncomfortable, as he remembered his grandfather. "My grandfather taught me many things in the Bible."

*That's your trouble.* John shook the thoughts from his mind, looking back at Will.

"What if I could prove to you that Marduk could be the Antichrist?" Will said.

"Well," John answered, not wanting to admit he was intrigued, "I guess you have a captive audience here."

"Okay," Will said, aiming a wary eye toward his passenger.

John sensed an excitement in Will's voice as he began to speak.

"First off, most people in the world today associate the Antichrist with the number 666. There is too much emphasis placed on that number, like he's going to appear on TV with that printed on his forehead or something. The fact is, in the book of Revelation, chapter 13, verse 18, when John the Apostle is foretelling about the Antichrist, he mentions the number 666, almost as an afterthought.

"For those who wish to study deeper and explore the identity of this Antichrist, he gave us a clue to his name. He writes that if you count up the numbers in his name, the total will be 666. Are you with me?"

"Yes," nodded John.

"Okay," Will continued, "the Apostle was writing in the first century, using the most widely used language of the time, Greek. Many of the books in the Bible were originally written in Greek, and back then they used the letters in the Greek alphabet for their numbers also."

Will pointed to a notebook on the seat next to a Bible. "Look on the inside cover of that notebook."

John picked it up and opened it to the first page, on the inside cover were three rows of markings.

| | | | | | | | | |
|---|---|---|---|---|---|---|---|---|
| Α | A | 1 | κ | K | 20 | ν | U | 400 |
| β | B | 2 | λ | L | 30 | ξ | X | 60 |
| χ | C | 20 | μ | M | 40 | ψ | Y | 400 |
| δ | D | 4 | ν | N | 50 | ζ | Z | 7 |
| ϵ | E | 5 | ο | O | 70 | θ | PH | 500 |
| ϕ | F | 500 | π | P | 80 | ϕ | TH | 9 |
| γ | G | 3 | ρ | R | 100 | χ | CH | 600 |
| ι | I | 10 | σ | S | 200 | | | |
| φ | J | 10 | τ | T | 300 | | | |

"The first column in each set is the Greek alphabet," Will said. "The second column is its comparable letter in the English alphabet, and the third column is the number designated in the Greek for that letter. Therefore, with this chart you can calculate the total sum of a person's name to what it would add up to in the Greek numbers. You still with me?"

"Yes, I understand."

"So, say we were going to add up the name Allen, it would go …

A … is 1

L … is 30

L … is 30

E … is 5

N … is 50

116, that name totals 116.

Now, you're probably thinking a lot of people's full names could add up to 666. However, I can tell you, through over ten years of adding up hundreds of different people's names, I've never got that exact amount, 666, from anyone's name." Will paused for effect. "Even when I tried to make up a fictitious name, trying to make it come out to 666, it always came out silly, or unrealistic."

"That is," Will said, looking straight ahead at the road, "until I read the name of a man previously unknown to me, who was voted

Secretary General of the United Nations last week."

Will shot a daring glance at John, "Look at my last entry."

John flipped through the pages until he came to the last written page, on it he saw the name he expected.

D ... 4
E ... 5
N ... 50
Z ... 7
E ... 5
L ... 30

M ... 40
A ... 1
R ... 100
D ... 4
U ... 400
K ... 20
= 666

"He's right on the money, isn't he?" John said, studying the figures.

"Yes," Will said, "that is his full name. He has no middle name, and have you ever heard anyone before named Marduk?"

"No, I always thought it was an unusual name."

"I'll say," injected Will. "Marduk is another name for Nimrod. He is the evil man in the book of Genesis who Satan uses to begin his counterattack against God's salvation plan for mankind. Nimrod is the one who builds the tower of Babel, the first large-scale resistance to God, and begins the ideologies that go against God's commandments. Marduk was the pagan name for Nimrod and was worshiped as a god down through the centuries. He was also worshiped as the sun, or the 'most Brilliant,' which is another name for Lucifer. In Roman times they called Marduk Jupiter, their most supreme god. The planet Jupiter has always played an integral part in the history of the pagan worship of Marduk."

"And by the way," Will added, "the Latin root word for Denzel is 'de intus' which means, 'an inhabitant.' And I don't have to tell you who the entity would be indwelling Denzel."

Will looked over at the skeptical face of John. "Not enough proof, intelligence man?"

"Rumor is," Will continued, "Marduk was born of a virgin, an important attribute for someone who will someday want to convince the Jewish people he is their messiah."

"Just suppose what you say is true." argued John. "What about what's happened today? You said the news reported he was as good as dead."

"Another sign in Revelation 13:3 is that the Antichrist will miraculously recover from a deadly head wound. The news bulletins are saying he has been shot fatally in the head."

"So, if somehow Denzel recovers, that would certainly be another nail in the coffin, so to speak," John said. "I can't believe that I knew him once, and that he could be what you're saying."

"John, I don't believe you and I just happened onto one another today," Will said, a premonitory tone lacing his words.

John's brow arched as he remembered then why he was going to Oak Hill. "If Denzel is the coming world leader," he speculated aloud, "he would need universal military troops in every country to take control." The thought sent a cold chill down his spine.

"I would imagine so," Will agreed.

"Have you seen any activity at the old army base in Oak Hill lately?" John asked.

"No, it's been deserted for over two decades, but then there's a lot of area no one ever sees. Why? Is that why you're headed in that direction?" he asked.

"Let's just say for now, I'm going to check things out," John answered, a look of determination on his Indian face.

A faded billboard announcing the town of Oak Hill, with a large red arrow pointing toward the right, appeared up ahead. "I'll take you by the church and you can call a tow truck for your car," Will said as they turned down the side road next to the big sign.

"I'll need to find a motel room," John said.

"No problem, there's only one in town."

"Thanks," John said, as the Power-Wagon moved down the road into town.

THE WIRY-BODIED DEMON FALSER sat perched on the top of the billboard next to the larger form of Executor. The smaller evil spirit pointed a black bony finger at Will's truck. "That's the hu-man I was watching when the two from the heavenly host attacked me," he said.

"And why didn't you stand your post against them?" Executor said, his deep voice dripping with venom. He knew the answer was that Falser would have been too scared, but he enjoyed watching this miserable one try to wiggle out of the truth.

Falser's eyes narrowed as he cocked his head in Executor's direction. "I knew you would want to know immediately about any heavenly hosts flying around the area." His lips smacked up some loose drool before it fell to the ground.

*Well, that much is true,* Executor thought to himself. Legion would want to be informed about any heavenly angels in the area. "So, where are they now?" Executor demanded, menacing the startled, red-eyed spirit.

"I don't know, probably hiding somewhere. How should I know? I've been here with you."

A powerful, black hand grabbed Falser around his neck and pulled him out into thin air. Executor angrily dangled Falser in front of him. Falser's red eyes bulged wide and his forked tongue grew out of his mouth in gasps.

"Listen, you little piece of dung," Executor said, his blood-colored eyes blazing in fury. "You go and inform everyone. I want to know where those angels are." He squeezed the neck even tighter, then threw Falser to the ground like a broken doll. "And I want to know now," he shouted, glaring down from atop the sign.

Falser lifted himself up painfully, slowly rubbing his neck and gasping for air. He glanced back up to where they had been sitting, but Executor had vanished."Thank golden calf," he whispered.

After a moment, Falser took off in flight to do what he'd been ordered.

WILL PULLED THE 4 X 4 into the parking lot of a simple, white wood-framed church with a steeple and stained glass windows. John and Will climbed out and started up the sidewalk to a side door of the building. As they approached, the door opened, and Billie Anderson walked out. The English teacher glanced at John for a moment, then turned to the preacher.

"Hi, Will," Billie said.

"Hi," Will replied, his face softening as he looked at her. "John, I'd like you to meet our part-time church secretary, Miss Billie Anderson."

"Billie, this is Major John Allen."

Billie smiled and held out her hand. John shook it lightly.

"Nice to meet you, Major," she said, unable to stop staring at him.

"Billie is an English teacher at the middle school here in Oak Hill," Will said, taking note that John and Billie were conspicuously staring at each other. Clearly, something had clicked between them that made the world nearby fade away. He was starting to feel as out of place as a clump of red hair floating in a punch bowl.

"Well," John said finally. "Maybe I'd have done better in English class if I'd had as pretty a teacher as you."

Will couldn't help rolling his eyes at that old line.

"Why, thank you, Major," Billie said, tilting her head, her eyes squinting coquetishly. "Well ... ah," she struggled as if trying to decide if she should ask, "has anyone ever told you, you look ... ?"

"Yes," John sighed, realizing he was still holding her hand. He let it go, slowly.

"Well," Billie said, taking a deep breath as she remembered she was late for a meeting. "I must run. Nice to have met you, Major. Perhaps I'll see you again."

"It would be my pleasure," John said, while thinking to himself: *Why couldn't I have said something more clever?* He had felt a sudden and strong attraction to Billie. The sensation was enough to overwhelm his tough emotional exterior for the moment.

"Bye, Will," Billie said, glancing at him quickly. The big red-headed man lifted a hand and wiggled four fingers slightly as he said bye. She turned and walked down the sidewalk.

"Nice lady," John said, as he and Will watched her get into her car.

"Yes," Will said, lost in his own private thoughts for a moment. He turned to John. "Come on in, Major. I'll show you where the phone is."

Billie got into her car and had a sudden mental block on how to start an automobile. She looked up at Will and John Allen as they walked toward the church office door. She fumbled with her keys and when she glanced at them again, they'd gone inside. *Why did I act like such a dope meeting John Allen?* she wondered. *He certainly is handsome, but good grief, girl, you acted like some starry-eyed teenager out there.* She started the car finally and thought, *Oh well, I'll probably never even see him again.* But as she put the car in gear a tiny voice in her mind suggested that he was here in town for a reason, and that they probably would meet again. As she drove out of the parking lot, she noticed her foot trembling slightly on the gas pedal.

After making his call to the towing company and letting them know where he'd be staying, John joined up with Will and together they walked down a hallway to leave the church. A man in his late fifties, with black hair and a mustache, appeared from a side door carrying a mop. When he saw John, he stopped and saluted. John reflexively returned the salute, and then wondered why. The man couldn't have known he was a military officer.

"John, this is Henry," Will said. "Henry meet Major John Allen."

"Nice to meet you," Henry said.

"Nice to meet you, too," John said, puzzled. Henry's eyes didn't show much life.

"I have to go to work at the school now." Henry spoke in a

childlike manner. He turned and walked down the hallway.

"What was that all about?" John said.

"Henry's a Vietnam vet," Will explained tenderly, watching the man walk away. "He came home a little messed up mentally. I'm sure you've seen it many times before, Major. He works as a janitor here and at the school. He is unable to drive a car or do many things a man his age should be capable of. He rides his bike to work and lives with his widowed mother."

John watched Henry walk down the hallway, and for a moment his heart went out to him in the kinship of one soldier to another who has experienced the horrors of war.

"I'm hungry," Will said, patting his stomach. "Ya wanna eat? he said, opening the door to the outside.

The white-robed angels, Garrett and Caleb, sat on a large limb in a big oak tree across from the church and watched Will and John drive into town. A moment later Henry came out of the church pushing a bicycle; he hopped on it and rode down the street.

"Do you know the story behind that one?" Caleb asked, watching Henry ride out of sight.

Garrett looked down at the ground and then said, "Yes, I do. All Henry Gardner had ever wanted as a boy growing up was to be in the military. When he turned eighteen, he fulfilled that dream by joining the army. He rose to the rank of sergeant and when the war in Southeast Asia began, he was sent there. He quickly learned jungle warfare in Vietnam. Those who didn't, didn't live long. Officers soon knew they had a natural warrior in Sergeant Gardner, and he was often sent on special missions. He earned the respect of his superiors, and the men he led into battle.

"When his first tour of duty was over, he signed on for a second and then a third.

"Then one morning, after a fierce gun battle in the jungle, Henry came up missing. The men in his platoon spread out and searched for him, fearing the worst. A short time later they found him, sitting in a stream, naked, frantically washing himself. He was mumbling something about not being able to wash the blood off, although he had no blood on him. His men had seen similar syndromes before, but would never have guessed it could happen to their battle-hardened sergeant. They gently brought him back to base, and soon after, he left Vietnam for good.

"After several years in military hospitals, the doctors let Henry's mother bring him home. There was nothing they could do to heal his broken mind." Garrett sighed.

"War is a terrible waste," Caleb said.

"Yes, it is," Garrett replied, sighing and intently looking into the sky. His eyes focused on several black beings flying around nearby. *Spiritual war*, he thought, *is coming to Oak Hill*. "I think it is time to report to Gabriel on the number of enemies concentrating here." He turned and looked at Caleb, "Let's go."

They disappeared.

After leaving the church, Henry rode his bike down the main street in town toward the school. As he rode along, he happily saluted everyone he saw. Most people just ignored the "town crazy." A few would even make fun of him. But then, there were some men who knew about Henry. When he rode by and saluted them, they would stop what they were doing and gaze solemnly at him, perhaps remembering a long ago, personal memory.

Those men couldn't help but salute him back.

The final period bell rang as Henry rode his bike into the school yard. Ahead of a flood of children, Donny and his buddies burst out the school's front doors headed for home. They were off in search of adventure. To them, that meant playing their fantasy role-playing games. Donny, Bobby, and David had been involved in these kinds of games since they were eight years old.

The picture on the game boxes and books — of wizards, warriors, and monsters — is what had first caught their attention years before. At first, they had played the games just for fun, rolling the pyramid-shaped dice, moving figures around a game board. They acted out battles between warriors, priests, wizards, and gods.

As the boys advanced in the games, they each picked a character and started to pretend to be that individual all the time. Then they could make up any kind of game scenario they chose to act out. Soon, each became that character 24 hours a day. This brought a new dimension to their everyday life. The game books taught that if they survived each game and kept advancing to harder games, they could gain the power to become "immortals." The heroic feats of the characters, the images they created in one's mind, made the games emotionally real.

As the three friends rode their bikes to Donny's house, they discussed the game they would make up today. When they arrived at the house, they went directly to Donny's room.

David was a warrior and Bobby was a priest, but since Donny was an advanced wizard, he was their leader. He took the book of rules off his shelf. On the outside cover was the picture of a red dragon.

John sat in an orange-and-green vinyl-covered booth across the table from Will and looked around the strange, little place called the Cactus Café. The walls were painted in desert scenery and the place was crammed with different kinds of cactus growing in planters and pots.

Will smiled as he watched John take in the place. "Kinda corny, I know. But they have the best food in town."

The two men had walked there from the motel, two blocks away. John had checked in after they left the church. It was an old run-down motel, but it was clean. John hadn't been able to read the name on the motel's sandblasted sign, but since the entire building was painted lime green, he'd decided he would call it the "Green Motel."

When their food arrived, Will bowed his head and said a blessing over it.

John stared at him, and then looked self-consciously around the room. No one seemed to notice. *This big guy is something else,* John thought.

The two men ate and talked, savoring the very good food.

After leaving the cafe, they started walking back to the motel.

The evening was pleasantly warm, and the stars looked brilliant and sharp in the desert night sky.

"I noticed that many people in the café greeted you tonight," John said as they walked along. "You're a well-known guy around here. Do they all go to your church?"

"No," Will said with a chuckle. "Our congregation is really quite small," his tone turning serious. "But you're right. Everyone in town always seems to know the preacher."

"Yours is the only church in town? Isn't that unusual for a place this size?"

"Yes, I suppose it is. Most people wander around this desert and town like lost sheep, John. Many of them following the wrong shepherd, instead of following the 'Good Shepherd.' I feel the time is near when the 'Good Shepherd' is coming to take his flock home."

"I don't understand," John said, a confused look on his face.

"The Bible says one day Jesus will snatch all the ones who love him — the Christians here on earth — and take them to heaven."

"Ah yes, the Rapture," John recalled. "When is that supposed to happen?"

"No one knows, not even Jesus. Only God knows. However, the Bible gives us clues to when the 'season' will be that our Lord returns. I believe we are living in that time frame, especially now with the appearance of Marduk on the world stage."

John walked silently for a while, rummaging through the thoughts in his mind. "You really believe in all of this, don't you?"

"Absolutely, John. I take the whole Bible as truth, or it might as well be just a fairy tale."

"What is truth?" John said sarcastically as they reached the motel and sat down on some lawn chairs near an old, empty swimming pool.

"The truth is ... that God created the earth and man," Will said. "Man is born sinful. But Jesus, God's Son, died on a cross so that man can choose to either live in sin, or accept the price Jesus paid for our sins with his perfect blood. Only His blood can wash away our sins, so that we can live with God when we die."

"Or, if you don't choose Jesus, you go to hell," John said. "That doesn't seem quite fair to me if you've tried to live a good life."

"Just trying to be good does not measure up to God's perfection. Jesus paid the ransom for us; his blood covers our sin in the eyes of God. All you need to do is have faith and accept him as your personal savior."

*That's your trouble.* The inner voice spoke once again to John's heart.

"How do you do that?" John asked.

Will looked intently at him. "Just pray to him and ask him into your heart. He is always there waiting just to hear from you. It is just a matter of believing in Him to begin with."

"You think I should do that, don't you, Will?"

"I just tell people the truth, John," the red-bearded man said, looking up at the bright stars. "I don't believe in pressuring someone into becoming a Christian. It doesn't work that way."

"What do you mean?"

"If you really desire to be a Christian, the Holy Spirit leads you. Then you have His help in letting God be in control of your life. Unfortunately, there are many people who profess to be Christians, but don't allow God to work His will in their lives."

"I don't know," John said, a disturbed look on his face. "I guess I'm going to have to think about it." The idea of turning your life over to God was one he'd rejected since boyhood, because he had blamed God for his parents' death. The truth Will presented made sense to John, but his stubborn pride honed over a lifetime of inner self-pity held him back.

Will looked at his new friend and said, "Don't put it off if you feel the spirit calling you, John. Tomorrow's Sunday. Why don't you come to church and I can preach to you some more?" Will said with a grin, the friendship for John apparent in his smile.

In spite of their opposite characteristics, or maybe because of them, the two men were becoming good friends, and Will had a definite feeling they were somehow in for an adventure together.

"Sure, why not," John answered dryly. "I'll come hear you preach ... and critique."

**11:38 p.m.**
Hopkins General Hospital
New York City, New York

FRANK PETTINATI WAS DEVASTATED. He stood at the window in a private room set up especially for Marduk. Frank stared out at the New York City skyline. Denzel lay in a bed with his head in bandages and a tube running into his nose. He had not regained consciousness since the shooting. Frank had been by his side for more than ten hours, watching the doctors working feverishly and listening to their fateful diagnosis.

Frank frowned and gritted his teeth as he looked at the lights of the city. How could this have happened? Everything was in ruin. He cursed to himself.

He felt like screaming.

All his plans, all his preparations, all had been in vain. Where had their lord been when that crazy woman attacked? Where was he now? Had he abandoned them? Frank felt enraged at everyone and everything.

He turned and stared at Denzel. He had raised him like his own son, had prepared him for the future events, and now he was going to die. The doctors had given up all hope. They had told him he probably would not last the night.

Frank sat down by the bed, put his head in his hands, closed his eyes, and cursed again.

He really didn't remember if it had been a couple of minutes or an hour, but suddenly he felt another presence in the room. With his head still in his hands, Frank peered through the space between his fingers to the front of the bed. What he saw startled him so much, he fell back against the chair in fright.

A red dragon stood at the front of the bed, its body seemingly filling the room. The grotesque head snaked close to Denzel's face. Then the dragon turned to look at Frank, the impious monster's yellow eyes blazing.

"It's time to wake him up," the beast snarled.

"Wake ... wake him up," Frank muttered. "He's ... dying!"

"He will not die," the dragon commanded as it stared at Denzel. "The time is near for him to rule the earth," Satan proclaimed.

Frank looked at the bandaged head of Denzel and could not believe he would live, much less rule anything. When he looked around, the dragon was gone.

"Wake up, Frank," Denzel said.

With a sudden start, Frank opened his eyes and stared at Denzel sitting up in his bed, pulling at the tube in his nose.

"Get a nurse and get this thing out of my nose."

Frank could not believe his eyes. He stood up and looked around, remembering the dragon. Had it been real, or just a dream?

"What are you looking at?" Denzel said. "I feel fine and I want to get out of here."

Frank stared in disbelief at Denzel. He seemed completely well. He was even his own haughty self. "You're healed" was all he could mutter.

"I feel fine, now get me a nurse," Denzel demanded.

"Yeah, sure," Frank said, walking around the bed, staring in mystification at Denzel as he headed for the door.

"Frank," shouted Denzel after him. "Who was that woman, the one who shot me?"

Frank stopped. "You don't have to worry about her. She's dead."

"Good. Now get me out of here."

The news that Denzel Marduk was completely healed stunned and baffled the doctors who had worked on him. They held a news conference and presented x-rays showing the damage to his head and brain. Everyone agreed the healing of Marduk had been a miracle. There was simply no other explanation.

The world suddenly began to look at Denzel Marduk as an individual of special merit and ability, a world leader with extraordinary powers bestowed upon him. He was certainly different from any man who had ever lived in the history of mankind.

And the entire world wondered after him.

*Who opposeth and exalteth himself above all that is called God, or that is worshiped, so that he, as God, sitteth in the temple of God, showing himself that he is God.*

— II Thessalonians 2; 4

# Chapter 10

**7:12 p.m., Sunday, September 12**
Oak Hill, California

.........................................

THE OPEN PIT IN THE SANDY GROUND loomed dark and dangerous as he slowly approached it. He peered uncertainly over the edge, and saw Denzel clinging with both hands to a wood beam.

"Help me. Please help me," Denzel's frightened face gazed up at him.

He felt uncertain as to whether he should help. Something in his mind told him not to.

Denzel's hands started to slip. "Help me!" he cried. His eyes pleading with disbelief at the possibility that his friend might not help him.

He stuck his hand down and caught one of Denzel's hands, their grasp secure.

Denzel looked at him with a smile of what he first thought was thankful relief. The smile turned wicked, matching Denzel's evil eyes.

Denzel savagely jerked him forward, pulling him into the dark pit ...

SOMEONE BANGING ON HIS motel-room door startled him out of the bad dream. Half awake, John stumbled across the room and opened the door to the glaring morning sun. In the doorway stood a short, portly man dressed in dirty overalls, torn shirt, and knit hat. All John could really focus on in the sun's glare was what had once been a cigar sticking out of the guy's mouth, surrounded by a stubble beard.

"You Major Allen?" asked the mouth.

"Yes," John said, trying to adjust his eyes to the brightness.

"I've got your car, just sign here and I'll drop her."

John squinted past the man to see his gray Ford hooked up behind a spotlessly clean and polished tow truck.

"What was wrong with it?" asked John as he signed the papers on the clipboard the man handed him.

"Not a thing, started right up. Seems to be running fine," the man said, as he handed John a copy of the receipt.

"Thanks," John answered slowly. *That's strange*, he thought as he closed the door. However, it was not nearly as strange as the newspaper headlines John read later, at breakfast, at the Cactus Café.

MIRACULOUS RECOVERY
OF U.N. SECRETARY GENERAL

Denzel Marduk's head wound had completely healed.

*Will was right,* the scary thought went through John's head as he stared at Denzel's picture on the front page of the newspaper. He recognized the handsome features grown older from their last encounter. Suddenly, John looked up from the paper, recalling another memory, one buried long ago.

John sighed and looked out the café window in deep thought. What would Will think, if John told him he had once saved Denzel's life?

Things were beginning to close in, inside John's heart and mind. He felt instinctive twinges of warning about hidden danger, like the silent sounds in the jungle before a deadly ambush. Denzel was the anti-Christ, of that John was now convinced. The friend of his teenage years was going to be and do all the horrible things foretold in the book of Revelation. The thought of it was frightening. Something, some sense of warning told him he was also going to be involved in Denzel's terrible destiny. *Shoot,* he thought, *I'm already involved — the Russian troops. They're part of the coming scenario, part of Marduk's plan to rule the world.* John looked out the café window, his blue eyes searching.

He needed to find those Russians, and soon.

John drove to Will's church for the 11 o'clock service and sat in a back pew. He nodded at Will who smiled at him several times during the meeting. Will's sermon that morning included many of the same things he had discussed with John the evening before, especially about God's love and his plan of redemption for everyone who would accept it.

John listened to the now-familiar words with guarded respite. As he looked around at the people sitting in the little church, he noticed Henry with an older woman, probably his mother. He noticed Billie, sitting with a young couple near the front of the church. As he continued his survey, he got a feeling of warmth and goodness from the folks seated here, something he wasn't used to feeling from the people of his world.

After the service, Will introduced John to several members of the congregation. When Henry and his mother came by, Henry looked at him strangely, not saying anything. It was a lost expression, and maybe a deep pain, that John saw in the man's eyes.

Henry saluted him, and John respectfully saluted him back. Henry's mother smiled and said "Hello," and the two of them silently moved on, their arms around each other. John felt a burst of emotion as he watched them walk away.

The simple-minded man called Henry might be pitied by most people, but John envied him right then. Envied the love and the touch Henry received from his mother. John's eyes narrowed in resentment. Something he had never known with his own mother.

Billie came by with the couple she had been sitting with earlier, breaking the spell John had cast himself into. John could not help but give her one of his rare smiles. He thought she looked very nice in a stylish white dress and heels. A small clump of violets was pinned in her hair.

"Good morning, Major," she said.

"Good morning," he replied.

"Major Allen, I'd like you to meet Ron and Sally Mitchell."

John shook Ron's hand. Ron was heavy set with brown hair and a jolly face. Sally said her hello with a smile. She was short, with curly blonde hair, and visibly pregnant.

"Are you a teacher also?" John asked Sally, trying to make conversation so they'd linger, along with Billie.

"Yes, I am," Sally said, looking at John in that you-look-like-someone-I-should-know stare.

"And Ron is in real estate," Billie added.

"Oh," John said, nodding quickly to Ron, his eyes traveling back to Billie.

"Well, nice to have met you, Major," Ron said, herding the two women along.

"See you," Billie said as they walked away.

As John watched them leave, he realized that his heart had been filled with so many new and strange emotions these last two days.

John watched as Will greeted each person leaving, always with some personal bit of news to share, receiving compliments or critiques on the service. Clearly, he liked his congregation and they liked him. The whole thing felt oddly like family, though John had little experience with that except, of course, his grandfather.

After everyone had left, Will began to gather up the hymn books and John quickly moved to help. When the books were stacked neatly at the end of each pew, Will turned off the air conditioning and lights. He waited for John to pass, then locked the church door behind them. Lightly, his fingertips caressed the smoothly painted wood before he turned with a smile to his newest congregant.

John said, "Billie seems like a nice girl."

"Yes, and I think she likes you, soldier boy."

"Is she dating anyone?"

"Not that I'm aware of."

John looked at his new friend. "You have feelings for her, don't you?" he guessed correctly. "Have you ever gone out with her?"

Will bit his lip and stared straight ahead.

"No," he finally answered, apparently embarrassed at the idea. "I've never had the nerve."

John looked at Will in amazement. This big man, who looked like some kind of a Viking warrior, and one he'd figured probably had more courage in his little finger than most men had in their whole being, was a pussycat when it came to women?

"Umph," John said, shaking his head. *Things sure are getting complicated around here.*

LATE THAT AFTERNOON, at the Mitchell home, Billie sat on a lawn chair in the backyard sipping lemonade, watching Ron cook hamburgers on a gas grill. Sally walked out the back door and handed her husband a plate of hamburger buns.

"Try not to burn them this time, darlin'," she said as she kissed him. Sally sat next to Billie, grabbed a carrot stick from a bowl on the table between them and started to nibble on it.

"All right, I want to hear everything about your friend, the Major."

"He's not my friend, Sally, for the umpteenth time. I only met him once at the church office with Will. I told you that."

"Yes, but you didn't tell me how cute he is," Sally said, her eyes squinting, trying to recall something. "He looks like that Indian chief in that TV series I used to watch when I was a kid. 'Broken Arrow.' What was that guy's name? Anyway, your Major is handsome.

"Didn't you think the Major was handsome?" Sally yelled over to Ron.

"Smashing, my dear, simply smashing," joked Ron.

"So what do you know about him, Billie?" Sally continued, looking back at her. "He didn't have a wedding ring on." Her eyebrows moved up and down several times.

"Oh, he probably hocked it," Ron said, eavesdropping on their conversation. "You know, to buy bullets or something."

"Ron, let Billie tell us about her friend," Sally exclaimed in a high voice.

"Sally, I hardly know him," Billie said sternly, "He's probably much older than I am anyway."

"See, you *have* been thinking about him." Sally said with wide eyes.

"Sally, if you weren't my best friend I'd soak you with this lemonade!"

"Hey, honey," Ron said from behind a cloud of black smoke, "do we have anymore buns?"

Billie watched Sally get up and playfully chew out her husband for burning the hamburger buns. She envied their marriage. *Oh Lord,* she sighed, *are there any other good Christian men out there like Ron?* No, probably not, at least not in this town. Well, of course there was Rev. Will. She had sensed for a long time that he liked her, but he'd never asked her out. At first she'd thought he was just shy. But maybe the truth was he simply wasn't interested in her. After all, who'd want a girl with a name like Billie?

She'd always felt embarrassed about her name. Her deceased parents, back on their farm in Iowa years ago, had wanted a son so badly. They had named their new baby "Billie" despite the fact that she had arrived as a girl. Living her life with a boy's name had not been easy.

Billie glanced at Ron who was pressing his ear against Sally's stomach listening to his "son." Just like her parents, he was hoping the baby would be a boy. Ron and Sally had refused the sonogram to learn their baby's gender. They wanted it to be a surprise.

Billie looked into the night sky. *Well, Lord, you know what is right for me,* she thought. Then she whispered a prayer she'd once heard. "When once we see and accept our Father's purpose for our lives to the extent that it becomes our will also, the time and details of His purpose cease to matter."

*I will always be happy with whatever You have in store for my life, Lord,* she thought. *Help me not to look at it from just my own perspective.*

Billie looked forward and sighed with a grin. *I'll probably end up an old-maid schoolteacher, wearing sensible shoes,* she laughed to herself.

Sally turned around from facing Ron, looked at Billie and said, "Hey, what's so funny?"

DONNY MATHEWS PEDALED HIS BICYCLE across the dark desert outside of Oak Hill, following a path he knew well, his thin body and knobby tire dirt bike silhouetted by the full moon's light.

Donny had the same feelings and fears as most thirteen-year-old boys. He faced the same problems all the other kids did that were becoming teenagers.

However, Donny had no guidance in his life. Both of his parents worked long hours so they could afford their new home in an up-scale neighborhood, as well as luxury cars to drive. They selfishly told themselves they were providing a good life for Donny. However, Donny's parents spent very little time with him. They were failing to rear him. Donny was literally rearing himself.

Because Donny had so few parental guidelines, no teaching about God or even about right and wrong, his young mind was open to sinister ways of thinking. He had fallen into the trap of role-playing games to give him purpose in life. Without contrary direction, he daily felt drawn to the world of dark spirits through hard-rock music, MTV, video games, and occult movies.

Tonight Donny was on his way to his secret hideout in the center of a cluster of large boulders about a mile from his house, deep in the empty desert. He went there often at night. Since his parents were seldom at home, he did whatever he wanted. They didn't seem to care.

Sometimes Bobby and David would come with him, but they had both said they needed to do homework tonight. Donny didn't feel like doing his homework.

When he arrived at his special spot, he jumped off his bike and let it drop. Moving around quickly, he placed some sticks of wood in the stone fire ring and started a small fire. He soon had a good blaze going and he sat down close by in deep thought.

*Man, if I could really cast spells, I would take care of that bully Chuck,* he thought to himself. He could think of all kinds of far-out things he would do to him. Donny's friends would think he was really bad then. So would Kathy.

He wouldn't do anything to really hurt him of course, just show him not to mess with the "spell wizard" — the god of Oak Hill and all its territory, he fantasized.

*Yeah,* he envisioned himself resembling the pictures he had of wizards with magical powers, lightning flashing from his fingertips. Now that was something cool — nothing corny like that Jesus stuff.

As Donny gazed into the fire, he continued to build the mental picture of himself as powerful wizard. The firelight reflected off his face in a yellowish glow as he watched sparks swirl upward into the darkness.

That's when he saw him, standing on the other side of the fire.

Donny's heart nearly stopped, his eyes went wide with fear. He felt frozen to the ground and the inside of his mouth tasted like metal. His brain could not believe what his eyes were seeing.

"How ya doing, Donny?"

The eerie words floated across the fire from an old, weird looking man. He was bald with a long, gray beard. He wore a red cape over a robe with a black leather belt around his waist. A large silver emblem, with strange markings on it, hung from a chain around his neck. He was leaning on a wooden staff with a dragon's head carved into the top.

Donny's first reaction was to run, but he was so frightened he could not will himself to move. The old man had appeared as if out of thin air.

"What's the matter, Donny?" the stranger asked sarcastically. "You ain't scared, are you?" His dark, piercing eyes frightened Donny.

The words stuck in his throat, but after a hard gulp Donny finally got them out. "Where did you come from?" he asked, wide eyed.

"Hey, Donny," the old man said, his brow arching. "Don't you know who I am? Don't you recognize me?"

Donny's only thought was that he looked like a skinny, evil, old Santa Claus. Then the boy's eyes grew like large saucers as it hit him; the old guy looked like one of the wizards in his game book.

"You're, you're … " the words stumbled as his mind reeled in amazement.

"Og," the old man said. "My name is Og. I'm an immortal, and I'd like to become your spiritual patron."

"Oh," Donny said. He knew what the old man meant — it was the highest level you could achieve. Spiritual patrons had unlimited power.

"You want to be my spiritual patron?"

"Sure, why not," Og answered. His manner changed. "Unless you don't want me too, in which case I'll just leave," Og said as he began to turn to go.

"No, wait," Donny cried out. "Don't go. Yes," he said thinking quickly, "I do want you to be my spiritual patron. What do I have to do?"

"Well, you know the rules," Og said, turning back, boring his eyes into Donny. "You have to prove your loyalty and courage, you know, like the Knights of the Round Table."

"How do I do that?"

"I can't tell you how, Donny. Everyone has to achieve it on his own. It is never easy, you know that."

Og, his dark, glossy eyes staring wildly, stretched out his hand as if to give something to Donny. "But if you do achieve it, your life can be filled with excitement, power, wealth" — he winked one eye at Donny — "girls."

*Yeah,* thought Donny, his eyes darting back and forth. *This is great. I can do it, I've come this far — I mean, look, Og's here isn't he, and willing to help me.*

His head jerked up and he studied Og. "How will I know when I've achieved it?"

"I'll come and see you again when you do." He vanished in a cloud of gray smoke.

Donny, still unable to move, stared at the spot where Og had been, visualizing the image of the old man. He sat there for a long time, chest heaving, open mouth sucking in the hot desert air. After a while he looked around wondering if the whole thing had been real or if he'd just imagined it.

No, it *had* been real.

The fire died down. Donny finally stood and looked around. The desert was eerily quiet. No living thing stirred. He hopped on his bike and tore off across the sand toward home. He would figure out a way to prove himself and win this game. No problem, he reasoned excitedly, he would really show everyone some real power.

He would really be a spell wizard.

**9:37 p.m.**
United Nations Building

New York City

DOCTOR DAVID ROTH sat patiently in the Secretary General's waiting room. He had just flown in from Israel and had come directly from the airport to see Denzel Marduk.

Dr. Roth was in his late sixties, a small diminutive man with a short, gray beard. He was Jewish and one of Israel's most respected archaeologists. For several months now, he and a few colleagues had been digging through a recently discovered tunnel near the temple mount in Jerusalem. The discovery of the tunnel — and their digging in it — was a closely guarded secret.

In recent years the Arab/Muslim world had stirred up much controversy over supposed tunnels undermining the holy shrines, the Dome of the Rock and the Al-aqsa Mosque. Even though Dr. Roth's tunnel did not go under any Muslim shrines, he had kept this new tunnel discovery a secret. There was no reason to inflame the situation and give the Arabs any more cause to protest.

*Now,* thought Dr. Roth with excitement as he sat alone in the empty room, *the "discovery" my team and I found yesterday will change everything.* He had in his possession digital camera prints of something that would indeed change the skyline of the city of Jerusalem.

Dr. Roth was a member of an organization that, over the last fifty years, had secretly made plans to someday rebuild the Jewish temple in Jerusalem. The blueprints had been drawn long ago. All the stone blocks needed to rebuild the temple had been cut and secretly hidden for decades.

The worship implements for inside the temple had been painstakingly reproduced and were also ready. The only problem had been the site where everyone believed the temple had to be built. The Arab Dome of the Rock was sitting there now. It was the third holiest shrine of the Arab world. To move or destroy it would cause the "sun to catch on fire" politically, and start a war with no end. Therefore, the people of Israel had waited patiently for a miracle to happen ... somehow ... some way.

That miracle was in Dr. Roth's pocket; he had come to Denzel Marduk immediately upon its discovery. The new Secretary General had secretly supported the doctor's quest from the beginning, with money and political help.

A door opened at the other end of the room interrupting Roth's thoughts. Frank Pettinati came into the room and held out his hand, faking a warm greeting.

"Good evening David. It is good to see you. To what do we owe this sudden visit? You know Denzel and I are going to be in Palestine next week and we could have met with you then."

"Mr. Pettinati," Dr. Roth exclaimed, "I have wonderful news! It could not wait. You will not believe it."

"I see," Frank said, his green eyes glowing. "It sounds intriguing — that's why Denzel has agreed to meet with you on such short notice, David. What with his recovering after being shot, well, you can imagine how tight his schedule is right now."

"Yes, it's a miracle," David said. "Is he really healed completely?"

"Yes," Frank said. "Completely."

The doctor thought for a moment, then decided to ask a question that had been bothering him. "Tell me, Mr. Pettinati, is it true, the rumor I've heard about Denzel? After this miraculous healing, it has made me wonder if it could possibly be true?"

"Rumor, David?" Frank said, looking at the manicured fingernails on one hand, his eyes then darting to David's. "What rumor do you speak of?"

"I feel strange asking about it," Dr. Roth said hesitantly, "but, is it true that Denzel's mother was a virgin nun?"

Frank smiled. He had begun to spread that story just recently, and he was pleased that it was getting around to the right circles.

"David," Frank said, "just between you and me, I can honestly tell you, that is a fact. I should know — I was there at the time."

The doctor's eyes grew wide. "Is it also true his mother was Jewish?"

"I have the documents proving it all."

The doctor looked away for a moment in deep thought, then turned back to Frank. "Do you know what this could mean to my people?" he asked in reverence. "He could be our messiah, the one we have waited for for so long."

"Why do you think he has helped you like he has?" Frank said.

Just then, Denzel walked into the room

"Hello, David," he said, shaking the doctor's hand. "Come into my office. We can talk there."

Once they were seated, the doctor pulled about a dozen pictures from his breast pocket and handed half to Denzel, half to Frank.

"Several days ago, we broke through a wall in the tunnel. We came across an ancient room with several drawings on the walls. The pictures you are looking at are of those drawings. They are actual maps of the city of Jerusalem that date back to King Solomon."

"I can see markings on them," Denzel said, "but I don't understand any of them."

"To put it simply," Roth said anxiously, "the Temple was not originally built where the Dome of the Rock now sits, as has been believed." He rose up and pointed to an area on the picture Denzel was holding. "It was built right here. It is an open area on the temple mount. No Arab shrine would be in the way."

Denzel shot a cutting look at Frank and then at Roth. "You're sure about this?"

"Without a doubt, this discovery will be bigger and more important than the discovery of the Dead Sea Scrolls," Roth said. "Once this becomes known, there is no reason the work on the Temple cannot start immediately. Isn't it wonderful?"

"Aren't you forgetting something, David?" Frank said. "The Arab world would never allow a Jewish temple to be built on what they consider to be their holy ground. And your own people would reject it unless the Arab shrines were gone."

Denzel looked at Frank and then spoke slowly as he turned to Roth. "What Frank says is true, of course, but I've been giving the conflict in Palestine a lot of thought lately. I believe I've come up with a solution to the problem there. I believe this discovery of yours, David, will help satisfy everyone once and for all.

"Who else have you told about this?" Denzel asked, his yellow eyes riveted on Roth.

"No one. Only two of my colleagues, and they are sworn to secrecy. I wanted to tell you first, so you could announce it to the world."

"Thank you, David, I would be honored to do that," Denzel said, "but I would like to wait a little while before I do, in order to put my plan of peace into motion."

Denzel leaned forward and looked Roth squarely in the eyes, "David," he asked, "who do your people think I am?"

Roth paused for a moment, his eyes darting around. "Some say you are a great leader," he said, "some even say you must have supernatural powers to be healed the way you were."

"Who do *you* think I am?" Denzel asked.

Roth glanced at Frank for a moment, thinking about their earlier conversation, and then back at Denzel. He looked into Denzel's eyes and felt power radiating from him — power unlike anything he had ever experienced from anyone. Yes, he felt he knew who this man was. His brain believed because of the facts, his heart believed because he wanted it to be true. Denzel was the Messiah, the long-awaited King who had finally come to lead his people.

"I believe you are the Messiah, the one my people have waited for, for so long."

"Trust me, David. When the time is right — and I promise you it will not be long from now — we will announce your discovery to the whole world. But you must have faith that I will choose the right time. Can you do that?"

"Of course. I will seal off the room until you are ready."

"Good," said Denzel standing up and shaking Roth's hand. "I will keep in close contact with you, David."

"All right. I will be waiting to hear from you soon," Roth said, turning to leave. As Frank ushered the Jew from the office, he turned and looked at Denzel. The smile on Denzel's face would have frightened a lesser man. Fortunately, the Jew didn't see when he winked at Frank.

The door closed and Denzel sat down at his desk, deep in thought. Things were working out fantastically. This was great news. Everything was beginning to fall into place in his elaborate plan for the seduction of the Jews and their ultimate destruction. Someday — soon — he would rule the world from their new temple.

"This calls for a celebration." He smiled to himself and rose from his chair. He picked up a package wrapped in brown paper from his desk and unwrapped it. It was a DVD that had just arrived from a friend in California. Denzel pushed it into the DVD player media center on the wall and sat down to watch.

It was of the latest gay parade in San Francisco. The video showed the parade from beginning to end, not just the censored parts that most people saw on the nightly news. The floats were covered with naked men doing all sorts of immoral acts and making all kinds of gestures. Some people walking in the parade were dressed in evil costumes, some depicting Jesus in different wicked and immoral acts. Some of the parade participants walked along chanting "kill the Christians" or "Christians to the lions." The debauchery and morally repugnant displays excited Denzel.

He watched as a long, flowing, rainbow-colored flag traveled down the street, held by many people. He loved it! The symbol of the gay-rights movement was the rainbow, which was also the symbol of the High God's promise to mankind to never flood the earth, after eliminating people who had been practicing this same kind of behavior in Noah's time.

Other displays in the parade used the symbol of a pink pyramid, another mark of the gay-rights movement. Denzel knew that this was another corruption of one of God's symbols. It was all so wonderfully deceiving!

Denzel set the re-play to watch it again, then again, and again. And why not? He did not get much chance these days to fulfill his own personal passions. He loved to go against the laws of God in any way he could, which was why he did not care for the affections of women.

> *Neither shall he regard the gods of his fathers, nor the desire of women, nor regard any god; for he shall magnify himself above all.*
>
> — Daniel 11:37

*Because thy loving kindness is better than life, my lips shall praise thee.*

— Psalms 63:3

# Chapter 11

**6:12 a.m., Monday, September 13,**
Desert Mountains, 5 miles
from Oak Hill, California

.................................................

THE BLUISH BLACK SKY was finally surrendering to the yellow glow of the new day. The sun poked its radiance over a distant jagged mountain range, lighting the rocky knoll where Will stood.

He came here often, usually on Monday mornings. His Sundays were always so busy, and by Monday he sometimes felt let down. That was when he felt the loneliness most. So, he would drive out to this spot, his favorite place to be alone with his Lord. He would talk to Him, right out loud, if he wanted too. He prayed to and worshiped his Heavenly Father, but even more, he could sing. Sing praises to his God, as loud as he pleased, and repeat the words as often as he wished.

Will looked at the new dawn, and felt its warmth on his face. And then he sang:

*My soul proclaims the greatness of the Lord…*
*And my spirit exalts in God my savior…*
*For he has looked with mercy on my loneliness.*
*And my name will be forever exalted…*
*For the mighty God has done great things for me...*
*And his mercy will reach from age to age…*
*And holy…*
*Holy...*
*Holy... is... His name.*

Will turned and looked to the west, over the flat plains to where Oak Hill sat, peaceful and quiet in the dawn. He felt a strong emotional feeling about the events happening in the world right now. He wondered what the coming days would bring. He knew the Lord was letting him know … something was coming.

"Use me, Lord," he prayed, "according to Your will. Watch over the people of my church, Father, and open John's heart to you." Will stretched out his arms and lifted his tear-stained face to the sky...

*And Holy …*
*Holy …*
*Holy … is … His name …*

The words rose up through the still desert air and were heard by Almighty God. It was like sweet incense to the Lord, and the Spirit of the Lord descended on Will…and filled him with His power!

LATER THAT MORNING John pulled his Ford in front of the main gate of the old Army base on the edge of town. The rusted iron gates looked like they had not been opened in decades. He switched off the car engine and read the barely legible sign on one of the gates.

**U.S. Army Installation**
**CLOSED**
**No Trespassing!**

John got out of the car and walked to the gate. He peered through it and saw a weed-infested blacktop road running through the center of the base. All he could see was abandoned buildings and an old water tower.

He stepped back, leaned against the hood of the car, and continued to study the base, pondering what to do next.

John had spent Sunday afternoon scouting around the town and the nearby area, avoiding the base on purpose. A good reconnaissance man always made a survey of the region before going after his objective. Even though he did not learn anything about what might be on the base, he had an understanding of the area, something that could prove useful later on. In a military sense, that kind of recon usually included monitoring the population also. Had he unintentionally used Will in that way? No, he considered Will to be a friend, maybe the best friend he'd ever had, and he had a feeling Will knew why he was there in Oak Hill.

From his rear pocket, John pulled out a map of the area and studied it. The base property extended along the road to his left, until it came to the school at the corner. There a highway ran north out of town, along the base's eastern side. John figured there must be a back entrance to the base somewhere, and that highway might lead him to it. He would check that out next.

He got back into the car and drove toward the school, glancing at the base every few minutes. Suddenly, a small movement in a far-off building caught his eye. Hard to tell from this distance, but he thought he saw activity. As he approached the school, he noticed that the military's tall chainlink fence ran parallel to the school's fence with a small strip of open ground between them.

John parked the car and began walking in the area between the two fences, thinking maybe he could see more activity from that direction. He became aware of children playing in the schoolyard, but his attention was focused on the base's buildings in the distance. Whoever was using the base had to be coming in from a concealed back entrance.

"Is it a habit of yours to hang around outside of schoolyards, Major?"

John turned around. Billie was standing on the other side of the school yard fence, watching him. She stood there with her arms crossed and an inquisitive smile on her face.

His first thought was how pretty she looked. "No, Ma'am." John said. "Just looking at the base." His second thought was how he couldn't stop smiling whenever he was around Billie. "You haven't noticed anyone over there lately, have you?"

"No, no one in town cares much about it any more, unless of course, the Army was going to open it again," Billie said as she walked over to the fence. "Are they planning to do that?"

"Not that I know of. But if I find out they are, you'll be the first to know," he said. He was grinning. He felt like he hadn't smiled for this long at one time since — just about forever.

Both stood there for a moment in awkward silence. Their words collided when they both started to speak at once, "I ... " "I ... "

"Go ahead," John said.

"I noticed you didn't have a Bible with you in church Sunday," Billie said.

"I ... I don't own one."

*That's your trouble.*

Billie tilted her head slightly. "Are you all right, Major?"

"Yes, I'm fine."

"Well, I thought if you didn't have one, I have one in my desk I can give you. You may have it, if you'd like."

"Oh no, I couldn't do that."

"Please, Major, I'd like for you to have it, and I know Will would also, unless you aren't interested"

John absorbed the sincerity and kindness in Billie's eyes; a man could lose himself in those eyes. Truth was, he was interested in reading some of the Bible these days.

"Okay," he said, "I'd be happy to accept your Bible, but only if you will please start calling me John, instead of Major."

She smiled. "Okay, John."

He started walking back to his car. "I'll be there in just a few minutes." He waved to her, and she waved back.

"Room 112."

Ten minutes later, John walked into Billie's classroom. It was between class periods and he had jostled his way through the crowds of kids in the hallways.

Billie was stacking books on her desk next to a vase of violets. "Your flowers are beautiful," he said as he walked up.

"Thank you. Violets are my favorite." She opened a drawer in her desk and took out a Bible that looked well used. When she handed it to John, their hands touched for a moment.

"Thank you. I'll take good care of it."

"Are you a Christian, John?" Her boldness disarmed him.

"Do I love Jesus, as Will would say?" he said with a grin. "No, I'm not." His vibrant blue eyes searched hers for a reaction.

"Well, then, I recommend you read this," she said, taking the Bible back and turning the pages until she came to a certain spot.

John stood there secretly enjoying just watching her.

"And I'd start here." She pointed to a verse and held the Bible out to John. "John, Chapter 3, Verse 16: 'For God so loved the world, that he gave his only begotten Son, that whosoever believeth on him should not perish but have everlasting life.'"

"Those are strong words," John said.

Kids were starting to file in now, and John knew he should leave. "I better get going. Thanks again for the Bible."

"You're welcome," she said, as she walked him to the door.

"Good-bye," he said with a smile.

"Good-bye."

As he turned to leave, he bumped into Sally. "Oh, Sally, please excuse me." John said, glancing at her enlarged abdomen, "Are you all right?"

"Yes, Major, I'm OK," she said, brushing back a strand of curly blond hair, looking coyly at Billie, then back at John.

"Good. I was just about to leave." He glanced once more at Billie, then walked down the hall.

Sally smiled impishly at Billie, and her mouth opened ...

Billie held up her hand, palm out."Don't even go there," she said to her best friend as she turned toward her class.

Back in his car, John drove out of town on the road that took him along the side of the base. Thirty minutes later, on a desolate backroad, he spotted another gate into the base. Inside the fence, next to the gate, stood an old wooden guard shack.

He pulled up to the gate, got out, and walked close to the fence. A man in U.S. Army fatigues, with sergeant's stripes, stepped out of the guard shack. He wore a .45-calibre H & K automatic sidearm.

"Can I help you, sir?"

John took out his military ID and flashed it so the guard could read it.

"What's going on here, Sergeant?" he asked. "Who is using this base?"

"I'm sorry, Major," the Sergeant said crisply. "I cannot tell you that. It's classified, sir."

"If you will look closely, soldier, you will see I have top security clearance on any U.S. military installation in the world."

"Yes, sir. I did see that, sir. I still cannot help you," the guard said, standing ramrod straight and gazing into the distance.

"Cannot, or will not, Sergeant?" John said, his eyes narrowing.

"Cannot, sir!" The guard's eyes held to the distant horizon.

*This Sergeant's exasperating,* John thought. Which was exactly what his job required him to be.

John studied the man's uniform. Other than his sergeant's stripes, it had no other markings to identify him. No one could trace him to any particular unit. John had done the very same thing himself at times, in covert operations.

John became aware of another man in the guard shack, trying to keep out of sight. A rifle was pointed toward him out of a small opening in a side wall.

"And ... I don't suppose you could call your commanding officer to speak with me, either?" John said, slowly eyeing the man.

"No, sir."

John sighed as he shoved his hands into his front pants pockets and looked around at the barren desert. He decided not to push it, "OK, Sergeant. Thanks for nothing."

The guard watched him get into his car and drive down the dusty road.

As John drove back to town, he thought about his next move. If his intuition had been stirred before, it was working overtime now. The gun poking out the side of the guard shack had not been U.S. military issue. John knew a Russian AK-47 when he saw one.

**1:43 p.m.**
Office of Frank Pettanati
United Nations Building, New York City

FRANK PETTINATI STARED AT the incoming e-mail messages on his computer monitor. He had read all but one, another one from that bogus account. *Must be some computer geek.*He cursed inventively and pressed a button to make the message appear.

HELLO SERGIO, MADE ANY MORE POISON GAS LATELY?

"You!" he shouted, his green eyes hot as melted wax. "Who are you?"

The screen could not reply.

Frank almost put his fist through it. "Damn." he said as he looked around his spacious office. When he got his hands on whoever was doing this — he uttered a line of profanity — he'd make them wish they had never heard of Frank Pettinati.

Frank's evil eyes burned into the words on the screen. What could he do? How could he find out who this was? His index finger drummed on the surface of the desk. If he brought in some computer experts to track it down, they would see the messages, so he couldn't do that.

Frank's eyes narrowed. He looked up from the screen and off into the distance. Suddenly the answer popped into his mind. He had other resources he could draw upon, a resource on a higher plain. A grin formed on his face as he got up and walked over to the window. He stood there in contemplation as he looked at the sun in the afternoon sky.

Someday soon, he would cause the people on earth to worship the sun, the moon, and the stars. Especially the "new star" in the sky. He would renew worship of the celestial bodies, a humanistic combination of a "New World Government" and the worship of Lucifer.

Frank was always aware of the supernatural powers bestowed on him by Satan. But he sometimes forgot about the supernatural resources available to him, on that higher plain, that spirit dimension. Unlike any other human who wished to conjure up a spirit from that dimension, Frank did not need to go through a series of rituals. He needed only to speak the name of the one he required.

Offscour." he imprecated clearly.

A few moments passed, while Frank continued to look out the window at the city. He heard a noise behind him, to his right, in the corner. A sound like leather stretching and a smell, not unlike an open sewer, assaulted his nostrils.

A low, throaty, raspy voice said, "I am here."

Frank turned around slowly to see what would have turned any mortal man's blood to ice.

The humpbacked creature, about five feet tall, stood in the corner of his office. Its thin, reptilian body and large wings were glossy black and covered with vertebrae-like bumps. It had claws at the end of its skinny legs and the fingers on its hands were long and bony. Above a cruel mouth, two hooded, iridescent red eyes blinked languorously.

Frank walked to his desk, sat down, punched up the unknown sender's e-mail message, and turned the flat screen in the demon's direction.

"I need to find someone," he said, looking the horrid creature in the eyes, "and I want you to do it for me, quickly!"

Offscour stepped awkwardly to the front of Frank's desk and grabbed a cigar from a humidor box. His head cocked in a playful manner as he bumbled with it, like a toy, with one hand.

Frank never ceased to be amazed at these supernatural beings. They could be so childlike, yet so deadly.

"Someone is sending me e-mail, and not signing it," Frank said, pointing to the message. "Find out who it is. I want his name, and where it's coming from."

Offscour lazily looked over at the message on the screen, then back at Frank. He put the entire cigar in his mouth and started chewing it whole, like a piece of candy — his leathery jaws moving around dramatically. Cocking his head sideways, he blinked his evil red eyes.

"What's in it for me?"

Frank sat back in his chair and formed his hands into a pyramid shape. "When our lord sets up his kingdom here on earth," he said, "I will need someone to be my executor." Frank's eyes shot up and met Offscour's. "That someone will be given much power."

The chewing stopped. Offscour's neon red eyes bulged at the thought, and he swallowed the cigar with a gulp.

Frank leaned forward and pointed to the message. He spoke in a fury. "Now go spread the word to all your nasty, little friends. I want to know who's sending me this ... and I want to know soon!"

The black spirit tilted back on his hind legs and lifted his head in exhalation. "I will report back to you quickly with what you seek." Offscour disappeared in a puff of gray smoke and a crackle of sparks.

Frank slumped back in his chair in an evil pout. He narrowed his eyes at the message still on the screen.

Whoever was sending this ... was as good as dead.

**6:03 p.m.**
Cactus Café, Oak Hill, California

"LOVE WILL KEEP US ALIVE" by the Eagles was playing on the juke box when John walked into the café and spotted Billie alone at a booth near the window.

"Hello."

Billie glanced up. "Hi, John."

"Is this seat taken?" He motioned to the seat across from her.

"No, please sit down. Have you had dinner? I recommend the chef's salad."

"Yes, I know," he said, sliding into the booth. "Since I've been in town, I think I have had everything on the menu at least once."

She laughed. He really liked her laugh.

"So … we meet again."

"I'm glad," John said. "I hate eating alone. Will has been joining me most of the time, but he wasn't home when I called this evening."

"Well, I guess you'll have to settle for his secretary tonight," Billie said shyly, her eyes dipping down.

"That's fine with me," John said, leaning closer to her. "I'd rather eat with a pretty lady any day, than with that red-headed hombre."

She laughed again … that laugh he liked.

Across the street from the café was a large billboard sign that read, "Got Milk?"

Garrett and Caleb sat on the top edge of the sign and watched John and Billie through the café window.

"I'm afraid John is headed for trouble," Garrett said.

Caleb looked at him and frowned. "I think Billie is a very nice Christian lady."

"I don't mean Billie. I'm talking about the U.N. troops."

"I wonder what he'll do when he finds them?" Caleb said, looking back down at John with concern.

"It is important that he does find them," Garrett said.

"He's having a hard time getting onto the base," Caleb said.

"Maybe we can help him find a way," Garrett suggested, slyly looking sideways at Caleb.

"Yeah," interjected Caleb, sitting up straight and looking mischevious. "Maybe we can."

After dinner, John escorted Billie to her house a few blocks away. As they walked and talked along the sidewalk of the quiet neighborhood, John couldn't recall ever meeting anyone like Billie. As they passed houses along the street, he thought of the families who lived in them. He had always figured he would marry someday and have a family. Now, he suddenly realized, he'd been pushing that someday away for a long time.

When they reached her house, Billie stopped and turned to him. He liked looking at her face, she was so pretty.

"What are you looking at?" she said.

"I'm looking at you, ma'm."

Billie gazed down for what seemed like a long time before she raised her eyes back to John's. "I should be going. Thank you for walking me home. Will you be in church Sunday?"

"Yes, if I'm still in town. I like to hear Will preach." John suddenly had a strange premonition that he might not ever see Billie again. The eerie sensation was like a cold finger touching his heart. He hesitated, then said, "I was thinking … could I call you and maybe have dinner again?"

Billie looked down at the ground and did not answer. John felt like kicking himself. She probably considered him too old for her.

"I'm sorry. Forget I said that."

She looked up at him and smiled. "Oh, don't feel bad. You didn't do anything wrong. It's just that — and please don't be offended — I don't date men who are not Christians. I would never want to fall in love with someone," her eyes darted away for a moment, "if they were not a Christian. It's called being unequally yoked."

"I understand," John said. Her strong convictions made him think that much more of her.

"Will's been talking to me about becoming a Christian," he said. "I like what I see in you, and him, and the others in your church.

I guess God and I need to get some things straightened out before I can make a commitment to Him."

"What things?" Billie asked. "Or is the question indiscreet?"

John looked at her as though his mind was somewhere else. "The question isn't," he said, "but the answer might be.

"Good night, Billie."

"Good night, John."

He turned and walked down the sidewalk.

Inside her house, Billie shut her front door and leaned against it, closing her eyes. *Well, girl*, she thought, *why don't you just let the hair grow on your legs and carry a big club around to beat off all the men.* A tear tracked slowly down her cheek.

*Oh Lord,* she prayed, *I only want to be in Your will. My life is Yours. Help me to understand and be patient as I wait on You. Help John to come to accept You. I love you, Lord.* When she opened her eyes, she felt better … much better.

John walked down the street from Billie's house in the warm night air, with Garrett and Caleb following a short distance behind him.

He had enjoyed his evening with Billie. He decided that, when he got back to the Green Motel, he'd start reading her Bible. He needed to study more about this God in heaven.

Garrett and Caleb both looked at each other with a smile, and nodded at that idea.

As John turned a corner and walked out of sight, five kids on bikes came into view, peddling down the street from the opposite direction.

Donny led the group. In back of him rode Kathy and her friend Stephanie. Bobby and David brought up the rear. Donny was not happy that Stephanie was with them. She was tall, with long black hair and, what seemed to Donny, accusing eyes. But she was Kathy's best friend, and Kathy wouldn't agree to come without her.

Donny had convinced them all to go out to his hideout tonight. He had told them they would see something more exciting than they had ever seen in their lives. He couldn't wait to see their faces when he conjured up Og. They were all going to see he really had mystical powers.

Twenty minutes later they arrived at the pile of boulders. Donny quickly got a fire going and instructed everyone to sit around it in a circle.

"OK, so what's the big deal?" Stephanie asked. "What are you going to show us?"

"It isn't anything scary, is it?" Kathy asked, looking around at the shadows the fire created against the large rocks all around them.

"The only thing scary Donny has is his last report card," David joked, laughing and showing off for the girls' sake.

"Yeah," Bobby said, curling over in a belly laugh, "is that what it is?"

Donny glared at his two friends. *Just wait,* he thought. *When Og appears, that will shut them up.*

Donny grimaced. He wasn't quite sure how to summon Og, but he figured that, if he called to him in his mind and focused real hard, surely he'd appear.

He squeezed his eyes closed and concentrated as hard as he could.

"What's the matter, Donny?" David asked. "You got gas or something?" That brought a roar of laughter from the two boys. Donny's eyes popped open, he felt his face turn beet red in front of the girls.

"Will you shut up, David. Can't you see I'm concentrating."

"Concentrating on what?" Bobby asked. "Can't you tell us?"

"You aren't trying to do any of that voodoo stuff, are you?" Stephanie said. "Our Sunday school teacher says Jesus doesn't want us to do that."

"Jesus, Jesus — is that all you girls ever think about?" Donny snarled.

Kathy and Stephanie just stared at him.

Donny was beginning to feel that this Jesus talk would ruin everything. Og wouldn't come around with them talking about that kind of thing.

"Listen, guys," Donny said, exasperated. "Just sit quiet for a few minutes, and close your eyes, OK? I promise you, you're going to see something really fantastic."

Everyone nodded and closed their eyes.

Donny sighed and nervously started concentrating once again. *Come on, Og,* he pleaded in his mind, *show yourself for just a minute. I'll do anything you want if you do. You gotta do this for me or everyone is going to think I'm nuts.*

David opened his eyes and looked around at everyone. They all had their eyes closed, waiting. He noticed a rock on the ground next to him about the size of a baseball. He quietly picked it up and then threw it against the boulder behind Kathy.

Donny heard the rock hit. He opened his eyes and jumped up. "Is that you, Og?"

"Og … who's Og?" Stephanie asked, frowning at Donny. They were all standing now, looking around, confused.

"Og is my friend, and he has magic powers," Donny explained in a rush of angry words. "And if you guys would just give me a chance, he'd appear."

"I'm outta here," Stephanie said in disgust. "Donny Mathews, you're crazy. Come on, Kathy, let's go."

Kathy stared at Donny as Stephanie grabbed her hand. "You shouldn't mess with things of the devil," she said.

David and Bobby picked up their bikes. "Are you guys leaving, too?" Donny said.

Bobby looked at Donny in surprise. "We can't let the girls ride through the desert alone."

Donny couldn't understand why his two best buddies were being so indifferent to him. "Some friends you are."

"Hey, chill out Donny," David said, trying to smooth things over. "Aren't you coming?"

"No. Come on guys, stay with me," he pleaded. "I know Og will show up."

"Well, if he does, bring him over to my house for some of my mom's cookies," Bobby said, "That's where we'll all be."

They all laughed, and rode off into the night. Donny just stood there, the secret still his alone. Tears streamed down his face, and he cursed.

"Why didn't you come Og?" he yelled "Og … Og …"

The name carried across the still desert night.

"Ogggggggggggggggggg!"

Later, after Donny had left, Og sat crouched on top of a large rock by the fire. He had been there the whole time, watching. He was in his natural form, large and black, with huge wings, and a hideous face. His evil red eyes watched Donny ride out of sight.

*It always turned out this way,* he said to himself. *These hu-mans are so simple-minded.* Og knew he had Donny on the edge of doing something now. He'd seen it happen like this so many times before.

By rejecting the most high God, Donny opened himself to Og's influence. It had to happen that way before Og could begin to control him. He could make Donny do almost anything now. Og's hooded eyes narrowed in thought.

It was only a matter of … when.

*Now the Spirit speaketh expressly that, in the latter times, some shall depart from the faith, giving heed to seducing spirits, and doctrines of demons.*

—1 Timothy 4:1

*But to which of the angels said he at any time, sit on my right hand, until I make thine enemies thy footstool.*

*Are they not all-ministering spirits, sent forth to minister for them who shalt be heirs of salvation?*

— Hebrews 1: 13,14

**7:30 a.m., Tuesday, September 14**
Oak Hill, California

........................................

# Chapter 12

JOHN RECEIVED A PHONE CALL from Will in his hotel room first thing in the morning. The big guy wanted to know if John was interested in going to an old mining ghost town up in the mountains and poke around for the day. John decided to go, since it was a chance to possibly get a good overview of the military base from a higher elevation. Maybe even see a place where he could sneak in and look around without being caught.

John packed a small canvas bag with a few items he might need, including a pair of binoculars. He pulled a Colt .45-caliber automatic from his suitcase and checked the magazine. Snapping the clip back into the grip, he put the gun into the bag also.

A horn honked outside his motel room and he grabbed the bag and a pair of sunglasses and hurried out.

Will waited behind the wheel of the Dodge Power-Wagon.

"Good morning," he said with his ever-present smile.

"Good morning," John said, climbing up into the cab. Will shoved the gearshift into first and they took off.

As they drove out of town and past the school, they saw Henry pedaling his bike to work, saluting everyone he saw. The salute for them he held an extra-long time as he watched them out of sight.

**9:45 a.m.,**
Oak Hill Middle School

BY SECOND PERIOD, DONNY could tell that every kid in school knew about his "imaginary friend, Og." He tried to ignore the teasing and remarks from everyone he met, but on the inside he was getting mad. He knew that stupid Stephanie had blabbed it to everyone.

When Donny noticed Kathy in the hall after third period, he turned around to try to avoid her.

"Donny, Donny, wait up." He heard her running after him.

He stopped and looked down at the floor.

"Donny, I've been looking for you all day. Are you all right?" she asked.

"Oh, I'm just great," he said. "Thanks to your friend Stephanie, the whole school is laughing at me."

"I'm sorry, I'm not laughing at you," she spoke warmly. "Try not to let it bother you."

"It's pretty hard not to," Donny said, "I think I'll just move away somewhere else — like the moon."

Kathy looked sideways for a moment. "Look, why don't you come to our Bible study with me after school today." She touched his arm softly. "It might make you feel better."

"I'm not interested in that Jesus stuff," he snapped, startling her. He glared at her with a confused look for a moment, and then turned and walked away.

**10:30 a.m.,**
Rock mountains over looking Oak Hill

THE CAVE WAS PITCH BLACK inside, except for a small fire burning in an open area about fifty feet from the entrance.

Legion sat on a stone ledge near the fire, resting, his hooded eyes closed. The fire's light reflected on his body and large wings, casting a silhouette of his shape against the stone wall behind him. Many red eyes glowed in the darkness around him. A black form moved occasionally among the shadows.

Executor hobbled near to Legion and waited silently, watching him.

Legion's eyes remained closed as he growled, "What is it?"

Executor swallowed a gulp of anxiety before he spoke. "We have not found the two from the heavenly host. I believe they have left the area," he boasted.

Legion's hooded eyes opened slowly, and for a long time he stared menacingly at Executor.

"They are still here, they are spying on us," he seethed as his head snaked toward the cowering demon. "They are much too clever for your mindless searchers."

Executor broke eye contact with Legion and looked sideways in exasperation and fear.

Legion's eagle-shaped head turned abruptly from Executor, his viper yellow eyes aimed at a pair of red eyes in the darkness of a nearby corner.

"YOU, come here," he commanded.

The red eyes floated closer in the blackness and became framed by a dark, hideous profile with folded wings standing against the light of the fire.

"Yes, my lord," Og said, bowing and giving Executor a quick sideways glance of contempt.

Executor returned the insolent gesture with a challenging glare.

"Make something happen to bring the two from the heavenly host out into the open," Legion ordered, his evil eyes set in determination. "I want to know who they are before I leave for Palestine this evening."

"As you wish, my lord." Og's sly mouth curved into a wicked grin as his body bent in respect, he turned around slowly and faded into the darkness.

"And Og ... " Legion's ominous voice traveled out after him.

The red eyes turned back in Legion's direction from out of the darkness.

"... do not fail me."

**11:07 a.m.,**
mountains overlooking Oak Hill

THE POWER WAGON CREPT up a rutted, narrow, winding road on the side of the rocky mountain. The truck's throaty engine growled in spurts as the 4x4 tediously bumped and crawled ahead. From inside the cab, John studied the military base on the flatlands far below, but he couldn't see much detail without the binoculars, that were still in his bag.

"What's on the base you're not telling me about?" Will asked. John stared at him questioningly, but Will had on dark sunglasses between that stormy red hair and beard, so John couldn't read his eyes.

With a sigh, John turned and gazed out the windshield, deciding to confide in his friend. "I have information there are thousands of Russian U.N. peacekeeping troops hiding there."

Will slammed the Power Wagon to a halt.

"What?" exclaimed Will. "Did you say thousands? Are they just visiting on maneuvers? Shouldn't you know about such things? Doesn't the Army know they're here?"

"Whoa," John said, holding up his hands in defense.

"They're not just visiting on maneuvers," he said, "What's more, there are thousands on other bases around the country. I believe that very few military people know they're here, and no citizens have been told. It's a very big, well-kept secret."

"You're kidding," Will said. "Why?"

John's demeanor and voice became deadly serious. "It's a conspiracy, Will, or I would have known about it. But I … and I'm guessing a lot of other people in the government … have been left out of the loop on this one."

John turned and looked out the windshield to the far horizon. "I'm here investigating on my own. I can't blow the lid off this thing until I have some tangible proof. The problem is, I can't even get onto the base without causing a ruckus." John explained about his experience with the guard at the back gate the day before.

"I see," Will said, nodding his head. "Do you have any idea why they might be here?"

"Yes, I do. I think it has something to do with our *friend* Marduk."

With a look of surprise followed by alarm, Will turned to John. "Yes, it makes sense. Well, so much for visiting the ghost town. What can I do to help you?"

"I can't let you get involved in this, Will," John said, shaking his head. "Like I said, I have no authorization myself to be investigating this, and it could become dangerous."

"I want to do something," Will insisted. "If Marduk is involved, you need my help, buddy."

"Why is that?" questioned John.

"Because we're talking about spiritual warfare here."

**12:07 p.m.,**
Oak Hill Middle School

AT LUNCH, DONNY SAW David and Bobby eating with Chuck — and he couldn't believe his eyes. They were laughing and joking around. Those traitors, he thought, as he dumped his uneaten lunch into the garbage pail.

As he turned to leave, he heard Chuck telling the group he was going to Bible study after school with Kathy.

Enraged that things were not going as he had planned, Donny left school right then — he'd had enough. As he rode his bike home, he cursed everything and everyone he knew. *Why didn't Og appear like he said he would,* he kept thinking over and over in his mind.

Suddenly he recalled exactly what Og had said — that the old man wouldn't come back to see him *until* Donny had proved himself, like in the games.

Donny stopped and sat on his bike trying to concentrate his mind in a cloud of confusion. He didn't know how to prove himself in this game. He didn't have powers, or a sword, or any weapon to battle anyone, like they used in the games.

Or did he...?

His mind raced with hatred, wait a minute, he ... could ... prove himself. He certainly knew who his enemy was: Chuck. Okay, he reasoned, getting a handle on his strategy. He also knew where he could find Chuck later today. Yes, and if he proved himself against Chuck, then Og would come and see him again, he just knew it. He would just scare the heck out of Chuck, and then he would advance to the next level. Og would become his spiritual patron, and everything would be okay again. Donny's body jiggled with hypertension and a demented smile crossed his face.

Yes, now he had a plan. He was experienced at planning and winning. Donny's eyes gleamed as he started pedaling once again down the street.

When Donny got home, he went straight to his parent's bedroom. Up on the shelf in the closet he pulled down his father's .38 pistol. He knew how to use it; he had fired it out in the desert once with his dad. The gun had a trigger lock on it, but Donny knew where the key was. It was all part of getting around the obstacles, just like in the games. It didn't take a lowly gnome to figure that one out.

And it certainly wasn't going to stop the "Spell Wizard."

**1:34 p.m.,**
Mountain overlooking Oak Hill...

JOHN AND WILL WERE LYING on their stomachs on

a stone ridge overlooking the Oak Hill Valley. The Power Wagon sat behind them at the bottom of the ridge.

John had been surveying the base with his binoculars for a long time when Will finally asked, "Ya see anything?"

"No, not yet," he answered, still looking through the binoculars. "What did you mean earlier when you said 'spiritual warfare?'"

"Well," Will said, "the Apostle Paul in the book of Ephesians, Chapter 6, verse 12, warns the Christians that we fight not against flesh and blood, but against principalities. There are powerful fallen angels of the devil out there that rule certain regions on earth. This verse points out that these rulers of darkness even rule the skies. They are part of thousands of the devil's demons that fight against God's angels on another dimension, invisible to humans."

"What are they fighting over?" asked John.

"The souls of man. The devil doesn't want people to accept God's salvation plan for mankind. He knows he can never live in heaven, and he doesn't want anyone else to be with God either. If he can stop them from accepting God's gift of eternal life before they die, then those souls will remain with Satan for eternity."

John finally turned his head away from the binoculars and looked at Will. "And you believe these angels are around you all the time and can effect your life?"

Will looked at John and grinned, "I certainly do, and I have no doubt."

"Hey, what are you fellows doing there?" came a voice from behind them.

Startled, Will and John turned around to see an old man standing behind them. John was unnerved for a moment, wondering how the old guy could have walked up on them without making a sound.

John and Will quickly stood, all the while studying the old man with guarded amazement. The old timer looked like a prospector out of a western movie. He was probably around seventy, with a long, gray beard that matched the hair under a cowboy hat that had the brim pinned up in front. He wore old overalls held up by red suspenders over a blue and white checkered shirt.

"Hi," John said in a restrained voice, fully recovered from the old guy's sudden appearance.

"Hello," Will said. He gave a friendly smile while his dark eyes studied the old man intently.

"Don't ever see too many folks up here," the old man said, his hands shoved into the front pockets of his blue jeans. "You boys lookin' for sumthin'?"

"We were just studying the military base down there," John said, nodding to the flat desert below. "Do you know this area around here?"

"Yep, me and my mule" He nodded down the ridge to a mule standing next to the power wagon. "Know every rock for fifty miles around."

Will glanced down the slope where the mule stood with packs and a pick and shovel strapped to its back. Apparently the old guy was a prospector. Will quickly brought his attention back to the old man and could not help staring at him in silent wonder. There was something about him that the preacher could not figure out. The prospector appeared normal, but a distant voice on the edge of Will's mind whispered an unrecognized revelation.

"Say, old timer," John said, opening up his map of the area. "If a person wanted to drive onto the base without going through any of the gates … " he paused, eyeing the old man slyly, "… I don't suppose a man who knew the area as well as you do would know any hidden ways in, would you?"

"'Course, I do," exclaimed the old guy, pushing out his suspenders with pride. "Why do you want to know?" he asked, a hint of curiosity mixed with accusation, turning his head sideways with one eye squinted shut.

John pulled out his Military ID and held it up. "I can only tell you it is a matter of national security."

"I believe ya," the prospector said, rubbing an ear with two fingers as his diamond blue eyes shot a look at Will. The red-bearded man perceived a message in those eyes but could not grasp its meaning. The old man's concealing stare drifted from Will, giving his attention back to John. He had not even glanced at the ID.

"Ya see that wash?" he said to John, his finger pointing to where the Power Wagon and the mule stood. "If you were to follow that all the way, you'd come to a place by the base no one knows about. It's surrounded by high mountain walls so the military never put up any fence there."

"Ah, perfect," John said. "Thank you, sir. You have been a very big help."

Will stood transfixed, an inquisitive look on his face, still enthralled at the old man.

"Well, gotta get." The prospector turned around abruptly and walked down the hill toward his mule. "You boys be safe now, ya hear?"

Will kept staring as the old man ambled to the bottom of the ridge. He suddenly yelled after him. "Hey, friend, what's your name?"

As if in slow motion, the old man turned for a moment and looked intently back at Will with eyes that seemed to sparkle.

And in that moment Will knew.

"They call me Caleb," the old man said with a smile, his diamond eyes looking intently at Will for a long moment before he turned and walked to the mule.

Caleb approached the mule, picked up the reins, and spoke quietly to the animal. "Time to go, Garrett." They both began walking away. "Next time, it's your turn to be the mule," said the mule to Caleb.

"Caleb? What kind of name is that?" John said to Will.

Will stood there watching the old man and the mule disappear behind some rocks. The whole, rapid exchange had a dream-like quality in his mind, yet he knew what had just happened had been a gift from God.

"You okay?" John asked, looking at him strangely.

"I'm great," Will said as he turned and looked at his friend. He could try telling him, but John would never believe it. "Now you know how to get onto the base. Let's call it a day and go home."

**4:00 p.m.,**
Oak Hill Middle School

Sally and Billie worked together arranging the chairs in a circle in the cafeteria for the Bible study. Several kids had already arrived and were talking by one of the many doors leading into the large room.

"I hope I do all right," Sally said, fidgeting nervously. "I've never taught a Bible study before."

"It won't be any different from teaching Sunday school," assured Billie, "and you've done that for years. Now don't worry, I'll be here, and I'll be praying for you, OK?"

"Have I ever told you how much your friendship means to me?" Sally said, stopping all of a sudden, holding her enlarged stomach, and looking at Billie with moisture in her eyes.

Billie smiled at her friend. "Now don't get sentimental on me. I don't have any Kleenex."

Other kids started arriving. Kathy and Stephanie walked in with Chuck. Henry came in and started sweeping the floor with a dust mop. As he moved around cleaning, he disappeared through an open door and was out of sight for a moment.

Suddenly a girl screamed and pointed her shaking hand toward the doorway. Donny stood there with a gun in his hands; it was pointed at Chuck.

Garrett and Caleb stood across the room and watched Donny. Three demons were hovering behind him. One was a spirit named Hate, one was named Murder. The third, named Og, hovered over Murder and Hate, inciting them on.

Sally spoke before she thought: "Donny, you put that gun down right now, you hear me!"

Donny swung the pistol around, pointing it at her. She stepped back with alarm.

"Don't tell me what to do," screamed Donny, his eyes glazed.

All the kids in the room quickly ran out the doors when Donny turned.

Billie stood terrified watching Donny take a step toward Sally.

"I hate you!" Donny screamed, his eyes darting around. He could see now the other kids had left.

Sally stared at him wide-eyed and instinctively putting her hands in front of her stomach. She froze as she realized she had brought Donny's wrath upon her and her unborn baby.

Caleb turned with alarm to Garrett. "Garrett, he's going to… "

Garrett watched intently and replied quietly, "I know… "

Donny pulled the trigger.

Garrett's eyes saw the bullet leave the gun barrel. He watched it as if in slow motion as it slowly twisted in its travel through the air toward Sally.

"No!" yelled Billie. Her scream echoed the sound of the gun blast as she leaped in front of Sally. The bullet slammed into her chest and she fell backwards knocking Sally down.

"Now," shouted Garrett.

He and Caleb quickly drew their swords and soared toward the demons. With frightened red eyes, two of the demons behind Donny suddenly noticed the charging angels and the two black spirits rocketed away in opposite streams of smoke. Og saw Garrett barreling down on him and he screeched a hateful war cry. He swung his sword menacingly at the heavenly angel. With a terrible swift blow Garrett's sword sliced through Og in a flashing arc before the demon could escape. Og screamed in horror as his body disintegrated in an electrical flash.

As Sally fell backwards, she hit her head on the edge of a table, knocking herself unconscious.

Billie watched her as she fell. Somehow she knew Sally would be all right. As Billie followed her down, her head bent sideways in prophetic realization; she also knew Sally's baby was a girl … and that Sally would name her Billie.

*Oh, no,* she thought, *not another little girl having to live with that name...*

She would have to talk to Sally about that later ... when this... was over.

Billie slumped to the floor next to Sally.

Henry had been behind the door. As he came around, he heard the shot. The sound was one he was familiar with in the jungle.

But he wasn't in the jungle.

He stopped, his dark eyes looking around as if he were seeing things for the first time.

He was holding a mop, standing in a strange room.

As he turned, the fog in his mind melted away. He saw a boy pointing a gun at two women lying on the floor. Instinctively, the sergeant swung the mop up hard and caught the boy between his arms; the gun flew from his hands and clattered to the floor.

Donny whirled and ran out the door with Henry chasing after him.

IT HAD ALL HAPPENED in less than thirty seconds.

Billie opened her eyes, her head lying sideways on the cafeteria floor. Her brown eyes searched unfocused for a moment; she thought she could hear church bells ringing faintly in the distance. *That's funny,* she recalled, *there aren't any church bells in Oak Hill.* She raised herself up on one elbow and then noticed two men squatting next to her. She didn't recognize either of them, but they were smiling at her like old friends.

Billie touched the side of her head with one hand, thinking she should be doing something but she couldn't remember what it might be.

*It's like when you graduate from high school,* she thought. *You look back over all the worldly things that had been so terribly important to you at the time, but then you suddenly realize that those things weren't significant at all, now that you were moving on.*

One of the men offered his hand and helped her up. They turned silently and walked outdoors, and she followed them. Outside, Billie searched with blinking eyes toward a bright light on the horizon, toward the sound of the bells. In the distance she saw a river, where the water was shining brightly.

There's no river near Oak Hill, she remembered. She looked at the two men. They seemed to understand what was going on.

"Why are you here?" she begged earnestly of them.

"We are here to take you to Jesus," Garrett said. "He's waiting for you." He nodded toward the river.

"Jesus?" Billie asked, her heart bursting with joy as she looked toward the river, feeling powerfully drawn in that direction.

"Jesus, oh how wonderful," she exclaimed as the bright light beamed upon her face, reflecting on the tears running down in streams.

Along with the golden bells ringing louder now, she could hear singing and rejoicing coming from the direction of the river. As the two men started walking that way, they turned and beckoned to her. They wanted her to go with them.

So she followed them.

# PART III

# The Apostasy

*How art thou fallen from heaven, O' Lucifer, son of the morning! How art thou cut down to the ground, who didst weaken the nations! For thou has said in thine heart, I will ascend into heaven, I will exalt my throne above the stars of God; I will sit also upon the mount of the congregation, in the sides of the north, I will ascend above the heights of the clouds, I will be like the Most High.*

— Isaiah 14: 12-14

**Tuesday, September 14, 5:49 p.m.,**
Mount Megiddo, Israel

# Chapter 13

THE MOUNTAIN STOOD TALL and magnificent, rising high into the sky with a tangerine-and-magenta-colored sunset as a backdrop. The silhouette of the mountain was cast like a stone monument in the midst of the flat Jezereel Valley and the plain of Esdraelon.

On a slope covered with orange trees, miles of expansive lowlands away from the mountain, stood the Messenger. The last brilliant rays of the sunset shot yellow gleams across his face. He wore his black Fedora, beneath which his piercing blue eyes stared at the mountain many miles away. He shoved his hands into his long dark coat as a chill wind blew around him.

**The Hebrew name for Megiddo is Armageddon. The rugged mountain commands the plains around it for two hundred miles. This area has been a battleground for many armies throughout the centuries. It has been said that more blood has been spilled around this site than any other place in the world.**

**It is Satan's favorite place on earth.**

Night came quickly as the hidden sun's last rays faded away. The growing darkness swallowed up the landscape on the slope, blotting out the figure standing alone among the orange trees.

THEY HAD BEGUN TO ARRIVE on the mountain, days before the meeting was to begin. From all over the world they came, millions of demons. From the least and insignificant through the ranks to the most powerful — the princes — they all came.

By nightfall, after much jostling and mischief, they began to settle down by rank in groups on the side of the mountain.

The gathering spread out across a vast area in a half circle around a high knoll. The princes moved to the front of each of their groups, formed in a pie shape according to rank, with aisles between each group. It made the whole gathering appear like an arena. Never before in history had so much evil gathered in one place.

At midnight, the dragon, Satan, appeared high atop the knoll. To the cheers of his unclean spirits, he stood brilliant, magnificent and powerful. As he gazed over his multitude of fallen angels, the princes each stepped out from in front of their commands and moved closer. They stopped in a close semicircle and bowed to their lord.

From an eerie greenish light shining behind the dragon, two human figures stepped into view on either side of Satan. Frank took the position to his left, Denzel to his right. Standing there, the three formed the shape of a pyramid.

Satan glared across the vast gathering in silent thought. He had just recently returned from the throne room of the Most-High God.

Even though no one except God knew the day of Christ's return for the ones on earth who worshiped him, no one was a better student of when the "season" of that return would occur than Satan. The "signs" of Christ's coming had all been fulfilled. And on this last visit to the throne of the Most-High God, a sense that Satan had honed over thousands of years told him the return and gathering must be close, very close.

It was time now for him to make his countermove, and strike first, playing upon the Most-High God's plans.

Satan's plan would bring world condemnation on the believers of the Most-High God. It would help cause those who would be left on earth, after the Christians were gone, to start hating God. That's how he would pave the way for Satan's man Denzel Marduk to take control of the world and, ultimately, pave the way for Satan's kingdom on earth.

Everything was set. Satan had spent over a half a century preparing the world for this next stage of events. He would be victorious, he knew, and soon the world would be his alone. His kingdom, forever.

Satan spoke, his deep voice echoing against the rock walls and across the horrible gathering. "The time is here. The season we have been waiting for is upon us. The deception we have been preparing for so long shall begin the day after tomorrow."

A wild exclamation arose from the vast demonic multitude at this long-awaited announcement. Excitement filled the air. A roar of anticipation moved across the group in a wave.

The princes standing before Satan eyed one another, vindicated in their surmise of the purpose for this unprecedented gathering. Now their primary concern focused on who among them would be the leader, who would rule over all the others in Satan's coming kingdom. Each had his own plan to vie with the others to be the one Satan would chose to be the most powerful.

One of the princes, called Baal, stepped forward boldly. This land they had gathered on was his territory. He had been a powerful prince longer than anyone here. The hu-mans who had first come to this land, even before Moses and his people, had all worshiped him. A few yards from where they stood now rested the ruins of a temple built in his honor by the king of Israel, Ahab, and his wicked queen, Jezebel. For centuries, hundreds of thousands of newborn babies had been sacrificed to him in temples just like this one.

Baal had taken on the "godlike human form" that resembled the pagan idol images, made of gold, that the hu-mans had always created to worship him. His body gleamed with a golden glow, and when he swung back his heavy purple cape, he revealed a large gold sword.

Baal spoke with confidence and authority. He knew most assuredly that he would be named the leader. "Has my lord chosen the one to rule at his side?" he asked Satan. "My lord knows of the innocent blood that has been sacrificed in my name over the centuries, in my name but for you."

"It is but a pitiful offering," growled a voice to his left.

Baal turned in fury toward the mocking voice of Legion as the eagle-shaped prince haughtily stepped forward.

"It cannot even compare to the countless millions of innocent hu-man babies slaughtered before birth in my territory, in just the last fifty years," Legion said with a smirk.

Baal glared at him as Legion gestured with a sweeping hand over the other princes while looking straight at Satan.

"Surely, my lord cannot compare the power I have wrought in America with anyone else here. I alone command the most power, and I can lead them for you, Master," he announced as he bowed slightly.

"I think not," a third voice bellowed to the left of Legion. Legion turned his head slowly to see where the challenge had come from.

A huge, winged, dark figure stepped forward; his body appeared as if it were made of glossy black armor. Two swords hung, one on each side, from a wide belt around his powerful body. On his massive left biceps, a swirling sun symbol, or swastika, glowed neon red. A silver death's head emblem glimmered in his forehead over angry hooded eyes.

His name was Odoacer, and he was the prince of Prussia. Directly responsible for the persecution of the Most High's chosen people down through the centuries, Odoacer prided himself on his reputation as a exceedingly cruel executioner. The black prince had gained favor with Satan in the middle of the last century for the slaughter of more than six million Jews, and the haughty Prussian was not about to let this upstart from America lead him.

Legion's eagle eyes were filled with rage as they riveted on the self-assured Odoacer as the black monster addressed Satan.

"The only thing this one is capable of leading," Odoacer snarled, gesturing in Legion's direction, "is swine!"

That brought a roar of laughter and back-slapping mischief from Odoacer's followers. The lesser of them, way in the back of the group, swirled around in the air in a crazed frenzy.

Legion uncoiled and struck like a viper, attacking with his massive sword visible only as a sudden blur catching a glint of light as it split the air seeking revenge. Its tip caught the astonished Odoacer under his chin, his claws caught hovering over his own swords in a failed response.

All the demons on the mountain suddenly held their breath in wary silence over the outbreak of savage disrespect in the presence of Lucifer. Every red eye locked on the terrible scene before them. No one dared move as they waited for the inevitable violence to erupt as the followers behind each prince inched threateningly toward the other.

With a slight raise of his arm, Legion triumphantly moved Odoacer's head up at an uncomfortable tilt.

"You are getting too feeble and slow, Odoacer, to think you could lead me," Legion said, his topaz eyes filled with vile contempt. The eagle-shaped demon seethed in barely controlled rage as he forced the point of his sword harder into the Prussian's throat.

"ENOUGH!" Satan roared in a voice not to be disobeyed.

Reluctantly, Legion released Odoacer's head and withdrew his sword. Odoacer glared at him with boiling hatred.

"I will choose a leader, after the deception is complete," Satan commanded, regaining the multitude's attention. The Devil's eyes searched intently over all the princes. "We will see who is worthy during the coming conflict."

*So,* thought Legion as his eyes darted around at the other princes, *this will be the test to determine which one of us will be chosen.*

"What is most important right now," Satan shouted, "is that the deception occurs." His voice grew in pitch and he glanced directly at Legion. "I will be watching everyone, so be sure that you do not fail. The day after tomorrow, start the deception," Satan commanded. "Soon *all* will know who is the god of this world, and soon my kingdom here on earth will begin ... *forever!*"

The millions of demons shrieked in battle cry, hailing allegiance to Satan over and over again.

Their shouting continued for hours ... it filtered up through the night sky ... traveling upon the wind currents floating across the flat plain ... until finally it drifted up a slope to a silent figure, standing alone in the shadows of an orange grove.

*Now learn the parable of the fig tree; When it's branch is yet tender, and putteth forth leaves, ye know that summer is near.*

*So, likewise ye, when ye shall see all these things, know that it is near, even at the doors. Verily I say unto you, this generation shall not pass, till all these things be fulfilled.*

— Matthew 24:32-34

**7:49 a.m., Wednesday September 15,**
Oak Hill, California

........................................

# Chapter 14

WHEN JOHN AND WILL RETURNED to town the previous evening and they learned about Billie's death, the shock was overwhelming.

They now sat in the Cactus Café, neither one able to eat the breakfast they had ordered. Both men were still stunned by the fact that Billie was gone. Each was lost in his own deep thoughts about the woman they had both loved.

"It's hard to believe. Why would God allow this to happen to her?" John said, finally breaking the silence. "Billie was such a sweet Christian woman." It was the same terrible question he had wrestled with his whole life. Why had God taken away the people he loved?

Will looked down at his untouched breakfast, then stared at nothing through the window beside their table. He was trying to gather his own thoughts.

John peered at him cautiously. He could tell Will was really hurting.

Finally, Will turned to John and spoke. "Becoming a Christian does not make you immune to the bad things in this world, any more than it makes you a perfect person. When you accept Jesus, and his gift of salvation, that leads you to the ultimate goal of living with Him in heaven. However, you still live in this world until you die. The difference is that, as a Christian, you begin to view things of this world from a higher plane, where Jesus is in control of your life. You begin to understand things from His perspective, not just your own. The world continues to be the way it has always been, corrupted by Satan. A Christian is one who is just passing through this world, as opposed to one who wants to reject Christ and live life any way they please, to be of this world only.

"Billie is with Jesus now, and for eternity. Sure, we feel sad, because we miss her. But there is rejoicing in heaven, because she is with the Lord she loved. People ask, why do bad things happen to Christians? They somehow expect them to be immune from troubles. Well, God does protect Christians at times, believe me, but the point is, we do not always understand why God works the way he does. Nevertheless, a wise Christian learns to understand that everything that happens is all in God's plan and He is always in control. If we put our trust in Him, He promises He will always be with us through anything. It is a hope that non-Christians do not have."

"I was beginning to have deep feelings for her," John admitted. "I find a good woman and suddenly she's taken away."

"God took her home, John," Will said. "His plan for her was not to be part of either of our lives. God has a plan for your life, too, John, if you allow Him."

John glanced at Will with uncertain eyes. He then turned and looked out the window at a billboard across the street that read "Got Milk?" It made him think, "Got Eternal Life?"

Garrett and Caleb sat on the "Got Milk" sign and watched Will and John in the café.

"I feel so sad when someone like John keeps stalling about whether to follow our Lord," Caleb said "Why can't he see that the truth will set him free from his pain?"

"Some people are just more stubborn," Garrett answered. "You know that."

"Yes, and some never accept our Lord," Caleb sighed.

"Then," Garrett said, "that is their decision that God has allowed them to have. It is an interesting concept called 'free will.'"

"Yes, but it's still so sad when someone rejects God. They never experience the wonder of His love," Caleb said as he lowered his head in dismay. He noticed something in Garrett's hand — an earth plant called a violet.

"What are you going to do with that?"

Garrett held the flower up, admiring it. "Oh, I promised someone yesterday I'd deliver it for them."

**8:55 a.m.,**
Oak Hill Middle School

DRESSED IN HIS LEVI'S SHIRT AND JEANS, cowboy boots, and gray Stetson, the Messenger stood on the sidewalk across from the school and watched the children arriving for class. Most were brought to school by concerned parents, this first morning after yesterday's shooting of a teacher in the cafeteria.

**The world did not pay much attention to the shooting here yesterday. So many similar shootings had happened in other schools across the country, it was not something new.**

**It had been good for the lead story on the local Los Angeles evening news. The commentators had talked about what a strange**

tragedy it had been. They linked it to the wave of other school shootings across the country. Moreover, like all those shootings, there seemed to be no explanation why this had happened in Oak Hill.

Why were young boys killing people in school? It was not gang-related, and there was no evidence of drug use, so what was causing it? The commentators would simply end their stories by saying it was a mystery.

Although no one appeared to be very interested in getting to the truth, the news people had actually given the answer. For the definition of the word mystery is "secret worship of a deity." Nevertheless, even if the truth were revealed, they dared not explain it on national television. If they seriously ventured into the world of the supernatural, of demons and the devil, they'd be giving credence to the fact that such beings exist. And if there was an adversary to God, then there must be a God. But anyone who is intelligent and worldly would be thought foolish to believe in God.

A janitor named Henry captured the shooter, a thirteen-year-old boy named Donny, on the front lawn of the school. He held the boy there until the police arrived. Henry was credited with stopping Donny from shooting anyone else and was being hailed as the town hero.

The police questioned Donny for many hours, but he would not give any explanation why he had done such a terrible thing. When the detectives questioned his parents and several of his friends, they mentioned that he was heavily into role-playing games but was otherwise a "normal kid." No one thought to make the connection to explain his actions.

Donny sat in a cell at the police station and wondered how everything had gone so wrong. He would never, ever, tell anyone again about Og. He knew that he was in serious trouble but overall he seemed unfazed, unlike most adults who are demon-possessed and commit murder. Adults usually cannot live with themselves and are driven to suicide.

**The Terminal Generation children's ability to feel guilt has been snuffed out through the daily feeding of violence and smut. They are saturated with movies, television, and hard rock music so evil that it should not be tolerated in a moral society, but it has crept in under the corrupted guise of tolerance for people's rights and free speech.**

**People are not interested in believing in the devil. He does not fit into the free-thinking, self-indulgent "selfism" that defines the popular philosophy of people of the Terminal Generation. In a world that has decided that God is dead, people will believe in anything, rather than have accountability to the living God.**

The Messenger turned from watching the schoolyard and gazed out past the town to the surrounding mountains.

**Sadly, for those who are looking for the devil and his demons, a simple Ouja board can open the door to that realm. Role-playing games open the floodgates.**

The Messenger turned and walked slowly down the sidewalk.

**3:00 p.m.,**
Oak Hill Church

WILL TOLD JOHN THAT, BECAUSE BILLIE had no living family, they would hold her funeral today.

John felt guilty and miserable. He wanted to try to sneak onto the base today, but he knew he had to go to Billie's funeral. His emotions were in turmoil as he walked into the church.

The memorial service was beautiful to John, and it had a calming effect on him. In these people of God who had come not only to say good-bye but to celebrate Billie's life, he could sense the deep feelings Will had talked to him about earlier.

Will read a verse during the service that touched John's heart considerably. It was Acts 20:24 : "But none of these things move me, nor do I count my life dear to myself, so that I might finish my race with joy, and the ministry which I received from the Lord Jesus, to testify to the gospel of the grace of God."

John thought those words had fit Billie perfectly — what a legacy.

After the service, John went over to Ron and Sally.

"I'm so sorry about your friend," he said quietly.

Ron held Sally closely, afraid she would break down under the strain.

Sally smiled at John, but her eyes seemed distant and far away. "She saved my life, you know," she murmured, "and my child's." Her eyes filled with tears. She bowed her head for a moment and then looked up again. "She was my best friend."

John looked at Ron, and they nodded slightly to each other, the way men do before Ron guided his wife away.

John turned and saw Henry standing with his mother. Instead of saluting, Henry boldly held out his hand and John shook it warmly with surprise on his face.

"My mother tells me I've met you before," Henry spoke in a new, confident voice. "But, well, I don't remember."

John could tell immediately that this was not the same, simple-minded man he had met before. Henry's mind was healed. He was the man he had been in Vietnam and before. It was nothing short of a miracle that he was normal again.

Henry must have presumed that John was a member of the church when he said, "I'm not a Christian, Major. I came to church for my mother's sake today. So you'll be seeing me here every Sunday, and maybe someday soon I'll do something about becoming a Christian, but I need a little more time to get things sorted out in my mind."

John knew that feeling all too well. "I'm not a Christian either, Henry," he admitted, "but I'm considering it, also. The people in this church have something I think is worth having."

Henry's mother looked at John and, smiling, said, "I have

prayed for my son's healing and his salvation, Major. The Lord has answered half my prayer in a mighty way." She put her arm around her son. "I know he will answer the rest. I will pray that you will come to know the Lord, too."

"Thank you, ma'am." John looked at Henry's mother and then back at Henry, envying their close, loving relationship.

Henry put his arm around his mother and they turned to leave. "See you around, Major," he said, with a slight wave so near yet so different from his former compulsion to salute.

As John watched them leave, he knew what Henry's mother must have felt after all these years: Henry had finally come home.

After saying good-bye to Will, John left the church and decided he needed to be alone for a while. Tomorrow he'd sneak onto the base and find out what was there.

**6:48 p.m.,**
Home of Ron and Sally Mitchell…

RON LOOKED OUT HIS KITCHEN WINDOW at his wife working in her vegetable garden. Sally had taken a few days off from teaching at the school since the shooting. It was good for her to be working in her garden. Tending God's earth always eased her troubles.

As he watched, she knelt and stared at the ground for a long time, not moving. Concerned, Ron came out of the house, walked up behind his wife, and knelt beside her. When Sally turned around, huge tears were running down her face.

"Hold me," she whispered.

As he held her, she spoke quietly, "Ron, I know the Bible says we are not supposed to try to communicate with loved ones who have gone on. But do you think they can see us, or can … ?"

"I don't know," he pondered. "Maybe."

"I miss Billie so much, but I know she is with Jesus," Sally said, sobbing.

She pressed the side of her head against Ron's chest and looked toward the sunset on the horizon, the sunset of Billie's presence in her life.

"Ron, can we name our baby Billie, whether it's a boy or a girl?"

"Sure, honey. I think that would be special." He held his wife close as the last bright streams of the sunset reflected on them.

Ron glanced down to see what Sally had been looking at so intently. His forehead wrinkled at first, for he could not believe what he saw. Then an understanding came across his face ... and he smiled.

In the dirt between a tomato plant and the beans, a good-bye from a friend had sprouted.

A single violet.

**11:38 p.m., San Gabriel Peak,**
Overlooking the Los Angeles basin

A DARK FIGURE DRESSED IN A LONG topcoat and Fedora stood on the highest peak of the San Gabriel Mountains looking upward at the night sky. The Messenger gazed at the firmament, clear and open for miles. Only the stars were visible, and they all seemed to twinkle in the silent darkness.

**For thousands of years man has looked into the night sky at the planets and stars, and wondered: Is there other existence out there in the universe? Does life only occur on earth?**

**For more than fifty years that question has been amplified by the sightings of unidentified flying objects (UFOs) in the skies around the world. An object in the air, that no one can identify or even prove really exists.**

**Is it a coincidence that this phenomenon began after World War II and its demonstration of the importance of air power in warfare? Since then, it has been hard for the government and the military to ignore these unknown intruders in the skies. Since no**

damage to military property or personnel has ever been reported, the military has taken the position over the years that UFOs pose no threat to the national security.

Although the government and many ufologists have made countless studies of UFOs, no one has ever come up with any proof to what they are.

This is mainly due to the fact that UFOs have always only been observed, not captured for study. Thousands of photographs and videos have been made to give strength to these observations, but no tangible proof has ever been presented to establish just what they are.

Conspiracy theories abound, saying that these UFOs have indeed landed or crashed countless times over the last fifty years. It is then suggested that the evidence is always secretly taken away and hidden by agents working for a government that wants the proof concealed for some sinister reason; even to the point of suggesting that the government is in league with the UFO entities.

Another aspect of the UFO mystery is the alien-abduction syndrome. People who claim they have been kidnapped and taken inside the UFOs say they are here with threatening motives, and that they may at some time snatch a large section of the population away all at once.

Polls in the last decade show that most Americans believe that UFOs are from outer space. This belief was almost nonexistent a half century ago. For the last fifty years, the Terminal Generation has been programmed through science-fiction movies and TV shows. Belief in interplanetary space travel has become commonplace in the minds of people.

There has been so much writing about interplanetary space travel for man that most people now believe that the reality of it is just around the corner. The fact is, science is nowhere near achieving such a feat. Mankind cannot produce materials to withstand the stress, nor has it developed the power source to create the velocities to perform the maneuvers that most UFOs

**are claimed to make.**

**Therefore, the question still remains: What are UFOs? Are they space ships from an advanced alien planet?**

**On the other hand, could the identity of UFOs be drawn more from the facts known about them? UFOs seem only to manifest themselves to the sense of sight; there is no tangible, touchable proof of them.**

**Over the decades, UFOs seem to have had no agenda but to have created a mindset in people about space aliens.**

**They appear, maneuver, and disappear as if by magic.**

**Is it possible that they could be a supernatural trick from the god of this world and ruler of its skies?**

**Could the explanation be part of a plan to help mock the belief in the true God? A device to create a false conception of aliens to a world ready to accept anything in the realm of science fiction, rather than the belief in God?**

**Could UFOs simply be a misleading illusion?**

The Messenger bowed his chin into his overcoat and his blue eyes searched the night lights in the many cities of the valleys below.

**The world has gone to bed this evening without any warning of what tomorrow will bring.**

**When the people of earth wake up, they will see objects in the skies they have never seen before outside of science fiction books and movies. Although they will not be prepared for it, in the backs of their minds they will know what these things are for they have been programmed to expect it. Some have even been anticipating it.**

**The people of the earth have forgotten how to think for themselves. They no longer seek after truth. They are too busy chasing after their own pleasures. Hollywood, the media, and the government have told them what the "truth" is.**

**Thus, the "Terminal Generation" has been conditioned ... to**

**accept a lie.**

The Messenger looked out over the vastly populated valley filled with countless lights and sighed deeply.

He vanished.

*Even him whose coming is after the workings of Satan with all power and signs and lying wonders,*

*And with all deceivableness of the unrighteousness in them that perish, because they received not the love of the truth, that they might be saved.*

*And for this cause God shall send them a strong delusion, that they should believe the lie.*

— II Thessalonians 2:9-11

**6:10 a.m., Thursday, September 16**

# Chapter 15

THE UFOS SUDDENLY APPEARED at daybreak. In the clear blue skies over exactly twenty cities in the United States, England, and Israel, twenty separate silver objects were sighted: three in Israel, four in England, and thirteen in the United States. The aircraft came into sight at about 3,000 feet. They were saucer shaped, about two hundred feet in diameter, with a domed top and upside-down-dish-shaped bottom. The sunlight reflected brightly off their silver metal, and other than what appeared to be windows or portholes dotting the base of the domes, the mysterious aircraft had no other visible markings.

They were flying saucers — except they were not flying. They hovered, motionless, soundless. Waiting. No gun barrels thrust from the porthold-like openings, yet their attitude and posture seemed threatening, aggressive in their silence.

It was shocking to everyone who could see the UFOs when they first appeared. People rushed from their homes to watch the "space ships," taking videos of the silver disks and expecting that they would go away soon. They did not leave.

They stayed, hovering, stationary.

Police phone lines were jammed with people calling to ask what were those things in the sky? Should they be afraid? Excited? Exalted?

No one could answer their questions, for no one knew. Soon the streets and freeways of the cities where the UFOs appeared clogged and came to a standstill. Many accidents occurred because people were watching the motionless silver disks instead of the road.

Confused, people gathered in groups everywhere, watching… watching… mesmerized by the UFOs. No one felt like working, nor even playing. Everyone just stared at the objects and wondered, with feelings of concern and anxiety. What was happening?

In the United States of America, the emergency alert system was used nationally for the first time since its creation. People heard the warning sound on their radios, which they had grown up hearing only during a test of the system. They were informed where to dial to hear a special emergency message, which came directly from the White House. The system had been set up in 1963, during the cold war, to alert the population in case of a nuclear attack. There had always been a prepared message ready for use, for almost any kind of national emergency. Yet, there was no pre-written announcement ready for what was happening now; no one had ever conceived of anything like this. So the message simply told people to stay calm and wait for further information concerning the UFO sightings.

People were not staying calm, however. Around the world, even in countries where no UFOs appeared, people began reacting to the mental shock of the strange sightings. Chaos, whether from fright, or just as an excuse for lawlessness and looting, spread like wildfire.

Emergency rooms in hospitals were filling not only with injured people but also with victims of heart attacks and suicides.

Trauma gripped the world, and the UFOs had only been visible, thus far, for less than an hour.

**7:12 a.m.,**
230 miles northwest of San Diego, California,
over the Pacific Ocean

The two F-22 Raptor fighter jets soared in close formation through the clear sky. Flying southeast over a calm ocean that stretched smoothly to the horizon, the stealth-shaped aircraft seemed to glow in the bright sunlight, each of the jets' canopies reflecting the sun with a bright gleam.

The plane was America's newest weapon in the sky, and the most advanced fighter jet in the world. Each jet's dual Pratt & Whitney F-119-PW-100 engines were able to push it at supersonic speeds for long distances, without using the fuel-consuming afterburner.

In the lead jet, Lieutenant Glen Hancock spoke into his helmet radio to his wing man and best friend, Clem Kidman.

"How ya doing' bro … ?"

"Jus' fine dude," Clem answered.

Based out of Edwards Air Force base in California, Lieutenants Hancock and Kidman were still getting used to their new fighters. Today they were out practicing maneuvers.

Glen's radio crackled as he heard a voice coming from his base. It was not the tower controller as usual, but his squadron commander instead.

"Lieutenant Hancock, this is Major Newcome."

"Yes, sir," Glen replied, wondering why his commander was on the line.

"Lieutenant, we've got an unidentified bogey in the air space over San Diego. It's going to be a few minutes before anyone there can respond, can you check it out?"

Glen could detect urgency in his commander's voice and knew

the reason for it. Hostile aircraft over Coronado Island Naval Base in San Diego Harbor would make the Navy very nervous. Especially with two nuclear aircraft carriers moored in the bay right now. Those carriers would be sitting ducks to any kind of an air attack.

"Sure commander," Glen answered, "we'll go stick our noses in it."

"Roger, Lieutenant, keep me informed."

Glen's helmet turned in the direction of his partner flying off his wing tip and even though their black visors hid their faces, Glen knew Clem was smiling at the thought of some real action.

"You hear that, bro?"

"Let's go take a look," Clem said.

The two jets roared as they increased speed and raced eastward. Glen watched his radar screen in front of him as the jet's sensors gathered, integrated, and displayed essential information for him. He could see the bogey was very close to the harbor.

*Whew, that's weird, the Navy is probably throwing a fit right now,* he surmised.

"Lieutenant Hancock," the commander's voice came over the radio once more, "do you have a fix on the bogey over the naval base?"

"Yes, sir," Glen said. "Four minutes 'til visual." A frown of dismay crossed Glen's face as he carefully monitored his aircraft's readouts; his instruments were unable to identify the bogey. His look changed to shock when he heard the voice on his headset crackle once again.

"Lieutenant, the Navy wants that bogey splashed now. I am ordering you to kill it. Now!"

Glen could hardly believe his ears. This was highly unusual. Firing on an unidentified aircraft, over a populated area in peacetime — it was unheard of. *It must be attacking,* he reasoned

Glen asked for verification of the order.

*What could it be?* he wondered. He had been watching the bogey on his screen and it was not moving. It had stayed in one place since his radar had picked it up. *Must be terrorists in a helicopter,* he concluded. *What else could it possibly be?*

His code verification for the order came through, confirming this was not a drill, that this was the real thing going down.

*Well, whatever it is,* thought Glen with mounting excitement, *it's going to be history in less than thirty seconds.*

Glen flipped several switches arming two AIM20A advanced long-range missiles. When his sensors locked onto the bogey, he fired them.

The two missiles blasted from below his wings in a stream of white vapor and quickly disappeared into the blue sky.

Glen watched on his screen as the missiles homed in on the stationary target.

10 … 9 … 8 seconds until impact.

Suddenly the bogey shifted incredibly fast in a 45-degree angle and shot away. Glen saw it happen on his screen, but could not believe it.

It was too late for the computers in the missiles to compensate. They flew through the open space where the bogey had been just seconds before and then beyond over the ocean.

Glen activated a self-destruct on the missiles so they would blow up without harming anything.

"What the … ?" exclaimed Glen.

Seconds later the bogey returned to its original position as quickly as it had left.

"I saw it, but I don't believe it," Clem shouted over Glen's headset. "I never saw anything move like that before. What is that thing?"

Glen had no idea, but the San Diego skyline was approaching fast. They would see it, whatever it was, in less than a minute.

"Let's take a closer look," Glen commanded.

The jets dropped down to the same altitude as the target and roared toward it. At first, the bogey floating in the distance appeared as a gray speck in the clear blue sky. Glen watched through his canopy, the bogey grew larger as they approached it. His eyes tried to focus on just what is was. A strange intuition reminded him of the dictionary definition of the word bogey: an imaginary image of an evil spirit. *Why,* he suddenly wondered, *is this object making me think that?* As the jets raced closer to the bogey it began to become clearer.

Glen couldn't believe his eyes. It was silver … and round … like a, oh, no … it couldn't be … a flying saucer! Like the UFOs from outer space you saw in the movies when you were a kid.

Only this one was real.

The two Raptor jet fighters roared past the hovering silver disk, one on either side

As Glen flew by it, he felt unnerved. What he had just witnessed was so surreal.

Nevertheless, it was real. He had not only seen it with his own eyes, but it was also showing on his radar.

"I sure hope our cameras are working," Clem exclaimed, "cause they're not going to believe this. That … that looked like one of those UFOs you see in pictures."

"I know," Glen answered with concern in his voice. "Let's try again to carry out that splash order, Clem. Use your short-range sidewinder missiles."

The jets swung around quickly and back toward the object. Clem fired two missiles at the silver disc.

Again, at the last moment, the UFO shot off sideways and avoided the missiles completely.

"I don't know how it can do that!" Clem shouted nervously as they circled around again. Glen couldn't figure it either. The technology of the silver disk was literally light years ahead of their own aircraft, the world's most advanced jet fighter.

"Let's try our guns," Glen suggested as they flew back toward the UFO. "We'll go in together, one on each side. He can't move sideways then."

"Yes, sir," Clem drawled. "Just like ol' times … "

When they came within firing range, the space ship suddenly darted straight up into the air at an incredible speed. The jets passed through the space where it had been without firing a shot.

When they banked around again, the silver disk had returned to its original position.

"It's just playing with us," Clem said. "How can we shoot it down?"

Lieutenant Glen Hancock watched the UFO hover in the sky, and one of his eyelids twitched slightly.

"We … can't." he answered slowly.

BY NOON, THE WHOLE WORLD was caught in the frightening grip of the mystery of the UFOs. The fact that each of the silver flying discs stayed in the same intimidating position, not moving, not giving any indication of their intent, scared people more than anything.

What were they? Could they be aliens from another planet? Most people agreed they must be.

Were they friendly, or was this an invasion of earth? No one wanted to dare speculate on that question.

All of the television channels were covering the story continuously. Through the marvel of satellite communications, the whole world could watch the UFOs from one of the three countries they had appeared over.

In America, the major TV networks were covering the UFOs with live coverage from each of the thirteen cities in the United States. Periodically they would switch to the four in England, and the three in Israel.

They carried stories about the effects that the appearance of the space ships were having on the nation. People everywhere were scared; many had left the cities to take refuge in the country. Rioting and looting were rampant in most of the large cities. Panic was snowballing into unbridled terror.

At 12:15 P.M. came the White House's announcement of a televised press conference at 1:00 P.M. The President would address the nation.

**12:32 p.m., Washington D.C.**
Outside the White House.

THE MESSENGER WAS SURROUNDED by thousands of people pressing up against the wrought-iron fence around the White House. Most of them looked scared and bewildered; many would glance eastward at different times, toward the UFO hovering over the city.

The Messenger, with his hands in his long coat pockets, stood next to the fence and looked at the White House through the iron bars.

**In 1979 President Carter signed into existence a new Federal Agency, called the Federal Emergency Management Agency, (FEMA). In times of disaster, like floods or hurricanes, FEMA is an agency that helps people by providing aid and help to those affected.**

**However, FEMA is also set up to control vital operations of the nation in the case of the President declaring a national emergency. Most Americans are not aware of the potential power this agency could have in a time of crisis.**

**Part of FEMA's emergency measures includes rounding up Americans redlined as potential activists, supporters, or sympathizers of terrorism in the United States.**

**Anyone who speaks out against the government declaring martial law or suspending Constitutional rights could be considered a "terrorist" under the powers granted to FEMA. This power was granted to the President by Executive Order No. 11490. It gives unlimited power to the President and unelected officials of FEMA. When the President declares a national emergency, FEMA can take control over: all electrical power, all farms and food reserves, all transportation, all health and welfare agencies, and it can require citizens to be drafted into a government work force.**

**The American people would be bound by law to submit**

**to anything the President decided must be done. This total government control could take effect over every United States citizen anytime the President decided to declare a national emergency.**

The Messenger turned to a man who was holding a portable radio to his ear. The man announced to the crowd that the press conference was starting. It grew quiet as he turned up the volume so people close by could listen.

**1:09 p.m.,**
White House Press Room...

THE ROOM WAS OVERFLOWING with reporters crammed in like sardines; security guards kept everyone else out. The people in the room were anxious and tense. They all knew they were covering the biggest story of the century, maybe of all time. The mood was electric and yet sober; the question on everyone's mind was: What was going to happen next?

Finally, the President walked into the room and quickly moved to the podium. The Secretary of Defense stood next to the President as he spoke.

The President looked down for a moment with concern at some notes he had brought with him. Then he looked up at his eager audience and smiled slightly before he spoke.

"I am going to read a statement," he began, "and then I will turn the podium over to the Secretary of Defense, and he will answer any questions you might have." He then began to read: "This morning, the people of the world were witness to the appearance of unidentified aircraft in the skies over the countries of Israel, England, and the United States.

"The origin, the purpose, or intent of these aircraft are unknown at this time," he read slowly. "These aircraft have not landed, nor has any physical contact been made with them, as of this hour. I would like to assure the American people that their government is doing everything possible to find out what the purpose is behind these aircraft. We are in constant communication with the governments of England and Israel over this crisis that is facing the citizens of these countries, and indeed the whole world. Because of this dire situation, I am announcing a national state of martial law to go into effect at 5:00 P.M. today."

This brought a gasp from everyone in the room.

"I believe that it is in the best interest of every citizen's safety and well-being that I announce this declaration immediately, until we resolve this situation.

"I have given a Presidential order for the Federal Emergency Management Agency to take over coordination of all Federal agencies during this crisis. Again let me assure you that we are doing everything possible to find the reasons for the presence of these aircraft. We will continue to keep the public aware of any new developments. Thank you."

As the President stepped back, the Secretary of Defense stepped up to the podium. "I will take any questions you have now ... "

The room exploded with reporters raising their hands and yelling his name.

The Secretary pointed to one and said, "Yes?"

The reporter stood up. "There have been reports that our military jets fired at a UFO. Will you confirm, have we shot any of them down, or have the UFOs fired on any civilian or military personnel?"

The Secretary pondered the question for a moment, and then seemed to answer with great reluctance. "As far as we know at this time, these UFOs, as you call them, have not shown any aggression. Several of them have been in or close to restricted air space and have been fired upon by some of our military forces. We have not shot any down nor have they retaliated in any way."

"Yes," he said, pointing to another reporter.

"Are you saying we can't shoot these things down even if we wanted to?"the second reporter said.

"No," the Secretary said, licking his lips. "I am not saying that.

And, frankly, until these aircraft prove hostile, I don't know that we should."

"Yes," he said again, pointing to another reporter.

"Do you believe these UFOs are from outer space … ?"

Were the UFO's an invasion force from another world? Were they filled with aliens ready to attack the earth and conquer it?

People were terrified! It was hard to deal with such an incredible mystery that threatened everyone in the world. People were forced to think about it, and they did not want to face the possibilities. They just wanted it all to go away. Some people acted crazy, while others were so stunned they could do nothing. Many tried to ignore the whole situation, but no one really could.

Still, the UFOs did not move nor go away.

They just hung in the sky, like a mute taunting.

Of the thirteen UFO ships in America, twelve were over large cities, scattered around the country from New York to Los Angeles.

Only one seemed out of character in its location. It had chosen to hover over a small town nobody had ever heard of in the California desert.

A place called Oak Hill.

**2:18 p.m.,**
Oak Hill, California

John was driving to the Oak Hill church when he was stopped by a police barricade. No one was allowed to drive any closer to where the UFO hovered. He parked his car and walked to the church, past crowds of people staring up at the silver disk shining brightly in the sunlight.

The aircraft was directly over the church building at about 3,000 feet, John guessed. He walked up to Will, who was standing on the front steps of the church staring at the UFO like everyone else.

John looked around at the hundreds of people pressing against the police barricade surrounding the church grounds. He counted seven television satellite trucks parked in the street.

"Some preachers will do anything to increase attendance," John deadpanned.

"I really wish it would just disappear," Will said, "but I'm sure glad to see you. What do you know about it, John? Have you talked to your people about this?"

"I've been on the telephone to my commanding general this morning. He didn't know I was up here," John added, eyeing Will. "But since I am here, I've been assigned here officially, to keep an eye on your flying saucer."

"How convenient." Will said.

"What's strange," John said, "is that out of all twenty of the space ships, yours is the only one that isn't over a heavily populated area."

"Quit calling it mine, will you," Will snapped with a frown.

"Well, buddy" John said, looking up. "It does seem to be dead center over your church."

**6:00 p.m.,**
press conference with Denzel Marduk,
Secretary General of the United Nations
United Nations building, New York City

DENZEL STOOD MAJESTICALLY and assuredly at the podium as he addressed the many reporters seated facing him. Frank stood off at one side and watched with intent interest.

The Secretary General looked calm and in control, unlike the other world leaders who had appeared earlier today.

Denzel pointed to a reporter to begin the questions.

"Mr. Secretary, what do you think the UFOs are?"

Denzel scanned the room slowly as he answered: "I believe a force unknown to any of us has invaded the earth."

The reporters all looked at one another in amazement. Here,

at last, was a world leader willing to go on record voicing what everyone was secretly thinking.

"I, also, am convinced," Denzel continued, "that if the people of this planet are to survive, we must unite immediately to withstand this threat to our planet, whatever it proves to be. If we do not all pull together," Denzel warned, "our great planet earth could end in ruin and anarchy because of this danger now posed against us."

Denzel's voice was calm and reassuring as he spoke. "I believe there will prove to be a rational explanation for these spaceships. It is obvious that they are from somewhere else in our universe. What their intentions are I do not know. However, I do know that the people of earth must stand together to meet this challenge. It is our only hope for a secure future. If we have no plan of action, no unity, only fear, then we could be destroyed.

"I have called a meeting of the General Assembly for tomorrow, to outline a plan to deal with this invasion to our 'mother earth.'"

The reporters looked up to the podium and stopped scribbling on their note pads — all contemplating the same thing: Denzel had a plan. No one else had even talked about a plan.

Denzel continued, "I invite you all to the General Assembly meeting tomorrow. Then I will announce my plans to the nations for combating this invasion. Thank you, that will be all for now," he said, signaling that the press conference was over.

BY 7:00 P.M. A CURFEW WAS IMPOSED on all of the major cities. Police and sheriffs, backed up by National Guard forces or Army troops, enforced it. The rioting and looting was finally coming under control with the severe measures taken by the increasing number of military troops in the cities.

At night, the silver disks could still be seen in the dark skies. Bright light radiated from windows or portholes that circled the lower part of each craft.

Many people stood outside their homes and watched them,

while others, not close to any UFOs, watched them on television. As the people of the world looked up into the night sky, their thoughts were different now than they had ever been throughout history. After thousands of years, the question now was not *what if*, but *who?* Where did these mysterious aircraft come from?

It seemed obvious now that man was not alone in the universe — there must be other life forms among the stars and planets. Today's events had turned the world's thinking upside down. Could it be that man was just a small part of some larger overall picture in the universe? Was the belief that life existed only on this planet now being exposed as a myth? To what extent, now in light of the appearance of the UFOs, would their revelation upset what man had believed, up until now, about a God? Had the people of earth believed in a fairy-tale existence of a God, like a child believes in Santa Claus, only to be shown one day it was only a make-believe fantasy? The established absolutes about God had already been on shaky ground to many people. Would the UFOs prove that man had been fooled about his existence, maybe even his origins?

Could there still be a God … now?

*Blessed are they who are persecuted for righteousness sake; for theirs is the kingdom of heaven.*

— Matthew 5:10

*CHRISTIAN: One who believes in the deity of Jesus Christ, that he is the Son of God. That His divine blood that was shed on Calvary's cross redeems them to God. That Jesus resurrected from the dead and ascended to the right hand of God. That He will return to earth someday, with power and glory, to reign as King of Kings and Lord of Lords.*

**11:28 a.m., Friday, September 17**
Kansas City, Kansas

.............................................

# Chapter 16

THE LARGE STONE CHURCH building sat on the corner of a downtown city block. The sidewalks were crowded with people watching the silver disc hovering overhead.

The UFO held its position directly over the church.

The Messenger stood silently in the crowd, his eyes focused intently on the church building as if he could see inside.

**In these times of the Terminal Generation, Christians are the only religious group in America for which it is politically correct to make fun of, discriminate against, or even hate its members.**

**In the modern world of positive thinking, most people look at**

**Christians as 'old fashioned.' Belief in God is something people used to hold dear, before man started to 'think' for himself, to move ahead in the realms of science and technology. Man has come to believe in himself rather than in God.**

**Today, the media lampoons Christians as weak, mindless, misguided poor folk who need a crutch to get through life. Christian-bashing is an art form, on TV and in the movies. Seldom is a Christian portrayed as a hero, or even a popular person. If a Christian is shown at all, it is in a demeaning manor, as dull, boring, someone without a real life. Because the Christian ethic is so unpopular in the eyes of the 'Terminal Generation,' the news media is quick to jump on any story involving a 'Christian' who is accused of being a con-artist, psychopath, or criminal of any sort.**

**Belief in God is not generally portrayed as a positive thing in the secular media. Christians are attacked in courts of law, movies, television, magazines, and even through the educational institutions. They belittle the idea of faith in God or traditional family values.**

**Many people do not like Christians because Christians hold onto the notion about 'sin.' To mankind, sin is an archaic concept that people who want to do anything they please would just as soon forget. Sin puts such guilt and bondage on those in the 'Terminal Generation,' those who want to do everything only if it 'feels good.'**

**Today, throughout the world, there is uneasiness about Christians. Many people are uncomfortable with Christians. In a world that has rejected the living God, Christians just do not fit in anymore ...**

The Messenger turned from looking at the church, and melted into the crowd.

THE PEOPLE OF THE WORLD woke up the next morning wondering if yesterday had been just a bad dream. It didn't take long for them to see that it had not been a dream. The UFOs were still there, all hovering in the same places they had first appeared the day before.

Newspapers were filled with close-up pictures of the "Space Ships," as some people were now calling them. These pictures, however, did not reveal anything new about the craft. All that was visible was the silver metal-like covering and the windows, or portholes around the bottom edge. Still no clue as to who or what they were, who or what waited inside them.

The networks continued to focus on the story, periodically cutting in on local broadcasts, but they had nothing new to report.

The emotional shock of the UFOs had not subsided in most people. The world was not normal any more. Businesses were not operating, and many normal activities were canceled. People just did not know what to do. The space ships had confused and mystified almost everyone.

Around noon, the news broadcasts started to mention a peculiar aspect about the positioning of the UFOs. It had been confirmed that all of them were hovering directly over specific kinds of structures.

Christian churches.

Was there meaning to this revelation?

After a day and a half, the world grew more anxious to have some kind of concrete information concerning the UFOs. Soon TV network reporters began interviewing pastors outside churches where silver disks hovered overhead. The big question asked, of course, was whether these pastors knew why every one of the ominous and strange space ships held its position only over churches. No pastor offered a reasonable explanation.

Before long, everyone knew that the space ships were somehow connected to Christian churches. Was it possible that the Christians had information they weren't willing to share with the general public? There had to be some reason why all the UFOs chose to position themselves only over churches. Was it possible the Christians were hiding some kind of religious secret about the aliens?

Stories soon started coming across the news wires about people witnessing strange happenings around the churches that had these space ships over them. People claimed to have seen church members walking into their churches and then seeing them "beamed up, or Raptured" into the UFOs. Others claimed they had seen Christians signaling the silver disks with lights from windows inside the churches, or that the alien ships had signaled the churches with lights.

Although none of these stories was ever proved to be true, so many of them were circulating that many people figured there had to be some truth to them.

Were the Christians of the world in league with the UFOs? Many people started to speculate on this theory.

Christian churches everywhere had suddenly become the objects of harassment and violence. Many required police protection to guard against crowds trying to destroy them.

**1:23 p.m.,**
Oak Hill Church

JOHN AND WILL SAT IN QUIET conversation in the pastor's study of the little church. They were tired of standing and watching the excited crowd that was growing outside the church.

"Will, I'd like to know your perspective on all of this UFO stuff," John said. He was seated across from the red-headed minister at his desk. "I have a gut feeling you know some truth about it that I just can't see."

"The only truth you'll ever get from me is God's truth," Will answered. "But I will tell you what I've been thinking, if you really want to hear it."

John shrugged. "I'm not going anywhere, and my job right now is to gather information."

"Well," Will began, gathering his thoughts. "The biggest part of being a Christian is believing in God, and one way God proves himself is through Bible prophecy. That is, telling man what is going to happen before it does. The Bible is full of prophecies that have been fulfilled over the centuries. It's a sign that God is in control of everything on earth.

"Many prophecies in the Bible deal with 'End Times,' the period right before, and after, Jesus comes back to earth to gather his church.

"Some of these foretold events, when they're fulfilled, can allow people to know when the time that Jesus is coming is drawing near. All of those prophecies concerning Christ's return have been fulfilled. I believe we are living in the generation that will see Jesus return to gather the ones who have accepted him and take them to Heaven. After that happens there will follow, according to the Bible, a period of seven years called the Tribulation, when God will bring judgment on the earth to those who have refused to believe in Him. After that time period, Jesus will come back to earth again to reign as King of Kings."

Will glanced at his hands folded on the desktop, looked back at John.

"The point I'm getting at is this: In these 'End Times,' before Jesus Raptures the Christians, the antichrist will be revealed. He will become a world leader, while in reality he's the devil's counterfeit to Jesus. The devil tries to imitate God by corrupting the good and wonderful things of God. Satan does this with many obvious things, such as by harming God's institution of marriage by encouraging sex outside of marriage and homosexuality.

"The devil also uses some things of God that are not so apparent. For example, have you noticed how often lately the pyramid shape is used in the logos of the media and business in this 'new world order' generation. The Bible says the great pyramid in Egypt will one day be a symbol and altar to the Lord during his kingdom here on earth. The devil has taken that and used it for the symbol of his kingdom. The all-seeing eye at the top of the pyramid on the back of our dollar bill is the mark of Satan taking the place of what God will someday be, the capstone that has yet to be placed on the pyramid. As such, the devil will empower this man I referred to earlier to be a counterfeit Christ, and he will work to set up his kingdom here on earth. This evil man — the Bible calls him the antichrist — will deceive the world into hating God, and God's people: Christians."

"Marduk?" John asked.

"I believe so, yes," nodded Will.

"All right, but where do the UFOs fit in?"

"I don't know exactly," Will said, "but they are definitely targeting Christian churches. Already, because of the UFOs, people are starting to fear Christians and are turning on them.

"Paul, in the book of II Thessalonians, talks about a 'falling away' of Christians that must occur before the Rapture. The Greek word is *apostasy,* which refers to an event that will happen quickly and will deceive many against God, even some who profess to be Christians. I've been thinking this UFO thing could be it. It's just the sort of hard blow that will separate the wheat from the chaff."

"But, Will," John argued, "those flying ships out there are very real. In my gut I have a definite feeling they are not of this world. They must be aliens of some kind. It's not just some magic trick."

"Ah, but I believe it is," Will exclaimed. "This magician is the most powerful the world has ever seen. Satan could very easily cause those images of space ships. The Bible says he has been given power over the skies. They could be demons metamorphosed to appear like space ships. Think about it. Why haven't any of them landed or communicated with the government? Where are the 'little green men' and why haven't they jumped out and made known their intentions?"

Will paused in thought. "All I'm saying, John, is that I believe that Satan, in the last days, will use some kind of deception, whether it's this UFO thing or not, to fool people into questioning whether or not there is a God. This deception will cause people either really to keep their faith in God, or to reject it. It will be a final test, the sifting of the chaff from the wheat, that God allows those who truly believe in Him to prove their belief. So there is no question of who goes with Him when He returns."

John considered for a moment. "What happens to those who don't accept Jesus before He returns, but realize the truth afterwards? Are they damned forever?"

"No," Will said, "the Bible says people will still accept Jesus during the Tribulation period, but it will not be easy living as a Christian during those seven years. With the church gone, and the power of the Holy Spirit diminished, the antichrist will not be held back. He will rain terror on anyone who professes their faith in God. His partner, the false prophet, will make everyone take a 'mark' that will claim allegiance to the spirit of the antichrist. No one will be able to buy or sell without that mark, so you can imagine trying to live in that kind of society. The Bible also says that those who do accept the mark are damned for accepting the devil as their god, and that many who become Christians during that time will be martyred."

Will looked at John. "You don't want to be there when that time comes, my friend. The Bible says it will be a time of unspeakable horror. If things are happening like I believe, the Lord could come back at any second. Would you be ready to go with Him?"

John couldn't look Will in the eyes. "I'm still thinking about it Will. I don't know if God will accept me, I've rejected Him for so long. Maybe I'm not even worthy."

Will shook his head. "None of us is worthy of God's love, John. You don't need to clean up your life before God will accept you. His grace covers you through the shed blood of Jesus. You only need to confess your sins and ask forgiveness and invite Him into your life. You don't need to understand every aspect of being a Christian before you receive Him into your heart. All you need to believe to begin with is that God sent His only begotten Son to die for your sins. He will then help you to understand more as you walk with Him and seek His will through His written word, the Bible."

John felt a tug at his heart. He felt emotions he had never felt before, but those old hurt feelings still held him back. "I need to think things through, Will. I'd better go check outside," he said. He turned to Will. "I'm sorry. That's all I can tell you for now."

"I'm praying for you," smiled Will.

"I'll be back," John said. He walked out and quietly closed the door.

Will stared at the door for a long time nodding his head in thought. "Lord," he prayed silently, "help John to come to know you, soon."

Will turned around to the computer by his desk and stared at the blank screen on the monitor. The desk was piled with stacks of folders that appeared to be very old. They were military files Will's dad had left to him when he died. Some of them had U.S. military markings on them and were dated 1945. Several of them had German titles and headings. One word seemed to be common on many of them … Nuremberg.

That evening, a television program had an interview with a man who claimed he had been abducted by one of the UFOs. He said the aliens in the ship had told him they were here to conquer the earth, and that it was fruitless to oppose them. They also mentioned they were in league with some earth people, but the aliens would not say who these people were.

Even though the man could not prove his story, it enraged many who believed it to be the truth. With the UFOs lingering over churches, it was easy for people to think they could be allied. Known Christians began to be looked upon with suspicion. Christian leaders appeared on television and radio denouncing all involvement with the space ships.

The fact remained, the alien ships still hovered above those Christian churches.

*And I beheld another beast coming up out of the earth; and he had two horns like a lamb, and he spoke like a dragon.*

*And he exerciseth all the power of the first beast before him, and causeth the earth and them who dwell on it to worship the first beast, whose deadly wound was healed.*

*And he doeth great wonders, so that he maketh fire come down from heaven on the earth in the sight of men.*

— Revelation 13:11-13

**1:00 p.m., Saturday, September 18**
Christian church, downtown Manhattan,
New York City, New York

.............................................

# Chapter 17

THE PRESS CONFERENCE had been called by Frank Pettinati, close friend of the Secretary General of the United Nations, Denzel Marduk.

The church had been the biggest attraction in New York City since the silver disks had appeared on Thursday. People from all over the New England area had flocked to see the "Alien Space Ship" hovering over the old stone building, on the corner of a busy intersection. The huge crowds were kept back by police barricades as everyone stared at the mysterious aircraft, intrigued by its mystery.

Approximately one hundred reporters stood in a group on the front lawn of the old church, near a stage that had been quickly erected for the news conference.

Everyone waited, silent.

A black limousine pulled to the curb in front of the church. Frank Pettinati stepped out and walked quickly to the stage. He wore a navy blue, double-breasted suit and a long, dark purple overcoat that swayed slightly like a cape as he bounded up the stairs. He moved to the podium, his intense green eyes assessing the crowd, the reporters and cameramen. *Perfect,* he thought with a hint of amusement crossing his face.

"I would like to thank all of you for coming here today on such short notice," he began quickly, scanning the crowd with an all-knowing glare. "On behalf of my friend, Denzel Marduk, I bid you welcome."

The crowd cheered.

"Denzel has asked me to announce a proclamation to the 'space invaders,'" Frank said, pointing high into the air toward the space ship as he looked dramatically around at the assembly.

"Although Mr. Marduk is a man of peace and wants only peace to reign on our mother earth," Frank said, his words echoing through the loudspeakers, "he is a man who will not be intimidated by any force that would try to attack our world!" he spat each word like a flung dart.

A ringing cheer answered him.

"Denzel Marduk is the one man our world needs to lead us. In any struggle. Against any force." Frank pointed again to the silver disk, making certain every camera focused on the skyship.

"The people of earth will no longer be intimidated by any force from space that is not friendly or means to do us harm."

Some of the newspeople glanced at one another with uncertainty, unsure whether they should continue to cheer with the others or return to their studio. What could this guy do against UFOs that no military force in the world had been able to do?

"Let it be known," Frank said, warming up like an old snake-oil vendor, "that all the countries of earth will stand together against this threat."

Again, the crowd roared in agreement.

Frank looked around slowly. His angry eyes narrowed as he growled, "If anyone tries to force their will on us … " His hands leaped into the air toward the east. "We will destroy them!"

For a moment the gathering grew silent, everyone seemed to be holding their breath in anticipation

Suddenly, the air filled with a roaring noise, like a thousand freight trains bearing down on the crowd. Everyone looked up with horror to see a huge ball of flame soaring from the heavens. Before anyone could think or move, the roaring fire crashed into the spaceship, completely engulfing it. For a few moments the silver disk crackled like tin foil. It wobbled and tipped as if in the throes of death, then exploded into nothing. No debris fell to earth; no one was hurt on the ground.

The UFO was gone.

Destroyed.

Utterly.

Some of the reporters glanced back to the podium where Frank had been. Too late. He slipped into the limousine before anyone could catch or question him. The car moved away from the curb and raced down the street.

Thousands of people on the sidewalks stood in mute shock, mesmerized, looking upward to the empty sky. A wild cheer erupted like a wave across the crowd, filling the streets with the sound of exaltation at the event that had just taken place and which they had all witnessed.

The UFOs could be destroyed.

What the world had wanted. Relief that no government had been able to deliver.

It could be done, and Marduk had done it. *He* had the power. People could put their hope in him.

The crowd streamed into the streets and waving at the limousine and shouting, "Marduk, Marduk, Marduk." Everyone suddenly felt like celebrating. The streets of Manhattan came alive with frolicking, dancing, and shouts of celebration.

On a nearby sidewalk, an old man wearing a long black coat stood motionless. The excited crowd ran past him like water flowing around a rock in the middle of a river. He turned and walked away from the dancing and rejoicing. The Messenger then stopped and turned again, a short distance from the partying crowd. He watched them with a great sadness on his lined face.

**The Terminal Generation has become weak-minded. They do not study, or remember history. They have not learned from the mistakes that repeat themselves over and over again. Instead of following the one true God, man is constantly running away from God. Ready to believe anything supernatural, or any false prophet that will arouse their senses and tickle their ears.**

**So, the children of earth have found a new "pied piper" to follow. Only this one is the most evil of them all. He will lead them dancing into an everlasting place of torment, without the presence of God, for eternity.**

The Messenger shoved his hands into his overcoat pockets, turned and began slowly walking down the sidewalk. His black form was soon swallowed by the crowds of people streaming past him, in the opposite direction, toward the growing street party.

**2:34 p.m.,**
Wooded area north of New York City

THE BLACK LIMOUSINE MOVED cautiously, traveling down an obscure dirt road through the dense New England forest. The many trees blocked out the afternoon sun, giving the sense of nighttime. Wide lines of sunlight slanted through the trees, illuminating patches of emerald green moss on the ground and rocks.

The car stopped and Frank stepped out of a rear door. He walked into the woods and out of sight. In a small clearing, he stopped and pulled a cigar from inside his trench coat. He placed the Havana between his lips and stared up through the trees for a moment, his large chest heaving a dramatic sigh.

"I haven't got all day," he seemed to say to the sky as he stood there waiting.

Accompanied by the crunching sound of dried leaves on the ground, a dark figure emerged slowly from the trees to Frank's right. The glossy black entity moved toward him, its identity revealed for a moment as it passed through a slanting shaft of sunlight, to stop hidden in the shadows about twenty feet from where Frank stood. Red eyes glowed from the silent and motionless form.

"Well, Offscour," Frank said impatiently, "do you have a name for me?"

"I have the name you seek," rasped Offscour, "I am your Executor now, am I not?" he demanded.

Frank's green eyes narrowed as his gaze turned threateningly to the demon. "The name?" he snarled, shifting the cigar to the side of his tight mouth.

The red eyes fell, searched the ground for a moment in indecision, then darted back to Frank. "The hu-man you seek is a minister," the demon said in a rush. "He lives in a village called Oak Hill in the California desert. His name is William Thompson."

Frank's eyes grew in hatred as he mouthed the name and seared it into his memory. "You are sure?" he asked.

"There is no doubt."

Frank's right hand swept up in the black spirit's direction. His fingers stretched out threateningly, an extension of his evil glare.

As the demon rose up straight from his crouch, his red eyes widened in confusion. "I did what you asked," he hissed.

"I couldn't have an Executor that was so demanding, now could I?" Frank said fiercely.

Offscour's hideous face turned into a mask of rage, his snarling mouth spewed a vicious roar as he took a swift step and began to leap at Frank.

A rumbling whoosh of fire shot rapidly from Frank's hand like a flame-thrower. Its burning glow lit up the clearing and reflected on the trees like yellow lightning. The ball of flame engulfed the demon in a fiery torch of combustion. Piercing screams of agony rent the silent forest until they died out and the flame from Frank's hand stopped. Frank stood motionless for a moment, his head tilted sideways. His arm was still outstretched as he slowly pulled his fingers into a fist, like a cat pulling in its claws. He grinned smugly as his arm fell loosely to his side.

Frank pulled the cigar from his mouth and studied it for a moment. Now, finally, he knew who the E-mail sender was. He decided to fly to California after the weekend. Monday morning he'd find this minister, this William Thompson, this pious antagonist who dared to taunt Frank Pettinati. He'd relish hunting this minister down, and then…

He would enjoy killing him.

Frank put the cigar back in his mouth. It lit mystically as he turned and walked back to his car. As he disappeared among the trees, the forest clearing grew quiet once more.

All that remained was a smoldering black spot on the mossy ground.

**5:00 p.m.,**
United Nations building,
New York City

THE OLD MAN WALKED THROUGH the doors of the building, and sat down on a couch in the foyer. *I'm getting to know this place quite well these days,* he thought to himself. The Messenger watched in silent contemplation as the throngs of people walked past him.

**In today's age, the world lacks good leadership. There are few who will take a stand for the good of the people. Those who are willing are rarely elected to high office. People with a higher standard are not allowed to climb the ladder to power. The evil power establishments behind the scenes hinder them.**

**Those who do not align with the world's secular thinking are**

**held back by the majority in the governing structure.**

**Because they have not demanded it, the people of "Terminal Generation" do not have good leadership. They think they have the freedom to elect anyone they choose, but little do they realize that the deck is stacked, by a force unseen.**

**All the choices have been selected by the rich and powerful, who in turn the men of the CIRCLE control. Therefore, no matter what party or candidate wins, they are all secretly following the same pre-arranged agenda. The platform of NO absolutes, NO adhering to the laws of God.**

**Like Esau, in the book of Genesis, who did not appreciate his birthright, the "Terminal Generation" has sold its freedom birthright for a bowl of fleeting prosperity pottage. Give the children of the "Terminal Generation" prosperity, so they can fulfill their lustful desires, and it does not matter to them if their leaders are immoral, or even if they are corrupt. All this generation wants, is peace, peace from the absolutes of a living God.**

**They want only leaders who will give them peace.**

The Messenger rose from the couch and followed the crowd filing into the meeting of the United Nations General Assembly.

**6:00 p.m.,**
Emergency Meeting of the General Assembly

ALL THE NATIONS OF THE WORLD had assembled to confront the great threat against them. For the first time in history, they had a common foe, this unknown force from outer space. The nations needed to put aside their differences, at least for the moment, to deal as one against the biggest threat the world had ever known.

No nation had been able to do anything against the UFO threat, but Marduk had. His man, Frank Pettinati, had destroyed one of the craft. Everyone in the assembly room was acutely aware of the enormous reality of that fact.

The auditorium was filled to capacity with a representative of every country on earth. TV cameras were set up to relay the speech by Marduk, via satellite, to every corner of the globe.

The people of earth were now ready for a strong leader, one who could fight the UFO threat and bring them together in peace. Marduk had proven he had the power to do it. He was the world's only hope.

He was their savior, if only they would embrace him.

Marduk entered the assembly hall with Frank walking steadfast by his side. He walked to the stage and stood at the podium as Frank sat on a chair behind him and to his right. Denzel appeared majestic and powerful. He looked around the assembly with an air of command and, as he stood motionless, the room grew quiet. He glanced down at the podium for a few moments, then slowly lifted his head, narrowed eyes glaring under a dark brow, as he began to speak, calmly, slowly, and deliberately.

"Until several days ago, the people of earth believed they were alone in the universe." He shook his head negatively. "We now know this is not true.

"What other beliefs — beliefs that man has held through the ages — are also not true in light of this revelation? I wonder ..." His words echoed through the auditorium.

"Whether we like it or not, we are all faced with a common enemy right now: one that, if it can, will destroy our way of life." He slammed the podium with his fist. "There is no place to run, no place to hide, because it threatens the whole earth!"

Denzel walked a few steps to his right and drew closer to his audience. He paused, studying the people before him.

"We can go on the way we have always before, fighting among ourselves, and thus face this invasion divided. Or," he paused, looking slowly from face to face, "we can ally ourselves and stand as one against this threat to our world."

Denzel walked across the stage, pointing his finger at the crowd. "Because of mankind's history, the enemy does not believe that we can stand together.

"I am convinced that to meet this threat, and to peaceably administer our world during this time in history, we must come together as one force united."

He again walked across the stage, lifting his hands in mock despair.

"Oh, I know, some will scoff at this idea, they will say it is impossible. It has been tried before and failed. This building is a testament to that." He turned dramatically and looked out at his spellbound audience. "But I tell you, my dear fellow earthmen, it is our only recourse if we are to survive. We can fight this onslaught on mother earth, and we will prevail."

Denzel scanned the room slowly. His threatening gaze passed over everyone.

"I know the force that is set against us, and it is a powerful one. It believes it is the omniscient power in the universe. Yes, it wants to conquer man and enslave him. It has been working its magic into mans' thoughts for thousands of years … " The fingers on Denzel's hand flew open and then suddenly clenched. " … making man believe there is a God, binding him into the chains of … religion." The words rolled distastefully off his tongue. "It hides its real intent behind a mask of goodness, and a fairy tale belief in an Almighty God."

Denzel glanced at Frank and then looked back at his audience and sneered. "For me, it is hard to believe in something that I cannot see. If there is a God, why doesn't He reveal himself openly to mankind? What is He afraid of, that we might see Him for who He really is? Could it be He is something He tells us He is not? If there is a good and mighty God, what is He hiding for? If there is a God, why isn't He here to help us now?

"I'll tell you why," he shouted, pointing a finger out across the audience, "because He is behind this to begin with!

"Are you ready, fellow earthmen, to be damned if we do not follow Him, believe in Him, follow His orders, as some on Earth already do?

"As for me, I think not," Denzel said with determination, "I am a man, and this is my world. The earth is mine to do with what I please, if I will only do it!"

The room was deathly quiet. Every eye was on Denzel. Every person in the auditorium spellbound.

Denzel looked down at the podium and paused for several moments in thought. There was a Force out there in the world right now, a supernatural hindrance that was keeping him from using all his powers he knew he possessed. That Force would be taken away soon. The UFOs had weakened that Spirit's influence tremendously already.

Many of the God believers were wondering about the truth of their faith. It had been a terrible blow to what had been an unquestioning belief to some.

Denzel knew that when that Power was removed, he would be able to gather the earth for himself and he would be able to make himself ruler of the world. He was now merely setting the stage for that time, and if in the meantime he could persecute any of the God-believers, well, so much the better.

Denzel's head lifted slowly and his once-blue eyes were now gleaming yellow, a change not visible to the audience. A power radiated from him that seemed to mesmerize everyone in the room. Denzel began to speak again. The audience was completely under his spell. They would agree to anything he suggested.

"I propose that we name this new organization of all the countries of our world 'Federation Earth.' Every nation on earth will join us in this supporting alliance to withstand any outside invasions, so that we may live in total peace!"

The lights started to grow dim in the auditorium. "I also propose that the emblem for Federation Earth, the seal of this great alliance, its 'mark' should be ... this." He gestured toward an image forming on the wall behind him in the now-dark room. It was a large circle filled in with the color green and inside the circle was a red pyramid. "The circle of green," he announced officially, "representing our mother earth, with the symbol of the pyramid, man's first great accomplishment on earth and his pillar of self-determination."

Suddenly a dozen floodlights mounted in the floor behind the stage came on; they threw streams of light skyward into the high ceiling. The effect was stunning and glorious, and the crowd leaped to their feet, cheering and wildly applauding Marduk.

Frank stood by Denzel and they raised clasped hands together, like a referee and the winner of a prizefight.

Denzel smiled and waved to the cheering people. *It will still take some time,* he thought, *but they all will follow me. It's now only a matter of time.*

Everything was going as his father had planned.

*And great earthquakes shall be in different places, and famines, and pestilence; and fearful sights, and great signs shall there be from heaven.*

*But before all these, they shall lay their hands on you, and persecute you, delivering you up to the synagogues, and into prisons, being brought before kings and rulers for my name's sake.*

— Luke 21; 11-12

**8:07 a.m., Sunday, September 19**
Christian Church, 1203 Maple St.,
Los Angeles, California

# Chapter 18

THE REVEREND PETER MADISON STOOD at his pulpit in amazement. As he gazed around he could not believe the crowd in the church sanctuary this morning. His congregation had been so large for several years now that he had held three services on Sunday mornings, but he had never had a standing-room-only crowd at the 8 a.m. service. Until today.

Peter would have liked to have credited this crowd to the outreach program of his church's ministry. However, he had to acknowledge this morning's large attendance was owed to the silver flying disc, that so called UFO, hovering over his church building.

It was apparent many of the people here were not members;

some may never have even been in a Christian church before. They were here out of curiosity. *Well,* thought Peter with a smile on his face, *it's a good opportunity to tell them the salvation story.*

Maybe something good, after all, would come out of all the negative publicity his church had suffered ever since the demonic apparition had appeared overhead.

Peter was about to welcome everyone, when the doors in the rear of the sanctuary burst open with a crash. A stream of uniformed men rushed through and ran down the wall aisles on either side of the sanctuary.

At first Peter thought he was dreaming, that this could not be happening, not here in the United State of America.

The men all wore military uniforms he did not recognize, but what was worse, they all held assault rifles. Everyone in the crowd looked around in mute horror as the soldiers lined up against the walls facing the people.

A woman screamed.

A man in uniform marched down the center aisle and stopped abruptly in front of the pulpit where Peter stood. From the trimming of his uniform and the smug expression on his face, Peter guessed this officer was in charge of this outrageous intrusion.

Born in Hondo County, Texas, the Reverend Peter Madison had a Texas temper. It flared at this moment, and Peter addressed the man who would dare interrupt the Lord's service in the way a true Texan would insult someone he disliked.

"What can I do for you, mister?" Peter shouted, his drawl emphasizing the word "mister," while he stared the officer straight in the eye.

The man glared at the minister, not understanding the insult inherent in his use of the word but recognizing the tone in his voice.

"I am Colonel Michael Rostov of the Russian Army," he shouted at Peter, "part of the United Nations Peace Keeping Forces for this sector, under the current state of martial law. You will cease this meeting at once, and you will leave immediately.

This building is to remain closed by order of the Operations Director for this sector. Anyone who remains in this building will be considered connected with the alien space ships and charged with terrorism."

Peter walked from behind the pulpit, never taking his eyes off the officer. He stopped on the platform near where the Russian stood. "Colonel," he said, "we have the Constitutional right as American citizens to worship wherever and whenever we please. You have no right to demand that we leave."

"You will leave immediately!" snapped the Colonel.

"And if we don't?"

"Anyone who does not leave immediately will be arrested and taken to prison," the Colonel said as he turned to face the crowd.

Peter watched calmly as many people got up and rushed toward the doors, but some remained in their seats in defiance. After several minutes the last of those who were leaving had gone, but around fifty men, women, and children remained sitting in the pews.

The Colonel turned to Peter. "Tell them to leave."

Peter looked slowly around at each individual — he knew them all very well. They were all members of his congregation, and he loved each one. As he searched into each face, they all mirrored his own look of defiance. *My God,* he trembled as he felt the Spirit swell inside of him, *I've never felt so proud to be a Christian.*

Peter turned to the Colonel. The man looked at him in amazement, anticipating what he was going to say.

"I will not," Peter answered.

"Arrest them all!"

**12:14 p.m.,**
Oak Hill Church, Oak Hill, California

THE MORNING SERVICE HAD BEEN uneventful, despite the crowds and television trucks surrounding the front of the little church.

John and Will walked out the side door and looked at the silver disc still hovering high above. "You don't have to go with me Will," John said. "It'll be dangerous once I get onto the base."

Will looked at John with a grin. "You need me, buddy. Besides, I wouldn't miss this for the world. I'll pick you up in about half an hour."

"Okay," sighed John, "but just remember, I warned you."

Garrett and Caleb sat on the roof of the church and watched Will and John depart in separate directions.

"John could be walking into a lot of trouble," Caleb said, "and taking Will with him."

"You and I will follow them," Garrett replied.

"We will be exposed to the enemy then," Caleb added. "And not that many of our forces have arrived. We will be outnumbered three to one."

"Inform those angels that are here to gather at the church while we follow Will and John," Garrett said, his eyes searching the grounds surrounding the Church. "The enemy will attack here, I am certain of that, most likely during this evening's service. Send one of our own to Gabriel for more reinforcements."

"And if the enemy hits here with all their force?" asked Caleb with concern.

"It will then be up to the people of this church," Garrett declared. "Their prayers, and their faith."

Forty-five minutes later, the Power Wagon was climbing up the same rocky mountain road Will and John had traveled on Friday.

John, dressed in his Army uniform, had brought along his 35mm camera and binoculars. His .45 automatic was in a holster on his belt.

When they arrived at the spot where they had met the old prospector, Will stopped the 4x4 and studied the wash they had been told would lead them onto the base.

"We won't be able to drive back out this way once we go down," Will said. "It's too steep and sandy."

"We'll find another way out," John said, tensely staring straight ahead down the wash.

"Just thought I'd tell you," Will said, as he put the truck in gear and they started down the incline. Overhead two bright lights followed the Power Wagon at a close distance.

"Did I tell you," Will said as the 4x4 disappeared down the gully, "I believe that old prospector was an angel of God?"

"Oh really?" John said, staring at the red-headed preacher.

Legion and Executor stood on a ridge overlooking the wash and watched the Power Wagon as it slowly descended below them. Executor's black bony finger extended out suddenly. "There," he said, pointing to the two lights that followed the 4x4. "Those are the two heavenly hosts who destroyed Og, and I just received a report that others of the heavenly host are gathered at the village church."

Legion's yellow eyes narrowed in thought for a moment as he watched the truck slip out of sight. It was time he made a move and started to show his power. His eagle head twisted abruptly to Executor. "Gather all our forces," he said. "We will go down to the church tonight. It is time to destroy the power coming from there. We will scatter those Christians like leaves. The deception is now working all over the world. The hu-mans are confused, and they are taking it out on the God-believers. They will be easy prey for us now."

After Will and John reached the bottom of the wash, they traveled along the flat desert floor for several miles. Will stopped at the crest of a ridge. Below them they saw a blacktop road. John knew then they were inside the base.

"Which way now?" Will asked.

"Follow that bus," John suggested, pointing left to a large green bus he suddenly spotted coming over a ridge.

As the vehicle passed, going west, they drove down from the ridge and turned on the road, following it at a distance. After several miles the bus turned into an area that was covered with concrete mounds dotting the desert floor for miles into the distance.

"What are those?" Will asked.

"Pull off here," John ordered quickly, his eyes staring at the mounds. "So that's where they're hiding."

"In those mounds?" Will shut off the truck engine.

"Yes," John said, nodding his head to a mystery solved. "Those are ammunition storage bunkers, and they can run underground for miles."

The two men watched as the bus stopped near one of the concrete mounds and several soldiers emerged.

"Come on," John said, jumping out of the truck. "I want to get closer." He snapped a picture of one of the Russian soldiers as he and Will crept foreword, staying behind other bunkers as they moved toward the bus.

The door of the bus opened and two Russian soldiers stepped out. John's eyes widened as he immediately recognized U.N. patches on their uniforms. *Bingo,* he thought. The two guards called out in Russian to two other soldiers standing near the door of the bunker. John noticed they were fully armed with AK47 assault rifles. John searched the area for more soldiers, but saw none.

People started to file off the bus — men, women, and children. It struck Will that they were all dressed so nicely, like they had all just come from ... his heart froze ... church.

The guards were treating the people in a very rough manner as they pointed them toward the door of the underground bunker. A mental picture of what was happening formed in Will's mind. It reminded him of pictures he had seen in his dad's files by his computer, scenes taken at the Nazi concentration camps.

"Oh Lord," he sighed as his eyes grew wide in unbelief, "not again."

John's blue eyes froze like ice as he watched soldiers poking and jabbing people with their rifle butts as they moved along in a line.

Suddenly, one of the Russians grabbed the arm of a young, blonde woman. He pulled her from the line of people and laughed as he said something in Russian to his buddies. John did not understand Russian, but the soldier's intent would have been clear in any language.

The air tensed as several men in the line stopped and looked angrily at the guard holding the woman.

Will turned with alarm to John as they crouched behind a concrete embankment. Will was worried. If the men in line challenged the soldiers, someone would probably die.

The Native American features in John's face had turned even more threatening than usual. "John," Will cautioned, shooting a glance at the volatile scene unfolding before them and then turning back to John. "If we try to do anything, we could bring the whole camp of soldiers down on us."

Something deep within John's being let loose — a fighting rage that was buried in his Indian blood. It was running hot through his veins right then. Like a tiger, he leaped up and bounded toward the Russian guard holding the woman.

"John, no!" Will cried, too late. "Oh Lord," Will prayed, "help us." He leaped up after him.

The Russian holding the woman never saw John's fist. It broke his jaw and he was unconscious before he hit the ground.

The other Russian swung his rifle toward the wild stranger who had just attacked his friend and was now bearing down on him like a runaway locomotive. His finger pressed the trigger of his rifle, which was pointed directly at John, but it would not move. The last thing he remembered was pulling against the trigger with all his strength. It was like someone else's finger was in the trigger guard blocking it.

Caleb held his finger in the rifle's trigger guard until a smashing blow from John's right hand put the Russian in the same kind of dirt nap as his friend.

The people who had been on the bus stood still in amazement at the scene before them.

Will snatched the rifle from the first guard John had hit. The red-bearded minister expertly snapped back the machine gun's loading bolt to full automatic. The distinct, sliding-metal sound rang through the air like a ominous warning, freezing two guards in their tracks who had run up from the nearby bunker. Neither of them raised their rifles when they realized that Will had them covered. One of them, wearing sergeants' stripes, stared in confusion at John's uniform.

"What's going on here?" John queried the Russian. "Who are these people?" He nodded toward the line of people.

Noticing John's rank, the Russian quickly saluted John and then looked back at the people as if he had just seen them for the first time.

"Oh, them, sir?" he answered in broken English. "They're Christians, sir."

John glanced at Will, who looked stunned, then back at the Russian.

"We've been rounding them up from the churches. They are in league with the UFOs," the Russian said. "Some of them have put up quite a fight."

"With what?" John asked. "Hymnals and offering plates?"

"Identify yourself," shouted a voice from behind the two soldiers. A Russian officer marched between the guards and stood in front of John.

The officer was as tall as John and he wore the uniform of a general. He had no hat on his bald head and a long scar ran down the left cheek of his cruel face. John disliked him immediately.

"Identify yourself," the general shouted again.

John's anger had not yet subsided; he spat out the words, "Major John Allen, US Army Intelligence, under General Alexander."

The Russian glared at John with distaste. "A salute is customary to a higher officer, Major," the general declared, looking around and assessing the situation, then staring back at John. "Even to one of the Russian Army," he said evenly.

"I want to know why these people are being detained," John demanded. "And why this soldier was not acting properly with a woman?" He pointed to the man lying on the ground.

The general started to reach into his pocket. He glanced at Will aiming the rifle at him, and then back to John. "May I?" he asked.

John shrugged his shoulders, eyeing the general balefully. The situation was very tense. With itchy fingers on so many weapons, it could easily turn into a blood bath.

The general pulled out a cigarette and quickly lit it. He blew out his first drag, staring at John the whole time. "I order you and your friend to surrender immediately," he commanded. "Under the authority of the U.N. Military Command, you are under arrest. Your situation is hopeless, you could not possibly get off this base."

In a tenth of a second blur, John's .45 automatic seemed to leap into his hand. He pointed it so it touched the general's forehead.

The Russian's eyes widened in shock, and the cigarette dropped from his lips.

"Let's get something straight," John said. "I don't care about your 'New World Order' authority, or for any of you who work for those goons at the U.N." John's vibrant blue eyes searched around at everyone as he paused for a moment. "We are leaving," he said, pressing the gun barrel against the general's forehead, "and you are coming with us, just so nothing bad happens to us along the way. On the other hand, we can all start blasting away at each other, and you die first. The choice is yours, General."

The Russian swallowed hard and sighed deeply as his eyes locked on John's. He then spoke to his men. "Put your weapons down on the ground," he ordered, "and tell them at the gate to let us through." The two soldiers put down their rifles and walked backward, toward the building.

"Are you happy now, Major?" the general asked. John slowly pulled the pistol back from his head, but kept it aimed at the Russian.

"I'm never happy," John admitted, shoving the general toward the Power Wagon in the distance. John looked at the people standing in line and then glanced at Will. He knew what Will was thinking. Yes, he wished he could take all of them now too, but they were pushing their luck as it was. In any minute the place would be crawling with soldiers.

A man stepped out from the line and addressed John. "Go on," he said. "We'll be all right. The Lord will watch over us."

"I'll be back," John answered. "I'll get you all out of here if it's the last thing I ever do." The man smiled and waved at John and Will as they turned and prodded the general toward the truck.

Back at the Power Wagon, John pushed the Russian into the seat between Will and himself.

Will started the pickup quickly, swung the 4x4 around in a circle, and roared down the road toward the back gate.

Inside the Dodge, the general could feel John's gun pressed against his ribs. "Are you going to shoot me once we are off the base, Major?"

"Not unless you make me," John replied, echoing the Russian's tone as he watched the road ahead. "These bullets cost thirteen cents apiece and, frankly, you're not worth wasting even one."

"Ah, I like the humor you Americans have," he said, apparently unfazed by the insult. He glanced at Will, then back to John, and said, "Allow me to introduce myself. I am General Volkof, commandant of Oak Hill Detention Center."

"You mean concentration camp, don't you?" Will said angrily.

"Why don't you ask your government agency, FEMA. They are the ones who built it and manage it," Volkof replied, feigning innocence.

"Why are Russian troops running it?" accosted John.

"We are part of the world-wide U.N. peace-keeping force, Major, made up of many different countries. Your country is under Marshal law right now, as are most countries in the world. The U.N. peace-keeping force is the most logical force to use. We are becoming a one-order government, Major; it is only a matter of time. The idea of a single-country patriotism is old-fashioned. We are all citizens of the world, especially since the space ships arrived, are we not?"

"Personally, I like being old-fashioned," John said, "and your buddy Marduk talks too much like a dictator to my way of thinking. I think you'll find there are still a lot of Americans who love their freedom."

"Then, they might have to fight to keep it," Volkof said.

"We're used to fighting for it now and then," John said, turning to the general. As their eyes met, both men felt destiny whisper in his ear: They would meet again someday.

They were coming to the gate now. It stood wide open, and the guards stood back, waiting. The Power Wagon raced through it and sped down the road followed by a cloud of dust.

"Tell me something, General?" Will asked. "Why are they putting Christians in the camps? How could anyone believe they are connected to the UFOs?"

"They are in league with the UFOs," Volkof claimed. "The space ships are only centered over certain churches. What more proof do you need? Only yesterday, your own military announced it has intercepted communications between churches and UFOs, using computers and a form of the hexadecimal code."

"That's crazy," Will exclaimed. "I don't believe it!"

"I haven't seen proof that any of these allegations are true," John said.

"Nevertheless," shrugged Volkof, "people believe it, and that is all that really matters, is it not?"

They were several miles from the camp now and John asked Will to pull over. When they stopped, John and the general stepped out of the pickup. "It is only a few miles back to the camp," John said. "I'm sure you can walk it easily, General."

As John started to get back into the truck, Volkof addressed him with a raised eybrow. "What are you going to do, Major? You must realize that your career is over. We will hunt you down. I will make it my personal business to see that you are captured."

John turned and glared at the general. "Don't bet any money on it, Volkof. I can be kind of a hard guy to find."

John shut the door and they sped away, leaving the general

standing in a cloud of dust.

On a high ridge overlooking the desert, the Messenger stood and watched as Will's 4x4 moved down the road toward Oak Hill.

**Is it possible that people who have a belief in God could be put in prison because of their faith, in this country? There are already 'hate crime laws' in some states that could put Christians in jail for simply expressing their first amendment religious rights, such as speaking negatively about a person's 'sexual preference.' If one group is selected out from a free society and persecuted for its religious beliefs, is anyone safe?**

**I am afraid for the children of the Terminal Generation. They have been lulled to sleep as history repeats itself, once again.**

As the Messenger looked over his shoulder to the eastern sky, his piercing blue eyes watched Legion's demons gathering in a large circle in the late afternoon sun.

It was time for him to go.

"What are you going to do now?" Will asked, as they drove into Oak Hill.

"Well, I'm not going back to Fort Chapin," John answered, wondering to himself just what he was going to do next. "And I'm certainly not going to turn myself in and then just rot in a brig somewhere. I've got to figure out a way to get those people out of that camp, and then expose to the nation somehow what's going on with these U.N. troops." John turned to Will. "What are you going to do?"

"About what?"

"Well, you can't let your congregation meet at the church," John said. "Sooner or later you will all be arrested just like the others."

Will smiled at his friend and shook his head. "You still don't understand what being a Christian is all about, do you, John? A Christian puts his trust in God, for everything in his life. If it is in God's plan for me to go to prison for my faith, then I will go. I'm not saying I'd like it, but I'd like it even less to be out of His will. The Bible tells me that if I deny Jesus before man, He will deny me before God. So I can't just be a Christian when it's easy. I also need to stand up for my faith when it's not popular. I'm sure some who say they are Christians won't go to church right now, all over the world, for fear of being arrested. But, as for me, I count it a privilege to stand up for my Lord, and I know many in my church will do likewise." Will paused, looking ahead as they entered town.

"I'll be informing everyone at tonight's service about our discovery today of the Christians being held at the base. Can I count on you to be there, John?"

John thought about what Will had said earlier that afternoon before they went out to the base. He turned and eyed Will. "I wouldn't miss it for the world.

**7:00 p.m.,**
Oak Hill Church

THE LIGHTS OF THE SILVER DISK SHONE brightly in the dark sky over the little church as people arrived for the evening service.

John walked in as the service was about to begin. He found a seat in the back just as Will got up to speak.

As Will paused and slowly looked around he saw that almost every member was present.

"I'm not giving a sermon tonight," he began, "because there's something I have to tell you, something you need to know. I've learned, just this afternoon, that government authorities are arresting Christians for allegedly being in league with the space ships."

The congregation gasped as one, glancing at each other in fear.

"I know for a fact that some of our brothers and sisters are in a detention camp at the old Oak Hill army base," he announced.

Another catch of breath rippled through the room.

"It is very possible that the authorities will come at any time, even tonight as we meet here, and accuse us of conspiring with the [quote] aliens [unquote]." In mocking fashion, he pointed a finger upward. "We must be prepared to realize it could happen, tonight, or anytime we meet in the future."

Members of the congregation looked at one another in earnest. Fear engulfed the room.

"I believe that thing hovering over our church right now is nothing more than a hoax of the devil," Will exclaimed, again pointing his finger into the air. "What you see is not a visitor from outer space, my friends, but a clever illusion created by Satan and his demons."

The night sky outside the church was clear, the desert air hot and still. Streams of yellow light from the church windows fell across the open sandy ground behind the building, fading into the murky darkness. Here, no movement could be detected by the human eye, but much activity was taking place on the supernatural level. Hundreds of demons had gathered near the back of the church. When fear and loss of faith grew inside, the demons inched closer and closer to the church.

Garrett, Caleb, and the few angels with them formed a thin line between the demons and the church building. The white-robed angels felt the power of the evil ones pressing in on them as they held their ground.

"Look," Garrett said, nodding to the large eagle-shaped figure emerging from the front of the line of demons. "That's Legion. This must be pretty important for him to show up."

"What shall we do?" Caleb asked under his breath.

"We are not empowered to do anything yet." Garrett kept his eyes trained on the swarm of evil in front of him. "It is up to the faith of the Christians inside now as to what will happen."

Will studied his congregation, sensing that they were feeling uncertain. "I know you are all fearful of what the world out there might do to us. I am afraid also," he admitted. The red-bearded man left his pulpit, stepping down into the middle aisle. "But remember, we are just passing through this world. We do not belong here forever. Our eternal home is heaven. While we are here, we must trust in the Lord, because he promises to be with us always."

Will paused for a moment and looked around at everyone. "Even in persecution, even unto death — for our goal is to be with Jesus in glory — it matters not what anyone might do to us here on earth."

Will opened his Bible. "I'd like to read to you what our Savior says to us in times like these, in Matthew 13:21: 'Yet hath he not root in himself, but endureth for a while; for when tribulation or persecution ariseth because of the word, immediately he is offended.'"

Will closed the Bible and looked around. "Are we going to be 'offended' if we are made fun of or persecuted by the world? Or, will we be like Paul who held onto his faith even after he was put in prison by the world? You folks are being forced to take a stand, right here, right now. I'm not here to make you do it. I am only telling you according to God's word, so you can make a decision one way or the other. There is no middle ground. You are either for the Lord … or you are against Him."

Outside, an invisible force seemed to stop the demons for a moment. The ones on the front line acted like they felt it the most, while the ones in the back jumped around, in anticipation of the kill.

Garrett and Caleb also felt the power increasing and knew that it was coming from the church.

"Come on," Caleb whispered to the people inside the church. "Stand up for your faith, the Lord is with you."

Inside, a man named Greg in the back of the room rose up and shouted at Will. "It's easy for you to stand there and preach to us about faith," he complained. "You don't have a family to protect." Greg looked around at the others. "I've already heard about those who have been arrested — some of my relatives in the city have been taken. I thought I could be strong about this. That's why I came here tonight. But I have a family to consider — a wife, kids, and a business I've worked hard for fifteen years to build." He looked back at Will. "Are you telling me to just throw everything away, not even try to protect my family?"

"I don't know what is in store for us Greg," Will replied. "All I am saying to you is to have faith in the Lord."

Greg looked down at his feet and then back at his family sitting next to him. "I can't do it. I'm sorry, Pastor, I can't risk the safety of my family. Come on," he said, guiding his family out of the church. Several others stood and walked sheepishly to the door, without uttering a single word.

The rest of the congregation looked at one another, and then at Will. Tears appeared in his eyes. John sensed that Will was not feeling hurt because the people were leaving him. It was because they doubted the Lord. The thought then occurred to John that he understood; he finally understood what it was all about. He looked around at the remaining people, and he felt like he was one with them. He no longer wanted to doubt God. Yes, trusting in the Lord was something he wanted for his own life. A tiny voice inside of him whispered that he should commit to the Lord — now. But he brushed it aside, thinking there was plenty of time, he would talk about it with Will, maybe tomorrow.

Outside, Garrett and Caleb felt the power subside from within the church, and the demons started to creep forward again. Looking around, Caleb whispered to Garrett, "Where are our reinforcements?"

"I have faith in these Christians," Garrett said. "Our reserves will be here when needed."

"I can't make any of you do what is not in your heart," Will said, looking around at his small congregation. "But for those of you who want to come, I am going to have a prayer meeting here every night until that demon apparition above us is gone."

"Amen!" shouted an elderly lady in the second row. That

brought a slight bit of laughter from everyone and relieved the tension in the room.

"You can count on us," added Ron, who was sitting next to Sally.

"And me, too," said Henry's mother, who was sitting next to a smiling Henry.

"I'll be there, pastor," shouted someone in the back. "You can count on me," announced another.

Will nodded his head, smiled, and lifted his voice in prayer. "Oh, Lord, we praise you, and we ask your blessing and protection on us, your children, here before you now."

Garrett and Caleb glanced at each other out of the corners of their eyes, not taking their attention off Legion, who stood before them.

This was it.

If the faith of the believers inside the church was not strong enough, Legion and his followers would go through them like a whirlwind, causing confusion and fear.

With evil yellow eyes under an arched brow, Legion stared at the two from the heavenly host; he was going to enjoy destroying them. He laughed haughtily. Then he would cause the hu-mans inside this insignificant church to lose any faith they might have left.

"You lose these," he snarled to Garrett and Caleb, pointing to the church. "I will destroy their faith and put fear into their hearts."

**"I think not,"** came a powerful, deep voice from behind Garrett and Caleb. The angels' eyes widened in amazement at the recognition of that voice. As they stood and watched Legion, they saw the smile fade from his face. Then they heard songs of praise to the Lord coming from inside the church.

Gabriel was here! Praise the Lord, the Christian's faith had come through. Oh, Glory, had it ever.

Gabriel walked slowly between Garrett and Caleb and stopped ahead of them, facing Legion. The Archangel was as tall as Legion and he wore a brilliant, white robe that glowed. His wings were magnificent; he looked strong and powerful. A large sword hung from a silver belt at his side, its scabbard gleaming like a thousand polished diamonds.

Garrett felt the presence of many angels filling the ranks behind him and Caleb. *Oh, this is going to be good!* he thought.

Legion's and Gabriel's eyes locked as they stood facing each other in silence. For a moment Legion remembered a time, countless ages ago, when they had known each other. He had thought that glory was forever forgotten.

His hooded eyes narrowed in anger.

The air turned heavy and tense as the two powers came against one another. Everything was still, nothing moved on either side of the opposing forces.

Legion looked at the one called the Messenger, and thought, *Gabriel, the mighty one from the heavenly host.* Now, this is where the battle they had been waiting for, for so many centuries would begin. Satan's great lie was sweeping the land, and their power was growing stronger. Legion would defeat this champion of the Lord God, and then his demon spirits would torment not only those Christians in this church, but also those across the entire land.

Legion felt stronger than he ever had. He would defeat this heavenly warrior easily, and it would finally make up for his embarrassment at Gerasene, so long ago, that had caused his banishment. This victory would assure him that Lucifer would make him commander over all the princes.

"The battle is ours," snarled Legion, his yellow eyes boring into Gabriel as hot, red air spouted from the huge demon's mouth. "The hu-mans of the earth are all under the spell and delusion of my lord. You have lost them to my lord, Satan, and now I will destroy you and your puny, feeble angels." Legion held his head high as he growled, "My lord's kingdom shall reign on earth, and I, Legion, shall be at his right hand forever." His dark wings rustled with a sound like leather stretching, and his eyes narrowed in hate.

His right claw moved slightly toward his sword's handle.

Gabriel's piercing blue eyes moved down and up Legion's massive body. He looked the monster squarely in the eyes. When he spoke, he acted as if he hadn't heard a word of what Legion had just spouted.

**"So ... you're ... Legion,"** Gabriel said, contemplating for a moment. His diamond eyes then shot quickly into Legion's. **"I've heard about you."**

Legion's head cocked slightly to one side, and he snarled, "What have you heard about me, Messenger?" he taunted.

**"I've heard that ... you like pigs."**

Later, Caleb would swear to Garrett that he saw Gabriel's mouth crack a small smile at that moment.

Legion's eyes widened with an evil fury as his claw flashed to his sword. Before he even touched it, Gabriel's sword was swinging in an arc through the center of Legion's body, slicing him in half.

Legion's arms lifted high in rage. His head snapped back with a piercing scream that filled the night with terror.

The ground cracked under Legion's feet, and streams of red glowing light shot up from below the earth's crust. The cracks grew wider and fire leaped up from the depths below, engulfing Legion. Suddenly, two black chains whipped up from beneath the surface, grabbing each arm and wrapping around him like snakes. They pulled him slowly down into the lake of fire. When he was out of sight, the cracks in the earth slammed shut like great iron doors.

Legion's demons were spellbound by the spectacle occurring in front of them: Their leader was gone. They stared mesmerized at the spot where he had stood. Then they all looked at once to the heavenly host, as they heard the sounds of swords being drawn.

"Attack!" yelled Garrett. The heavenly angels, with drawn swords, moved toward the horde of black spirits. Immediately the demons fled in retreat, swarming crazily in a rout, slamming into each other, trying to get away as fast as they could.

The demons swarmed like bats emerging from a cave. They flew into the night sky above the church, past the area where the

UFO had been, now mysteriously vanished.

The heavenly angels chased after them in hot pursuit as they flew off into the darkness. As the last of them disappeared, the sounds of singing could be heard coming from inside the little church in Oak Hill.

*I have decided to follow Jesus...*
*I have decided to follow Jesus...*
*I have decided to follow Jesus...*
*No turning back, no turning back...*

*And the devil that deceived them was cast into the lake of fire and brimstone, where the beast and the false prophet are, and shall be tormented day and night forever and ever.*

— Revelation 20:10

**6:23 a.m., Monday, September 20**
Oak Hill, California

. . . . . . . . . . . . . . . . . . . . . . . . . . . . . . . . . . . . . . . .

# Chapter 19

JOHN WOKE UP TO THE KNOCKING on his motel room door. When he opened it, there stood Will and another, strangely familiar man.

"Come on in," he offered, as he let them in and sat down on his bed to try to wake up.

"John, I'd like you to meet Reverend Peter Madison. He's the one who spoke to us yesterday out at the base."

John shook Peter's hand in astonishment. "How did you get out of that concentration camp?"

"Well," Peter said, "I just drove myself out this morning."

"What?" exclaimed John, suddenly fully awake.

Will grinned. "Peter has quite a story to tell, John. Did you feel the earthquake last night?"

"No," John shook his head, frowning as he thought to himself. Earthquakes were quite common in California, and he generally slept through those that occurred at night.

"Well," Peter said, "we sure had one out at the base last night. It was different from any I've ever experienced before. All of us were locked up in different rooms in those underground bunkers. Around midnight, we all were awakened by the sound of rushing air filling the hallways. Then the ground started shaking, and all the locked doors opened by themselves."

"What happened to the Russian guards?" John asked.

"They all ran away, jumped in some trucks and took off," Peter said. "We haven't seen hide nor hair of them since."

"Kinda reminds me of what happened to the apostles Paul and Silas in the book of Acts, chapter 16, verse 26," Will said. "Wouldn't you agree, Reverend Madison?"

"Oh, I have no doubt about it," Peter said. "It was the Lord's doing. There is no other explanation."

John could see these two ministers were about to burst with joy at what had happened, and he couldn't blame them. Their story was amazing.

"So what you're telling me is that you believe that God caused the earthquake, and scared away the guards?" John asked. "Do you think it had anything to do with the UFO disappearing over your church last night?"

"I don't know about that," Will replied. "All of the other eighteen UFOs are still in place. Ours is the only one that's gone, besides the one Pettinati destroyed. But I do know the Lord is working in a mighty way around here right now."

"So where are all those hundreds of people now, Peter?" John asked.

"Still at the base. I came to town to find a church and met Reverend Will. He has agreed to help us all get back to our homes."

"I sent Henry and some others out to the base already," added

Will. "We were just on our way back, and I knew you'd probably want to come too.

"Give me five minutes to get dressed," John said.

When they arrived at the bunkers on the base where John and Will had been the day before, they found many people milling about, getting ready to leave.

As John stepped out of Will's truck, Henry walked up to him. "How ya doing, Major?"

John was glad to see him and shook his hand. "Fine, Henry. What's going on?"

"We've rounded up some buses," Henry replied. "We've found some drivers to take these folks back to their homes in L.A."

"Have you seen any of the U.N. troops?" John asked

"Nope, I think they've gone for good. They sure left a lot of equipment and supplies here. And, Major, they left some paperwork I think you should take a look at."

John suddenly turned his head to Henry: "Show me."

In what appeared to be a command center in one of the underground bunkers, Henry showed John what turned out to be a wealth of information on the U.N. peacekeeping forces, including their orders for taking over and controlling the population.

As John read through the documents, his heart raced at the implications of the plans that Denzel Marduk had initiated, plans for taking over not only America but the whole world.

"Some pretty nasty stuff here," Henry said as he watched John reading over the papers.

"Yes," John said. "I'm going to make sure the American public gets to read all this."

"Good," Henry said. "I'll help you pack it all up."

Later, after John and Henry had put the incriminating papers in boxes and put them in Will's pickup, the Reverend Peter, Will, John, and Henry stood together and watched the buses leave with the former captives.

"Most of my people and I are not going home," Peter said.

"What are you going to do? Will asked.

"We feel there is no reason to go back," Peter said. "We'll only be arrested again. I believe we're only seeing the beginning of Christians being persecuted. The spirit of the Antichrist is growing. I have an airline pilot in my group who informed me that all known Christian pilots are being grounded for security reasons. There are others in my church who are losing their jobs for the same reason. I'm going to take those who want to go and head up into the mountains here."

He nodded toward the rugged mountain range north of them.

"The Lord has told me to do this, so I must."

John looked up toward the mountains, then turned slowly back to Reverend Madison.

"How will you live?" Will asked.

"Oh, we have some outdoorsmen in our group, and I'm going to load up all the supplies I can from here on the base into some trucks," Peter said. "Otherwise, the Lord will provide for us."

"Sounds like you've made up your mind, Reverend," John said, his blue eyes widening in approval. "We'll help you get going."

By noon, about seventy people had packed up seventeen military ten-wheelers with food, supplies, and equipment. They were ready to leave.

Henry took John aside. "I'm going home to get my mother and go with these folks."

"You're not a Christian," John said. "You don't need to run off to the hills."

"It's not just Christians who are going to end up fighting for our freedom," Henry said.

"Yes," John said. "I believe you're right about that, Henry."

"Come with us, Major. We're going to need someone to lead us, to help us when we need to defend ourselves."

John looked silently at Henry for a moment, "Maybe I will. But I need to do something first. You go on ahead. You have the savvy to protect the Reverend and his people. He'll be happy knowing that you're with them."

"Okay," sighed Henry, shaking John's hand. "I'll be watching for you. Take care of yourself, and I'll set us up someplace you'll be able to find us. Just go where you would set up a safe place and we'll be there."

"Good luck," said John, "I'll see you soon."

A short time later, Will and John watched the trucks pull out — loaded down with the Reverend Madison and his people, Henry and his mother — headed down the road to the mountains.

"What are your plans now?" Will asked John.

"I'd like to use the copier at your church to make copies of some of these papers I found here today," John said. "Then I'm going to mail them to every news organization I can think of."

"Sounds like a lot of work to me. You want some help?"

"I'd like that."

"Well," Will said, putting his arm around his usually impassive friend and leading him toward his pickup. "You're gonna have to feed me first."

**2:14 p.m.,**
Oak Hill Church

ONCE BACK IN WILL'S OFFICE, John selected twenty pages of the U.N. plans for controlling the American population. That, along with a cover letter he had written, made up a nice package to send out. He was sure many news organizations would jump on this proof and expose it to the American public before it was too late.

Will and John set up a little assembly line copying the pages and packaging them for mailing.

After about an hour, Will looked up from the copier. "We're out of paper," he announced. "I'll run down to the store and get some more."

"Okay," said John, putting papers into a manila envelope. "Pick up some more envelopes too."

"Be back in a few minutes," said Will as he walked out the door.

The street outside the church was deserted. The reporters with their TV trucks and crews had left when the UFO disappeared. A slight breeze blew, scattering bits of trash the crowds had left behind on the sidewalks and street. That and some waving streams of yellow police-barricade tape were all that remained. Everyone was gone.

A black limousine pulled up to the curb in front of the church, and Frank Pettinati slowly stepped out.

From the roof of the church, Garrett and Caleb watched Frank as he stood at the curb, glaring. They looked at each other solemnly and then back at Frank.

Frank examined the deserted street, and then checked out the little wooden church building. His eyes narrowed with hate. So this was the location of the preacher who had been sending him E-mails. It was good there was no one around, no witnesses.

The side door of the church suddenly opened and Will walked out looking down at a page of paper in his hand.

*Perfect,* thought Frank. He knew immediately this was the preacher. He would kill him quickly and then leave.

Will was walking and reading a U.N. document, when he suddenly looked up to see the Beast standing at the curb. He had stopped for a moment when he first saw Frank. He stepped a few paces closer and looked straight into evil, sinister, green eyes.

Frank lifted his head high and snarled: "Why do you torment me, preacher?"

"The Lord God commanded me," Will answered with authority.

Frank's eyes narrowed. He glared at Will. "How did you know about my past?"

Will paused before he spoke, silently praying to the Lord for help.

"My father was in Army intelligence during the war. He prosecuted many of your 'friends' at Nuremberg," Will said. "He wanted, more than any of the other war criminals, to bring you to trial. However," Will shook his head slowly, "he could never get enough evidence to arrest you. I read all about you in the papers that he left me."

"And so you think you had to pick up where your dear father left off, is that it?" Frank's words dripped with venom. He was already tiring of this conversation. It was time to end it. All of a sudden, Frank felt an overwhelming but invisible force assault him from behind. A mask of rage fell over his face as he bowed his head slightly, keeping an eye on Will. He stole a quick glance over his shoulder.

Across the street stood an old man wearing a black topcoat and hat, his face hidden by the shadow from the hat's brim.

Will also noticed the seemingly sudden appearance of the man. Though he could not see the face, the eyes gleamed like bright stars.

Will looked at Frank, and he knew immediately what to say. "The Lord has told me, oh ye false prophet, that your days are numbered."

Frank stared at Will in a crazed fury.

Will lifted his arm and pointed a steady finger at Frank. His eyes blazed, and his red hair seemed to glow and wave like a flame in the wind.

"I know who you are, thou beast!"

Across the street, the Messenger watched in fascination as Will confronted the beast. It reminded him of another red-headed man of God he had watched over several thousand years ago, at a place called Mount Carmel. That man's name had been Elijah. He and Will were very much alike.

"You will deceive for a short time those who want to believe you," Will said, taking a step forward. "You will keep your power, but not for long. And, as for the promise that your lord Satan made to you, that you will live forever, well, that will happen. You and that man of perdition, and your lord Satan — you all will be tormented forever, in the lake of fire."

Frank, his green eyes burning like melted emeralds, had heard enough. He raised his head in defiance. His mouth quivered in hatred as he thought about Will's statement. Lake of fire, huh — he would show this preacher a lake of fire.

Will let his accusing hand drop. He stood and confronted Frank in silence. He had seen Pettinati on TV, destroying the UFO in New York with fire, and he knew he was probably going to try to kill him the same way now. However, he had no fear of death. His only concern was that he had done what the Lord had told him to do.

A voice suddenly came into Will's head from the man across the street. The angel of the Lord said unto Will, "Fear not, thou shalt not die today."

Frank's arm shot up and his fingers slowly stretched out in Will's direction. Fire streamed from his hand with a loud, deep, rumbling noise. Instead of going toward Will, the flame curved up into the air. It returned to earth behind Frank, engulfing his limousine. Frank whirled in astonishment. Where the car had been was now only a black smoldering wreakage in the street.

Facing Will, Frank saw two men dressed in white robes standing on either side of the minister. Frank turned and stared at the man in the black coat standing across the street. He took a threatening step toward the stranger but stopped abruptly as the head of the old man tilted up slowly, revealing the face. Frank's eyes opened with fearful recognition as he gazed motionless at Gabriel.

Frank swung around once more to Will, his brow creased and his evil eyes narrowed. "You win this battle, preacher," he growled, glancing back to the old man and then straightening the knot in his tie. But I will win the war," he said haughtily, combing back his black hair with one hand. With that said, he turned and began walking down the sidewalk toward town.

Will studied Frank as he walked out of sight. His heart began to beat once again. He looked over to where the old man had been, but saw no one. Will sighed, and grinned deep in thought. Falling to his knees, he prayed, "Thank you, Lord. You are so great."

A short time later when Will returned from town with the paper and envelopes, he told John what had happened. John was amazed that Frank had been here in Oak Hill, trying to kill Will.

The event only added to the many things already on John's mind, things that kept him awake and restless most of that night.

*How shall we escape, if we neglect so great salvation, which at the first began to be spoken by the Lord, and was confirmed unto us by them that heard him.*

— Hebrews 1:3

# Chapter 20

THE SUN HAD RISEN in the eastern sky and presented the world with a beautiful day. Most people on earth had adjusted to the UFOs hovering in the air. Although the uncertainty about them remained, people were beginning to get back to a semi-normal routine. Rumors floated around about certain religious groups that had been accused of conspiring with the UFOs. However, it was nothing for most people to worry about — the government was taking care of things. Moreover, that man, that leader of the New Federation Earth, Denzel Marduk, seemed to have the situation concerning the UFOs under control. There was really, it seemed, no reason not to go on with their daily life. Things would work out for the best.

**8:34 a.m., Tuesday, September 21**
Oak Hill Church

John walked into Will's office and sat down in a chair across from the preacher, who was studying his Bible.

Will looked up and smiled. "Good morning. Did you sleep well?"

"No," John answered, sighing heavily. "I've got a lot on my mind."

Will nodded his head. He understood. "Well, you mailed your packages to all of the news organizations. What are you going to do now?"

"I don't know. I've been thinking a lot about Frank being here yesterday, and about Denzel. I never told you, but I saved Denzel's life once, when we were teenagers."

"So?" Will shrugged.

John looked at him in alarm. "Don't you see, I'm responsible for him being around, doing all that he is doing, and what he is going to do."

"Don't beat yourself up over that," smiled Will. "God has allowed Denzel to live and to be where he is to fulfill prophecy. Just like yesterday with me and Frank, it is not yet his time to die. Believe me, your saving Denzel's life once did not change history."

John looked as if he had just had a huge burden lifted from his shoulders. "Yes, I guess you're right. I still wish I could do something about him now, though."

"Listen, John," Will warned in a serious tone. "Don't ever go up against Denzel unless you are empowered by the Lord. Denzel's supernatural powers would destroy you. And you can never have the power of the Spirit of the Lord until you ask him into your heart."

"I know," John admitted, looking down at the floor. *Why am I being so stubborn about doing that,* he wondered. It probably came from his rejection of the idea for most of his life, feeling like he hated God for taking his parents, not feeling like he needed the Lord.

John would always remember Will's smile as the red-headed man looked at his friend and said, "I hope … "

Somewhere in the vast heavens … God had been watching the events of the past, present, and future on the earth he had created. He knew now, right at this exact moment, the world had gone on long enough.

Will disappeared!

One second he was talking to John, and the next second he had vanished.

John froze, then quickly looked around the empty room and back at the empty chair Will had been sitting in only seconds before. A horrible, frightful dread flowed over him as he stared at the empty chair.

In a heavy wave of shock he knew what had happened.

"Oh, God!" he exclaimed. "Oh, no … why did I wait?"

Everything that had seemed so important to him these last few days suddenly seemed so unimportant now. He had wasted his time fooling around when he should have been doing the one most important thing in his life, asking the Lord into his heart.

John fell to his knees and cried out like a wounded animal. "Oh, Lord, forgive me. I am so sorry I waited. Please forgive me of my sins and come into my heart. I know it is too late to go with you now, but I promise I will do your will from now on. Even … if it means I shall have to die for your name's sake."

Immediately the Spirit of the Lord came into John, and he knew without a doubt that the Lord loved him and saved him from his sins. He was confident that he was now a child of God.

John sat on the floor struggling to remember what Will had told him about what was going to happen in the coming days. Things his grandfather had also tried to explain to him.

There was going to be a period — a certain time — a time of horrible events on earth before the Lord came back again. Seven years … yes, seven years of — John looked up in remembrance —Tribulation! A time of turmoil, when it would be extremely difficult to live as a Christian.

John lay down on the floor and prayed. "What do you want me to do now, Lord? Tell me, and I will do it."

The Lord put His thoughts into John's heart and mind.

Sometime later, John got up and walked into the church's sanctuary. He was drawn there by the sound of someone crying.

In front of the stage, near the pulpit, a man was kneeling and sobbing intensely. John recognized him. It was Greg, the man who had walked out of the Sunday-night service with his family after confronting Will.

Greg turned toward John. He stopped sobbing and stood up wide-eyed, running to him.

"You … you're still here?" he cried.

"Yes," John answered calmly.

"Do you know what's happened?" Greg asked "They're gone, everyone's gone. My wife, the kids, they just disappeared," he said hysterically. "I don't understand, I mean … I don't know why I didn't go, too." Greg grabbed John by the shoulders and looked at him with great fear in his eyes. "I mean, I always tried to be a good person. I never did anything really bad. I always thought I was a Christian, I even joined the church and came every Sunday with my family. I even gave money! Why didn't I go, too?" He suddenly stepped back and looked strangely at John. "Why didn't you go?"

"Because," admitted John, "I never asked Jesus into my heart. I never asked for his forgiveness of my sins. I never asked him to save me."

"Oh, that," Greg murmured, rubbing a shaky hand through his hair. "Well, I thought I was okay if I was just a good man. I mean, how could a good and loving God ever condemn me if I tried my best to be good?"

"It doesn't work that way," John said remorsefully, remembering Will saying the same thing to him once. "You must accept His plan of salvation, His way, if you want eternal life with Him."

"Well, that doesn't seem fair," Greg mumbled. He took a few steps backward and looked around, bewildered.

"You can still ask the Lord to save you, Greg," John said. "He is always ready and waiting for that."

"I don't know," Greg said. He stepped back again and looked at John strangely. "You know, I'd better go check on my business." He turned and dashed out the door.

John followed Greg outside and watched him run down the street, apostasy's child running back to his Godless world.

John noticed a car sitting motionless at a corner stop sign, its engine running but the driver missing. Standing in front of the little white church, he had the sinking feeling of being terribly alone — and an extreme sense of loss.

The whole atmosphere seemed filled with a sad, despondent wailing of many voices, moaning in grief and pain. The loud weeping could be heard coming from every corner of the earth.

John began walking down the middle of the street toward town. He knew where he must go now.

The UFOs had disappeared, all of them, gone without a trace. They had left Tuesday morning about 8:30, leaving as they had come — without warning. They had apparently taken many earth people with them. Millions of people from all over the world had disappeared moments before the UFOs disappeared. It was not just a random abduction. All those who were gone were people who had claimed to be Christians.

Denzel Marduk had been right. Those Christians had been in league with the silver space ships all along, the proof was undeniable now. Why else would only Christians have been taken? The fact that governments, under the recommendation of Denzel Marduk and his new Federation Earth, had grounded Christian airline pilots and removed other Christians from sensitive positions had been a wise move. It prevented what could have been mass accidents and destruction when the Christians disappeared. As it was, many terrible accidents in the streets and highways were caused by the disappearance of drivers, but it could have been so much worse.

The people of the world were very happy that the UFOs and those traitorous Christians were now gone.

The shock of the abductions was not as traumatic as the initial appearance of the space ships had been. Federation Earth announced that it was making plans to combat the aliens should they ever return again, reassuring everyone that things were now under control. People were happy that it now appeared that the scare was over and they could get back to living a normal life again.

**10:39 a.m., Wednesday, September 22**
United Nations Building, New York City

John walked into the front office of the Secretary General of the United Nations, which was now also the office of the President of Federation Earth, Denzel Marduk.

When he told the secretary at the front desk he wanted to see Denzel, she informed him that he was to busy today for any appointments.

"Just tell him John Allen is here to see him," he demanded with determination.

She told him to have a seat and she would let Mr. Marduk know that John was waiting to see him.

John sat down and thought about the reality that he was actually here at the U.N., all the way across the country from California. He had driven to Los Angeles and boarded a plane to New York. No small feat in itself, considering the mass confusion everywhere over the millions of people suddenly vanished. Also knowing that at any moment he could be arrested because of his U.N. warrant. Indeed, this was quite an achievement and miracle.

Nevertheless, the Lord had compelled him to come and see Denzel and, although he was not quite sure why, he knew he had to come. It had been something he had wanted to do even before he felt the Lord leading him. Now that he was here, he did not know just exactly what he was going to say to Denzel. But he had prayed about it on the plane, and he was sure the Lord would give him the words when the time was right.

This was a whole new experience for John, doing things that

the Lord led him to do. It felt good, even though he also realized he might not walk out of this place alive. But that didn't bother him or even cause him to be alarmed. John was quite comfortable, knowing that his life was now in the Lord's hands. No matter what happened to him, now or in the future, he resolved in his heart to listen to God always and follow His leading.

The secretary called John back to her desk and informed him, with surprise in her voice, that Mr. Marduk would see him now. As John walked toward Denzel's office door, he whispered a prayer, "Oh, Lord, reveal to me what you would have me do and say."

When John walked into the spacious office, the first person he saw was Frank, standing by expansive windows overlooking the city skyline. The large man showed no signs of aging since the last time John saw him, when he'd left for boot camp. Frank turned and smiled secretively, walking over to shake John's hand.

"John," he said. "It's so good to see you. You look great." He turned to Denzel sitting at a large desk, "Look, Denzel, it's your old friend, John."

John gazed at Denzel; it had been more than twenty years since he had seen him. The change in his appearance was dramatic; he looked tall and filled out and very handsome. He was a man, full-grown and mature, with an air of authority and power. It seemed to John, as they stared at each other in those first few seconds, that they had known each other before only in a dream. John felt something else: an overwhelming sense of evil radiating from Denzel.

"John," Denzel said as he rose and went around the desk to shake his hand. "Why haven't we kept in touch all these years?" When their hands touched, John looked intently into Denzel's eyes. Was it his imagination or did he really feel like he was shaking hands with the devil?

John thought that Denzel reacted strangely as their grasp ended. Denzel sat on the corner of his desk and said, "I've done some quick research on you, John. You're in Army Intelligence. I always knew you'd do well.

"Frank," Denzel exclaimed, "did I ever tell you that John saved my life?" Denzel's smile was weird as he kept looking at John.

"No, when was that?" declared Frank in surprise.

"Oh," he waved his hand around indecisively, "you remember those old mine shafts in the hills you told us never to go near. Well, I fell into one once. I would have been killed by a bunch of snakes if John hadn't risked his own life to pull me out." Denzel's eyes bored into John's with an almost accusing stare.

"Well, I never knew that," Frank said with what seemed to John to be sarcasm.

"You know, John," Denzel said, "I could use a man with your experience in the Federation Earth's military police force that we're forming. Why, the man who saved my life could make general right away, don't you agree, Frank?"

"You bet," exclaimed Frank.

John eyed Frank, and then looked at Denzel and said solemnly, "I don't think that could happen, Denzel. There's a warrant out for my arrest by your U.N. people right now."

"Oh, don't worry about that," Denzel said, waving his hand away. "I can take care of that. Just think, John. I can make you a general, and give you a command over all my intelligence forces."

"You could always buy me, Denzel," John admitted. "You could buy the uniform, but you can't buy my soul, and one without the other isn't any good."

"Your soul?" Denzel questioned fiercely.

John studied Denzel for a moment, but he did not see the boyhood friend he once knew. He only saw something very evil and a powerful adversary to the Lord and to those who believed in God.

He also understood now what his mission in life would be and what he should say to Denzel. "That's right, Denzel, my soul. It has been redeemed by the blood of the Lamb, the Son of God, Jesus."

Denzel winced at the word, *Jesus*.

"Who do you think you are coming in here like this?" Frank demanded. "You can't just ..."

"It's all right, Frank," Denzel said, seething while holding his hand up to Frank. He looked at John with narrowed eyes. "I want to hear what my old friend has to say."

"I'm a Christian, Denzel," John declared.

"I thought all the Christians got beamed up with the UFOs," Frank said.

"You know better than that, and so do I," John said, looking over at him with cold eyes. "You might be able to sell that bill of goods to most people, but you and I both know the Lord came and took the Christians. The UFOs were just a deception, part of your plan to cause the world to hate Christians and lift you into power."

"If you're a Christian, why didn't you go too?" Frank sneered. "Forget to tithe one Sunday?"

"I just became one, after the Rapture. I also have the feeling many more people will become Christians, as time goes on." He turned and stared at Denzel. "We will band together, Denzel, and we will fight you every step you try to take. The Lord will be with us, and we will have his power to stand against you. That is why he sent me here, to tell you that. In the end, Denzel, the Lord Jesus will triumph over you, and he will be the King of Kings on earth. I'm going to be around for the next seven years to remind you of your fate."

Frank had heard enough. "You're dead!" he growled, pointing a finger at John. "You will never leave this room alive."

"I'm afraid Frank is right," Denzel said, slipping off the corner of the desk and stepping back out of the way. "It's too bad, John," he said. "You could have been part of my great kingdom here on earth. But you've decided to believe all those Bible fairy tales. I really thought you were much smarter than that."

Frank began raising his arm in John's direction. He lifted his head and an evil grin spread across his face.

"And," Denzel added with venomous insincerity, "we really can't have you running around spreading all those lies about us." Denzel stood with his hands clasped and his head raised exaltedly. "Now can we?"

Frank's arm stretched out toward John and his fingers began to spread open …

"Good-bye, John," Denzel said with a laugh.

John disappeared!

The laughter melted off Denzel's face as it drained into shock.

Frank looked startled at the spot where John had stood, then stared at Denzel with uncertainty and wonder.

Denzel turned to Frank with a deep gasp and said, "Damn!"

**1:45 p.m.,**
Oak Hill Church, Oak Hill, California

ONE MOMENT JOHN WAS LOOKING at Frank in Denzel's office, wondering if he was going to die, the next second he was standing back in Will's office at the church in Oak Hill.

John stood still for a moment, amazed, regaining his bearings, and then his thoughts. *How did that happen?* he asked himself in shock. It could have only been the Lord. "Oh my," John whispered to himself.

If he'd needed any more proof that he was now in God's will, he had just received it. Later, he would read in his Bible, in the Book of Acts, Chapter 8, about the Spirit of the Lord moving the Apostle Philip from one place to another, in the very same manner that he had just experienced. John humbly fell down on his knees and gave thanks to the Lord.

John walked into Will's office and sat down in Will's chair.

He knew it would not be easy. There were troubling days ahead for him and anyone else who became a Christian; but he knew there was a job out there for him to do: To tell everyone he could about Jesus, and to fight Denzel relentlessly, so that whomever he could convince would not be damned by Denzel's lies.

John looked around at the shelves of books in Will's office, he knew he had a lot of studying to do. He was sure Will wouldn't mind him using his books. John suddenly realized how much he missed Will. He had been the best friend he'd ever had. Someday he would see him again, in heaven.

*Thank you for showing me the way ol' buddy,* John thought.

*And, oh yes, Will … I do love Jesus.*

*And he causeth all both small and great, rich and poor, free and enslaved, to receive a mark in their right hand, or in their foreheads.*

— Revelation 13:16

**11:39 p.m., One week later**
Mountains overlooking Oak Hill California

.....................................

# Epilogue

THE MOON REFLECTED brightly off the old Dodge 4x4 Power Wagon as it crawled up the dirt mountain road through the forest. At a curve on the mountainside, the driver stopped the pickup, stepped out, and walked to the edge of the side of the mountain.

John stood for a long time gazing at the lights of Oak Hill twinkling in the darkness of the valley below.

The change in John's countenance was dramatic. The chiseled sharp lines of his Indian face still presented an expression of strong self-possession, but the look was not generated from the man-centered "selfism" that he had tried to persevere his whole life. John's appearance now was one of meekness, but not "meekness" in the sense of a weak character as is the definition of the word nowadays. But rather he was indwelled with the Holy Spirit in the true meaning of the word: enormous power under control. John's personal integrity was now also joined with a driving desire to serve God. The result was the powerful look of determination on his face.

His thoughts now were about all that had happened in the last week.

He'd spent most of that time in Will's office at the little church, reading and learning from the many books Will had collected over the years. John was a little wiser in spiritual matters now. He was quickly learning how to become "strong in the Lord" and to trust in Him for everything. It was part of the growing faith that he was certain he would need in the coming days.

He had packed all of Will's books and brought them with him, so he could continue to study.

As John looked down at the lights of Oak Hill, he thought about the last two weeks he had spent there, and the people he had known, Billie, Ron and Sally, Henry, and of course Will. He had learned a lot in a short period of time, about himself, and about the Lord.

John then lifted his intent blue eyes upward. In the clear night sky, he could see a giant star hanging in the darkness, its brightness seemingly unnatural. The abnormal light had appeared several days after the UFOs vanished. The new star was so bright it could be seen even in the daytime. Many people believed it was a sign, an announcement of the beginning of a new age and of a New World leader — Denzel Marduk.

Yes, the folks of Oak Hill and all the rest of the people of the world, it seemed to John, were feeling that things were going to be better from now on. Marduk claimed to have defeated the UFOs and the Christians. The consensus was that the world was a lot better off without those "believers in God."

John could see the whole picture of what had happen as clearly as he could see the outstretched valley below him now. Will had said the signs of Christ's return were all fulfilled, they were living in the last days, a culture of love of self and loss of character, gender conflict, religious confusion and the rejection of God. The world was certainly prepared and ready to accept the coming lie. The UFOs had been a clever deception orchestrated by Satan to completely turn people of the world against God, and to cover the miraculous and spiritual Rapture of the Christians. It had worked brilliantly, and it was now helping Denzel to become ruler of Satan's kingdom on earth. It was what Will had called the "apostasy," and it had all happen so terribly fast.

And now, in the last week, more disturbing events had occurred.

John had watched the news continually, hoping to see announcements concerning the U.N. military papers he had sent out. However, they were never mentioned. TV and newspapers ignored the facts about the U.N. forces in America. John knew then that Marduk had control over all media. The evil tentacles of Denzel's new-world-order Federation Earth had already slipped in and taken over. It was a force that John was destined to reckon with in the future.

Denzel had traveled to Israel several days ago. He'd made an important announcement about an archeological discovery that would mean the Jewish temple could be built in Jerusalem, without any conflict with Arab shrines there. The rebuilding of the Jewish temple had caused quite a joyful celebration in Israel. Some people claimed that, with the announcement of the building of the temple, and the appearance of the new star in the sky, Marduk was the long-awaited Messiah.

John had watched Denzel on the television news the previous night, riding a white horse through the streets of Jerusalem. Marduk was promising to bring a final peace to the Middle East through the power of his Federation Earth Organization. A peace treaty between Marduk and the Jewish people was in the making, to be signed shortly. When John heard about that treaty, he knew from reading his Bible, that the signing would trigger the beginning of the seven years of Tribulation. The knowledge of the terrible things that would happen on earth during the coming seven years sent a chill through him.

*And then,* sighed John, there's Frank Pettinati. The prophet of Federation Earth had been going around the country holding "Revival Meetings" at abandoned churches. He was spouting some kind of "New World Religion," with Denzel as the god of the Earth, and Frank the spiritual leader. He was proclaiming to everyone that they could have their own heaven here on earth, and that it was all right to do anything you wanted to do, as long as it didn't hurt others.

Frank would cause fire to come from the sky and burn down church buildings. He would then invite those who wanted to take the symbol, or "Mark," of Marduk's new Federation Earth on their hand or forehead, they could do so in the light of the burning church. He told the people that if they took the Mark, they would not be abducted by the "God UFOs," like the Christians had been.

John saw right through all their evil hype, but most people, from what he could see on the news and in the papers, were ready and eager to swallow it all.

John turned and, looking around the wooded forest, his eyes fell on Will's old pickup. He had gone back to the Oak Hill military base that morning and found the complex still empty. There was no one around to stop him, so he loaded the Dodge with supplies, guns, ammo, anything else he could find that might be useful in the days ahead. He then headed for the mountains. He knew he had stayed around Oak Hill too long, assuming Denzel's New World order soldier's were probably looking for him. He had decided he would follow this road into the mountains, where he knew he would eventually find the Reverend Peter's hideout. John knew Peter and the Christians who had left with the minister were gone in the Rapture, but maybe some were still there, maybe Henry.

John suspected that, even if none of these had been left, others would be coming in the days ahead. New Christians would run from Marduk's persecution, and John would have a place they could gather and be safe. It was what God had commanded him to do. With the Lord's protection, Christians could wait out the Tribulation in that place.

John looked across the wide-open desert, past the lights of Oak Hill, and realized the world was in for terrible times. His job was to help others come to know the Lord, and then help them to survive the agonizing years.

John took one last look at Oak Hill, lying peaceful and still in the desert night. He turned and climbed back into the driver's seat. He began driving the truck up the incline. The only sound in the forest was the truck's engine as it rumbled up the road.

Soon, all you could see in the darkness were two red tail lights, and two very bright white lights following above it.

*Coming soon from Bill Copeland …*

## *The sequel to* The Apostasy: **Petra, America**

Tribulation Date: Day 543 …

The earth has barely survived a world-wide nuclear war. The people of the world are now suffering under the terrible judgments foretold in the Book of Revelation.

The antichrist, Denzel Marduk, rules over most of the earth from his capital in Babylon, while his prophet of propaganda, Frank Pettanati, preaches the message of the New World Order around the globe. But for Marduk to defeat his Asian enemies and completely destroy God's chosen people so he can rule from the new Jewish temple, he must complete a secret weapon of mass destruction before time runs out.

In America, it has been eighteen months since the Christians of the world disappeared, and the New World Government blames their disappearance on the ever-present UFOs flying the skies.

Christian revival is sweeping the land, even though Christians are labeled terrorists and are put into concentration camps or martyred.

A young Christian woman from Oak Hill, California, goes searching in the mountains for a refuge she has heard about on the Internet.

An ex-Delta Force veteran soldier roams the backroads in the mountains searching for the same place.

A mysterious young man, dressed in western clothes and wearing a six-gun in a fast-draw holster, walks out of the desert looking for a Christian stronghold in the mountains.

They are but a few who are looking for a place they have heard about, a place called Petra.

Petra, America, is the continuing saga of The Apostasy, and of a former U.S. Army Intelligence officer, Major John Allen. Amid the backdrop of the terrible judgments God is raining down on earth, John has made a place of refuge for Christians during the Tribulation. Now, with the supernatural help of God, John must fight the human and demonic forces of the devil, to protect the people of Petra.

Denzel Marduk wants John dead and has sent a two-pronged attack against him. Marduk is getting ready to set up his image of the devil's kingdom on earth in the newly rebuilt temple in Jerusalem, an abomination reflecting an event that happened once before in Jewish history. An object from that first defilement of the temple more than 2,000 years ago, buried in a grave for more than two millennia, along with the prayer of one man from that time, will circumvent over twenty-two centuries to help John fight the forces of the antichrist.

Made in the USA
San Bernardino, CA
23 June 2019